Allison's Journey

**Center Point
Large Print**

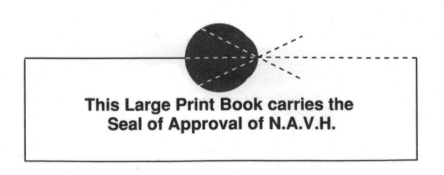

**This Large Print Book carries the
Seal of Approval of N.A.V.H.**

Allison's Journey

WANDA E. BRUNSTETTER

CENTER POINT PUBLISHING
THORNDIKE, MAINE

This Center Point Large Print edition
is published in the year 2008 by arrangement with
Barbour Publishing, Inc.

All scripture quotations, unless otherwise noted,
are taken from the King James Version of the Bible.

The text of this Large Print edition is unabridged. In other
aspects, this book may vary from the original edition.
Printed in the United States of America.
Set in 16-point Times New Roman type.

ISBN: 978-1-60285-279-2

Library of Congress Cataloging-in-Publication Data

Brunstetter, Wanda E.
    Allison's journey / Wanda E. Brunstetter.--Center Point large print ed.
    p. cm.
    ISBN: 978-1-60285-279-2 (lib. bdg. : alk. paper)
    1. Large type books. I. Title.

PS3602.R864A79 2008
813'.6--dc22

2008016985

DEDICATION/ACKNOWLEDGMENTS

To Leeann Curtis,
who makes beautiful faceless Amish dolls.

And ye shall seek me, and find me,
when ye shall search for me with all your heart.
JEREMIAH 29:13

Chapter 1

*W*ith a sense of dread, Allison Troyer stepped into the kitchen. Today was her nineteenth birthday, but she was sure Aunt Catherine wouldn't make a bit of fuss over it. In the twelve years Papa's unmarried sister had lived with them, she had never made much over Allison's or any of her five older brothers' birthdays. Allison figured her aunt didn't care for children and had only moved from her home in Charm, Ohio, to Bird-in-Hand, Pennsylvania, because she felt a sense of obligation to Allison's father. After Mama's untimely death, Papa had been left to raise six children, and it would have been difficult for him without his sister's help.

Allison glanced at her aunt, standing in front of their propane-operated stove. She was a lofty, large-boned woman with big hands and feet. Aunt Catherine's gray-streaked, mousy brown hair was done up tightly in a bun at the back of her head, and her stiff white *kapp* was set neatly on top.

The wooden floor creaked as Allison stepped across it, and her aunt whirled around. Her skin looked paler than normal, making her deeply set blue eyes seem more pronounced.

"Guder mariye," Allison said.

"Morning," Aunt Catherine mumbled, her thin lips set in a firm line. "You want your eggs fried or scrambled?"

"Whatever's easiest."

"It's your birthday, so you choose."

"I prefer scrambled." Allison offered her aunt a faint smile. So she hadn't forgotten what day it was. Maybe this year she would bake Allison a cake. "Would you like me to set the table or make some toast?"

"I think it would be best if you set the table. Last time you made toast, it was burned on the edges." Aunt Catherine's pale eyelashes fluttered like clothes flapping on the line.

If you'd let me do more in the kitchen, I might know how to do things better. Without voicing her thoughts, Allison opened the cupboard door and removed four plates and glasses, placing them on the table.

"I thought I might make a batch of peanut brittle after the chores are done," Aunt Catherine said as she went to the refrigerator and withdrew a jug of milk. "Your brothers and their families will probably join us for supper tonight. I'm sure they would enjoy the candy."

Peanut brittle? Allison felt a keen sense of disappointment. She liked peanut brittle well enough, but it wasn't nearly as good as moist chocolate cake. At least not to her way of thinking. Sally Mast, Allison's best friend, always had a cake on her birthday. Of course, Sally's mother, Dorothy, was still living and cared deeply for her eight children. Allison didn't think Aunt Catherine cared about anyone but herself.

Allison had just set the last fork in place when her father and her brother Peter entered the kitchen.

"Hallich gebottsdaag," Papa said, giving Allison a hug.

"Jah. Happy birthday." Peter handed Allison a brown paper sack. "I hope you like this, sister."

Allison placed the sack on the table, reached inside, and withdrew a baseball glove. She grinned at her blond-haired, blue-eyed brother. *"Danki,* Peter. This is just what I needed."

He smiled and squeezed her arm. "Now you'll be able to catch those fly balls a lot easier."

"Fly balls—*puh*!" Aunt Catherine mumbled. "Baseball's such a waste of time."

Papa cleared his throat real loud, and Allison and Peter turned to face him. "I have something for your birthday, too." He handed Allison an envelope.

Allison smiled and quickly tore it open. If there was money inside, she planned to buy a new baseball to go with the glove, since her old ball was looking pretty worn. She pulled a piece of paper from the envelope and stared at it, unbelieving. "A bus ticket?"

Papa nodded, his brown eyes shining with obvious pleasure. "It's to Seymour, Missouri, where your aunt Mary and uncle Ben King live."

Aunt Catherine's thin lips formed a circle, but she didn't say a word.

Allison's forehead wrinkled as she studied the ticket. Why, she was supposed to leave in two days! Tears sprang to her eyes, and she sank into the closest chair.

"Aren't you happy about this?" Papa asked, pulling his fingers through the sides of his thinning brown hair. "I figured you'd be excited about making a trip to Missouri."

"I—I had no idea you wanted to send me away."

"*Ach*, Allison," he said kindly as he took a step forward. "I'm not sending you there for good. It's just for the summer."

That bit of news gave Allison some measure of relief, but she still didn't understand why her father wanted her to be gone all summer. With the garden coming up, it was Allison's job to keep the weeds down, and it was one of the few chores she actually enjoyed and did fairly well. "Why do I have to go to Missouri for the summer? Can't I stay right here in Lancaster County?"

Papa glanced at Aunt Catherine as if he hoped she might say something, but she turned her back to them as she cracked eggs into a glass bowl.

I'll bet this was Aunt Catherine's idea. She probably asked Papa to send me to Missouri so I'd be out of her hair. Allison squeezed her eyes shut. *She doesn't like me; she never has!*

Papa touched Allison's shoulder, and her eyes snapped open. "I thought you might enjoy getting to know your *mamm*'s twin sister and her family. Mary's a fine woman; she's so much like your mamm. You probably don't remember her well, but Mary's a fine cook, and she can clean a house like nobody's business."

10

Allison swallowed around the tears clogging her throat.

"From the things Mary has said in her letters over the years, it's obvious that she has a way with the sewing machine, too," Papa continued.

"Not like me; that's what your *daed*'s saying," Aunt Catherine spoke up. "I've never been able to do much more than basic mending, because I . . . " Her voice trailed off, and she started beating the eggs so hard Allison feared the bowl might break.

"Because why?" Allison asked. "You've never really said why you don't do much sewing."

Aunt Catherine turned to face Allison. Her lips pressed together, deepening the harsh lines in the corners of her mouth. "Before my mamm died, she never spent much time teaching me to sew." She pinched her lips even tighter. "Used to say I was all thumbs and that she couldn't be bothered with trying to show me things on the sewing machine because I kept making mistakes."

Allison felt a stab of compassion for her aunt. Apparently, she'd had a difficult childhood. Even so, was that any reason for her to be so sharp-tongued and critical all the time?

Allison shook her thoughts aside and looked up at her father. "Are you sending me to Missouri because you think I should learn to cook and sew?"

Papa motioned to the baseball glove lying in Allison's lap. "Thanks to being raised with five older *brieder*, you've become quite a tomboy. Truth is you'd rather be outside playing ball than in the house doing womanly things."

Peter, who had wandered over to the sink to wash his hands, added his two cents' worth. "Allison always did prefer doing stuff with me and the brothers. Even when she was little and the girl cousins came around with their dolls, Allison preferred playing ball or going fishing with us."

Allison grunted, her defenses rising. "What's wrong with that? I enjoy doing outdoor things."

"Nothing's wrong with fishing or playing ball, but if you're ever going to find a suitable mate and get married, you'll need to know how to cook, sew, and manage a house," Papa said.

"Maybe I won't get married. Maybe I'll end up an old maid like—" Allison halted her words. She knew she'd already said more than she should.

Aunt Catherine's face flamed as she stomped back to the refrigerator to put the eggs away.

The lump in Allison's throat thickened. As much as she didn't want to leave her home and spend the summer with relatives she couldn't remember, she didn't wish to seem ungrateful for Papa's unexpected birthday present. If her learning to cook and sew was important to him, then she would try to act more willing. But she doubted she would ever find a husband. Because none of the available young men in her community seemed interested in marrying a tomboy, unless she learned to be more feminine, she'd probably never catch any man's eye.

Allison forced her lips to form a smile as she looked at Papa. "I promise to make the best of my time in Missouri." *But I'll do it for you, not because I want to.*

Allison had a difficult time eating breakfast that morning. Every bite she took felt like cardboard in her mouth. All she could think about was the bus ticket lying on the counter across the room. Was Papa really sending her to Missouri so she could learn to manage a household? Or was the real reason to appease Aunt Catherine? Allison's cranky aunt rarely had a nice thing to say, but since Papa needed his sister's help, he'd probably do most anything to keep her from leaving—even if it meant sending Allison away for the summer.

When breakfast was over and the menfolk had gone outside to clean the milking barn, Allison and Aunt Catherine began cleaning up the kitchen.

"That was some birthday gift your daed gave you, wasn't it?" Aunt Catherine asked as she carried a stack of dishes to the sink.

Allison followed with the silverware. "Jah, I wasn't expecting a bus ticket to Missouri."

Aunt Catherine placed the dishes in the sink and ran water over them. "Your daed thinks going there will turn you into a woman, but if you don't listen to your aunt Mary any better than you do me, I doubt you'll learn much of anything."

Allison winced, feeling like she'd been slapped in the face with a dishrag. "I . . . I listen to you."

"You may listen, but you don't do as I say." Aunt Catherine grunted. "You've always had a mind of your own, even when you were a young *maedel*."

Allison silently reached for a clean dish towel.

"If you want to be a woman, you can do that right here," Aunt Catherine continued. "My *bruder* shouldn't have to spend his hard-earned money on a bus ticket to send you away so you can learn from your mamm's sister what you could learn from me."

Allison bit her tongue in order to keep from saying anything negative. Maybe being gone for a few months would be good for her. She picked up a glass and poked one end of the towel inside. *It will be a welcome change to be away from Aunt Catherine's angry looks and belittling words.*

A knock sounded on the back door, and Allison hurried to answer it. She found her friend Sally on the porch, holding a package wrapped in white tissue paper.

"Hallich gebottsdaag," Sally said, handing the gift to Allison. "Has it been a good birthday so far?"

Allison swallowed against the burning lump in her throat and gave a quick nod. She couldn't let on to Sally that the day had begun so terribly. Not with Aunt Catherine standing a few feet away at the kitchen sink.

"Danki for the gift," Allison said. "Won't you come in?"

Sally smiled, her blue green eyes fairly glistening. "Of course I'll come in. I want to see if you like the gift I brought."

Allison pulled out a chair at the kitchen table and offered Sally a seat.

"Aren't you going to sit with me and open your gift?" Sally asked.

Allison glanced at her aunt to get her approval. They were supposed to be doing the dishes, and she knew better than to shirk her duties.

Aunt Catherine grunted and gave a quick nod. "I guess it'll be all right if you finish drying the dishes after you're done opening Sally's gift."

I'll bet Aunt Catherine only said that because Sally's here and she's trying to make a good impression. Any other time, she would have insisted that I finish the dishes before I did anything else.

Allison took a seat next to Sally and tore the wrapping paper off the package. She discovered a book about the Oregon Trail inside. "Danki, Sally. This is very nice."

"You're welcome." Sally smiled. "Since you've always shown an interest in history, I thought you might enjoy reading about the pioneers who traveled to the West by covered wagon."

"I'm sure I will, and it'll give me something to read on my trip."

Sally tipped her head. "What trip is that?"

"I'm going to Webster County, Missouri—just outside the town of Seymour," Allison answered. "Papa bought me a bus ticket to Seymour for my birthday."

"Why Seymour?"

"My mamm's twin sister and her family live there, and Papa thought—"

"He thought Allison could learn how to run a household better there than she can here," Aunt Catherine interrupted. Her forehead wrinkled, and she pursed her lips. "Guess my brother thinks his wife's sister can teach Allison things I'm not able to teach her. He obviously thinks Mary King is more capable than me."

"I don't think Papa believes his sister-in-law is more capable," Allison said in her father's defense. "As he mentioned before breakfast, Aunt Mary knows a lot about sewing, and—"

"She can cook and clean like nobody's business." Aunt Catherine grunted. "That's exactly what Herman said."

"How long will you be staying in Missouri?" Sally asked, touching Allison's arm. "I hope not indefinitely, because I would surely miss you."

Allison shook her head. "I'll only be gone for the summer, so you shouldn't miss me too much. Besides, you'll have my bruder to keep you company while I'm gone."

Sally's cheeks turned as red as her hair, and she stared at the table. Peter and Sally had begun courting several months ago. Allison figured it was just a matter of time before they decided to get married.

"I hope you'll write me while you're gone," Sally said.

Allison smiled. "Of course I'll write. I hope you'll write, too."

Sally's head bobbed. "I'll be looking forward to hearing about all the fun you have while you're in Missouri."

Allison swallowed around the lump in her throat. *I doubt that I'll have any fun.*

When the bell above the door to the harness shop jingled, Aaron Zook looked up from the job he'd been assigned—cutting strips of leather. His best friend, Gabe Swartz, stepped into the room, carrying a broken bridle.

"Hey, Aaron, how's business?" Gabe asked as he dropped the bridle to the workbench.

"Fair to middlin'," Aaron replied. "Business always seems to pick up in the summertime."

Gabe glanced around. His hazel-colored eyes seemed to take in the entire room. "Where's Paul? I figured he'd be up front minding the desk while you were in the back room doing all the work." He chuckled. "Isn't that how it usually is?"

Aaron grimaced. He knew Gabe was only funning with him, but the truth was Aaron's stepfather did like to be in charge of the books. There were times when Aaron's father was still alive that helping in the harness shop had seemed like fun—almost a game. But when Aaron first began helping the man who eventually became his stepfather, he'd always felt like he was stuck with the dirty work. Now working here was just plain hard work—but at least he was getting paid for it.

"Paul, Mom, and my sisters, Bessie and Emma, went to Springfield for the day," Aaron said. "Bessie had an appointment with the dentist. Paul said they'd probably do some shopping and go out to lunch while they're there."

Gabe pushed a wavy brown lock of hair off his forehead. "What about your brothers? Didn't they go along?"

"Nope. Joseph and Zachary went to the farmers' market in Seymour. Davey's visiting one of his friends."

"Which left you here at the shop by yourself all day."

"Jah. Somebody has to keep the place open." Aaron stared wistfully out the window. "I do like working here, but on a sunny morning like this, I'd rather be fishing than working."

"Me, too."

"So how are things at your place?" Aaron questioned. "Has Melinda taken in any new critters lately?"

Gabe grinned. "Almost every week she finds some animal that's either orphaned or injured. Just yesterday she found a half-starved kitten out by the road. The pathetic little critter had one of those plastic things that holds a six-pack of soda pop stuck around its neck."

"Will the kitten be okay?"

"Jah. Melinda will see to that."

Aaron fingered Gabe's broken bridle. "Guess there's never a dull moment in your life, huh?"

"That's for sure." Gabe's eyes narrowed as he stared at Aaron. "When are you going to settle down and find a nice young woman to marry?"

Aaron's ears burned. "I'm not interested in marriage. I've told you that plenty of times already."

"Wouldn't you like someone to keep you warm on cold winter nights?"

"Rufus is good at that. He likes to sleep at the foot of my bed."

"*Puh*! No flea-bitten mongrel can take the place of a flesh-and-blood woman." Gabe poked Aaron's arm and chuckled. "Besides, think how nice it would be to have someone to cook, clean, and take care of you when you're old and gray."

"It'll be a long time before I'm old and gray, and I don't need anyone to care for me."

"What about love? Don't you want to fall in love?"

Aaron stiffened. Why did Gabe keep going on about this? *Is he trying to goad me into an argument? Or does he think it's fun to watch my face turn red?*

"I know you're dead set against marriage," Gabe continued, "but if the right woman came along, would you make a move to court her even if you didn't have marriage on your mind?"

Aaron shrugged. "Maybe, but she'd need to have the same interests as me. She'd have to be someone who isn't afraid of hard work or getting her hands dirty, either."

"You mean like your mamm?"

"Jah. She and my real daed worked well together in the harness shop. She and Paul did, too."

"I wonder if your mamm misses working here now." Gabe motioned to the stack of leather piled on the floor a few feet away. "I heard her tell my mamm once that she enjoyed the smell of leather."

"It's true; she does. So did my daed. He loved everything about this harness shop." Aaron picked up the bridle and ran his fingers over the broken end. "I love the feel of leather between my fingers. I'm hoping to take this shop over someday—when Paul's ready to retire."

"Do you think that'll be anytime soon?"

Aaron shook his head. "I doubt it. He seems to enjoy working here too much."

"Maybe he'll give the shop to you, the way my daed gave the woodworking business to me after Melinda and I got married."

Aaron squinted. "Are you saying I'd have to find a wife before Paul would let me take the place over?"

"Not necessarily."

"My real daed wanted me to have this business. He told me that more than once before he was killed."

Gabe leaned against the workbench. "You were pretty young back then. I don't see how you can remember much of anything that was said."

Aaron dropped the bridle, moved over to the desk, and picked up a pen and the work-order book. "I was barely nine when my daed's buggy was hit by a truck, but I remember more than you might think."

"Like what?" Gabe asked as he followed Aaron across the room.

Aaron took a seat at the desk. "I remember how the two of us used to go fishing together. I remember him teaching me to play baseball." Before Gabe could comment, Aaron glanced back at the bridle and said, "How soon do you need your bridle?"

"No big hurry. I've got others I can use for now."

"By the end of next week?"

"Sure, that'll be fine." Gabe moved away from the desk. "Guess I should get on home. Melinda and I are planning to go to Seymour later today. We want to see if the owner of the bed-and-breakfast needs more of her drawings or some of my handcrafted wooden items for his gift shop."

"See you Sunday morning at church, then. It's to be held at the Kings' place, right?"

"Jah." Gabe started for the door. "Maybe we can get a game of baseball going after the common meal," he called over his shoulder.

Aaron nodded. "Sounds like fun."

The door clicked shut behind Gabe, and Aaron headed to the back room to dye some leather strips. After that, he had a saddle to clean. Maybe if he finished up early, he'd have time to get in a little fishing. At least that was something to look forward to—that and a good game of baseball on Sunday afternoon.

Chapter 2

Allison stared vacantly out the window at the passing scenery as the bus took her farther from home and all that was familiar. She would be gone three whole months, living with relatives she didn't really know, in a part of the country she'd never seen before—all because Papa thought she needed to learn to be more feminine while she learned domestic chores.

Allison glanced at the canvas bag by her feet. Inside was the book Sally had given her, as well as some of Aunt Catherine's peanut brittle, which she planned to give Aunt Mary and her family. Allison's faceless doll was also in the bag. She'd had it since she was a little girl. Papa said Mama had made it, but Allison didn't remember receiving the doll. All her memories of Mama were vague. She'd been only seven when Mama died. Papa said a car had hit Mama's buggy when she'd pulled out of their drive-way one morning. Allison had supposedly witnessed the accident, but she had no memory of it. All these years, she'd clung to the bedraggled, faceless doll, knowing it was her only link to the mother she'd barely known. Allison had named the doll Martha, after Mama.

Allison reached down and plucked the cloth doll from the canvas satchel. Its arms had come loose long ago and had been pinned in place. Its legs hung by a couple of threads. Its blue dress and small white kapp were worn and faded. "Mama," she murmured against the doll's head. "Why did you have to leave me? If only I could remember your face."

Allison was sure if her mother were still alive, she would have mended the faceless doll. Whenever Allison had mentioned the doll to Aunt Catherine, the crotchety woman had said she was too busy to be bothered with something as unimportant as an old doll. But even if Aunt Catherine had been willing to fix the doll, she'd admitted the other day that she couldn't sew well.

As Allison continued to study her doll, she noticed a spot of dirt on its faceless face and realized that she felt as faceless and neglected as tattered old Martha. Tears blurred Allison's vision and trickled down her hot cheeks. *My life has no real purpose. I have no goals or plans for the future. I'm just drifting along like a boat with no oars. I have no mother, and Aunt Catherine doesn't love me. She doesn't care about anyone but herself.*

Allison had spent most of her life trying to stay out of Aunt Catherine's way rather than trying to learn how to run a home. Maybe a few months of separation would be good for both of them. Aunt Catherine would probably be happier with Allison gone.

More tears dribbled down Allison's cheeks. *I've never been to Missouri before. What will Aunt Mary and her family be like? Will I make any new friends there? Oh, Sally, I miss you already.*

Allison returned her doll to the satchel and reached

for the book Sally had given her. If she kept her mind busy reading, maybe she wouldn't feel so sad.

"Did you get Allison put on the bus okay?" Catherine asked Herman as he stepped onto the porch. She was shelling a batch of peas from the garden.

He nodded and took a seat beside her. "It was sure hard to see her go."

"Then why'd you buy that bus ticket for her birthday?"

"You know why, Catherine. I want Allison to have the chance to know her aunt Mary better and to learn to cook, sew, and keep house."

"Humph! She could have learned those things from me if she'd been willing to listen." *Plink. Plinkety-plink.* Catherine dropped several more peas into the bowl braced between her knees.

"You don't sew very well; you said so yourself." Herman pulled at a loose thread on his shirt. "Let's face facts, Catherine. You and Allison have never hit it off. I believe that's why she hasn't learned as much as she should have under your teaching."

"And you think she'll take to her aunt Mary better than me?"

"I'm hoping she does." Herman gave his beard a quick pull. "I'm also hoping Mary relates so well to Allison that she'll want to give up her tomboy ways and become a woman."

"Jah, well, I could have related better to the girl if she hadn't been so set on doing things her own way."

Catherine gave an undignified grunt. "Never did understand why Allison preferred to be outside doing chores with the boys when she should have been in the house learning to cook and clean."

"It might have helped if you'd been willing to let Allison try her hand at cooking more."

"I didn't like the messes she made." Catherine shrugged. "Besides, it's quicker and neater if I do the cooking myself."

Herman leaned heavily against the chair and closed his eyes. The morning sun felt warm and helped soothe his jangled nerves. He hadn't wanted to send Allison away. It had nearly broken his heart to see his only daughter board that bus, knowing she would be gone for three whole months and might even decide to stay in Missouri if she liked it there. But watching Allison turn into a tomboy and realizing that if she didn't learn some womanly things she would never find a man to marry had made Herman decide it was time for a change. If Allison stayed in Pennsylvania under the tutelage of his sister, she would never learn the skills of a good homemaker.

Herman grasped the arms of the chair and clenched his fingers. That was another reason he'd sent Allison to Missouri. She needed some time away from Catherine. He'd seen how frustrated she'd become the last few years, having to deal with his cantankerous sister. He'd even thought about asking Catherine to leave, but she'd been with them so long and really had no place else to go. His and Catherine's folks had been dead a good many years, and their siblings, who used to live in Ohio near Catherine, had moved to a newly established community in Wisconsin. Since Catherine had never married, Herman felt responsible for her. After his wife's death, he figured Catherine felt responsible for him and the children, too.

"Are you sleeping?"

Herman's eyes snapped open. "Uh . . . no. Just thinking, is all."

Catherine lifted the bowl of peas into her arms and stood. "Jah, well, you can sit out here and think all you like. I need to get inside and start fixing our meal."

Herman nodded. "Call me when it's ready."

With a weary sigh, Allison reached for her canvas tote and stood. It had taken a day and a half to get from Lancaster, Pennsylvania, to Springfield, Missouri. From Springfield, the bus had headed to the small town of Seymour, where someone was supposed to pick her up at Lazy Lee's Gas Station. Allison had slept some on the bus, but the seats weren't comfortable, and there wasn't much leg room. She hadn't rested nearly as well as she would have in her own bed.

Allison glanced down at her dark blue dress. It was wrinkled and in need of washing. She knew she must look a mess. Unfortunately, there was nothing she could do about that now, for the bus had just pulled into Lazy Lee's parking lot.

Allison gathered up her satchel and stepped off the

bus. She spotted a young Amish man with red hair standing beside an open buggy on the other side of the building. When he started toward her, she noticed his deeply set blue eyes and face full of freckles.

"You must be Allison," he said with a lopsided grin. She nodded. "Jah, I am."

"I'm your cousin, Harvey King." He motioned to the suitcases being taken from the luggage compartment in the side of the bus. "Show me which one is yours, and I'll put it in the buggy for you."

Allison pointed to a black canvas suitcase, and Harvey hoisted it and her small satchel into the back of his open buggy. Then he helped Allison into the passenger's side, took his own place, and gathered up the reins.

"My mamm will sure be glad to see you," he said as they pulled out of the parking lot. "Ever since your daed phoned and said you were coming, she's been bustling around the house doing all sorts of things to get ready for your arrival. She hasn't seen you since you were a little girl. I'll bet she'll be surprised to see how much you've grown."

Allison smiled. "Is your telephone outside in a shed?"

Harvey shook his head. "No, but they have one at the harness shop. From what I was told, your daed and Paul Hilty know each other from when Paul worked in his cousin's harness shop in Pennsylvania. Since Uncle Herman knew Paul had put a phone in at the shop, he called there and asked Paul to get the message to us that you were coming to visit for the summer."

"Ah, I see."

"I hope you don't mind a little detour, but I need to stop by the harness shop before we go home," Harvey said. "I would have done it on my way to Seymour, but I got a late start and didn't want to miss your bus."

"I don't mind stopping," Allison assured him. "I've been sitting on that bus so long, it will feel good to get out and move around."

"I figured you'd probably just want to wait in the buggy while I ran in and picked up my daed's new harness. But if you'd like to go into the shop or walk around outside the place, that's fine by me."

She nodded. "I like the smell of leather, so I think I'll go inside with you."

Harvey cast her a sidelong glance but made no comment. He probably figured she was strange for liking the smell of leather. He'd probably think she was even stranger if he knew all the tomboy things she liked to do.

"Are you finished pressing those rivets into that harness yet, Aaron?" Paul called from the front of the shop. "Ben King said his son would be over sometime today to pick it up, and it should have been ready this morning."

Aaron frowned. Why did his stepfather always have to check up on him? Did Paul think he was incapable of getting the job done on time? He clenched his teeth to keep from offering an unkind retort. Truth was, when Paul first came to Webster County for his brother's funeral and had stayed to help Mom in the harness shop, Aaron had resented Paul. He'd been worried that Paul wanted to marry his mother and take over the harness shop. Then when Paul had rescued Aaron from the top rung of the silo ladder, he and Paul had established a pretty good relationship. Paul had eventually married Aaron's mother, and things had remained fine between them—until recently, that is. For some reason, ever since Aaron had become a man, Paul had become kind of bossy, and for the last few months, he'd started talking to Aaron like he was a child again.

"Aaron, did you hear what I said?" Paul called, pulling Aaron's thoughts aside.

"I heard. The harness is almost done."

"Good, because I see Harvey pulling up outside."

Aaron snapped the last rivet into place, picked up the harness, and headed to the front of the shop. He reached Paul's desk just as the front door opened. In walked Harvey with a young Amish woman Aaron had never seen before. Her hair was the color of dark chocolate, she was of medium height and slender build, and her nose turned up slightly on the end. Had Harvey found himself a new girlfriend? If so, she wasn't from around here. Aaron knew all the young women in their small Amish community. Maybe she was from one of the towns near Jamesport, where a good number of Amish people lived.

"Afternoon, Harvey," Paul said with a friendly smile. "Your timing is good; we just finished your daed's harness."

"Great." Harvey turned to the young woman at his side. "This is Allison Troyer. She's my cousin from Pennsylvania, and she'll be staying with us for the summer."

Paul took a step forward. "You're Herman's daughter, aren't you?"

"Jah," Allison said with a nod.

"I haven't seen you since you were a little girl."

Allison opened her mouth as if to say something but closed it again.

"You came to my cousin's harness shop with your daed a couple of times."

"I . . . I don't remember."

"You were pretty young." Paul smiled. "Anyway, I took the message when he phoned to say you were coming."

How come I didn't know about it? Aaron wondered. *I had no idea Harvey had a cousin living in Pennsylvania.*

Paul took the harness from Aaron. "Here's what you came for, Harvey. I hope it's done to your daed's liking."

"Looks fine to me," Harvey said with a nod.

"Where are my manners?" Paul motioned to Aaron. "Allison, this is my son Aaron."

Stepson, Aaron almost corrected, but he caught himself in time. "It's nice to meet you," he mumbled.

She smiled, kind of shylike. "Same here."

"Are you related to Isaac and Ellen Troyer, who live not far from here?" Aaron asked.

"No, I don't know them," she said with a shake of her head.

"Guess I'd better settle up with you and get on home." Harvey moved over to the desk. "Mom's probably pacing the floors by now, waiting for me to show up with her niece."

As Paul wrote out the invoice and Harvey leaned on the desk, Aaron ambled over to one of their workbenches and picked up a piece of leather that needed to be cut and dyed. He was surprised when Allison followed.

"It smells nice in here," she said, tilting her head and sniffing the air.

"You really think so?"

"I sure do."

"Most women don't care much for the smells inside a harness shop. Except for my mamm, that is," Aaron amended. "She used to work here with my real daed when I was a young boy. Then she took the place over by herself for a time after he died." He glanced over his shoulder at Paul. "After Mom married Paul, she kept working in the shop, but then my grandparents' health started to fail, so she had to give up working here in order to see to their needs."

"I see."

Aaron's ears burned with embarrassment. He didn't know what had possessed him to blab all that information to a woman he'd only met.

31

"I can see why your mamm would enjoy working here," Allison said, motioning to the pile of leather on the floor. "This looks like a fun place to be."

"Some might see it as fun, but it's a lot of work."

"I'm sure it would be." Her fingers trailed over the end of the harness. "I'd like to know more about harness making."

Aaron was about to comment when Harvey sauntered up, holding his finished harness. "Guess we'd better get going," he said, nodding at Allison.

She gave Aaron a quick smile. "Maybe I'll see you again sometime and you can tell me more about harness making."

"No maybe about it. You'll see him at church tomorrow morning." Harvey winked at Aaron, but before Aaron could think of a sensible reply, Harvey and his cousin walked out the door.

"She seemed like a nice person, didn't she?" Paul asked, as Aaron resumed his work.

"Huh?"

"Harvey's cousin, Allison. She seemed real nice."

Aaron shrugged. "I guess so."

Paul thumped Aaron on the back. "How come your ears are so red?"

"Must be the heat. Summer weather makes its way indoors pretty quick on days like this."

Paul nodded and picked up a piece of leather lying on the workbench near him. "Just never saw your ears turn so red before."

Aaron just kept on working.

While Harvey guided his horse and buggy down Highway C, Allison sat in amazement, studying her surroundings. Everything looked so different from what she was used to seeing in Pennsylvania. There were no rolling hills—just a multitude of trees with Amish and English houses built on the land that had been cleared. Most of the homes looked old, and many were a bit rundown. Few had flowers in abundance, the way most Amish places did back home. The two-story gray and white home that loomed before them as they turned onto a graveled driveway was an exception. A bounty of irises danced in the breeze near the vegetable garden growing to the left of the house, and two pots of pink flowers graced the front porch.

Harvey had no more than guided the horse to the hitching rail when the front door opened. A middle-aged woman followed by a young boy and a girl hurried over to the buggy.

Allison climbed down and was surprised when the woman gave her a hug. "I'm your aunt Mary, and these are my youngest children: Sarah, who is twelve, and Dan, who's ten."

Allison noticed immediately that Aunt Mary had the same dark hair and brown eyes with little green flecks that she had. Since Allison barely remembered her mother, she couldn't be sure her mother's sister looked like Mama, but Papa had said they were identical twins. Mama probably would have looked much like Aunt Mary if she were still alive.

"It's nice to meet you, Aunt Mary," Allison said. She turned to face the children. "You, too, Cousin Sarah and Dan."

"Actually, we have met before," Aunt Mary said. "I came to Pennsylvania for your mamm's funeral."

Allison stared at the ground, struggling to remember the past. "Sorry, but I . . . I don't remember."

"You were quite young then, so I don't expect you would remember." Aunt Mary put her arm around Allison's shoulder. "Shall we go inside and have a glass of freshly squeezed lemonade? It's turned into a real scorcher today, and nothing cools a parched throat quite like cold lemonade."

Allison licked her lips, realizing that they were parched and she was rather thirsty. "That would be real nice."

"I'll put the horse away and bring in her luggage," Harvey said as Allison, Aunt Mary, and the two younger children headed for the house.

"Sounds good. When you're done, come join us in the kitchen," his mother called over her shoulder.

Allison began to relax. *Aunt Mary seems so pleasant—much different than Aunt Catherine. Of course, I'd best wait until I get to know her better to make any decisions.*

As Allison sat around the supper table that evening, she was amazed at the camaraderie between family members. Aunt Mary made no sharp remarks—only smiles and encouraging words. Uncle Ben was kind and friendly, but then Papa and her brothers had always been that way, too. It was Aunt Catherine who had made Allison feel as though she could do nothing right. No jokes were tolerated at Aunt Catherine's table, and she often hurried them through their meals, saying more chores needed to be done.

Allison had never been able to talk about her feelings with Aunt Catherine, either, and Papa sure didn't have much time to listen. Here, everyone seemed interested in what others in the family had to say.

She glanced at Cousin Harvey, who sat beside his fifteen-year-old brother, Walter. The younger teenaged boy had been in the fields with their father when Allison had arrived. This was the first chance she'd had to meet him. Both Harvey and Walter seemed polite and easygoing, and so did Dan and Sarah. Could the whole family be as pleasant as they seemed?

"Allison brought us some peanut brittle," Aunt Mary said to Uncle Ben. "Since it's your favorite candy, I hope you'll let the rest of us have some."

He chuckled, and his crimson beard jiggled up and down. "I'll share, but only a *bissel*."

"Ah, Dad," Walter said with a frown, "don't you think we deserve more than a little?"

Uncle Ben jiggled his eyebrows playfully. "Well, maybe." He smiled at Allison. "It was sure nice of your daed's sister to send the peanut brittle. She must be a very *gedankevoll* woman."

Allison almost choked on the piece of chicken she'd

put in her mouth. If Uncle Ben knew Aunt Catherine the way she did, he might not think she was so thoughtful.

"Are you all right?" Aunt Mary asked, patting Allison on the back.

"I'm fine. I almost choked on a piece of meat, but I'm okay." Allison reached for her glass and took a gulp of water.

"I met your aunt Catherine at your mamm's funeral," Aunt Mary said. "You said earlier that you don't remember me being there, right?"

Allison nodded. "I was only seven when Mama died, so I don't remember much of anything about that time."

"Are you saying you don't remember your mamm at all?" Uncle Ben asked with raised eyebrows.

"I have a few vague memories of her from before the accident, but that's all."

"Martha and I were so close when we were growing up," Aunt Mary said in a wistful tone. "It was hard on both of us when I moved to Missouri. We kept in touch through letters until her passing. I sure miss my twin sister."

"What made you move to Missouri?" Allison asked, not wishing to talk about her mother's death.

"That was my fault," Uncle Ben interjected. "I wanted to get away from all the tourists in Lancaster County. Since I had a brother who'd moved to Missouri, shortly after Mary and I got married, we packed up our things, hired a driver, and moved here to Webster County."

Allison wondered if her life would be any different if Aunt Mary and Uncle Ben still lived in Pennsylvania. Aunt Catherine wouldn't have needed to move in with them after Mama died if Aunt Mary had lived closer. She took another sip of water. *Oh, well. As Papa always says, "Since you can't change the past, you may as well make the best of the present." So I will try to enjoy my summer here,* she resolved.

Chapter 3

Before church the following morning, Allison stepped into the Kings' barn and was surprised to see how few people filled the backless wooden benches. At home, twice as many people would have attended, but then this Amish community was much smaller than hers in Lancaster County.

As she lowered herself to a bench on the women's side, someone touched her arm. She glanced to the left. A young, blond-haired woman smiled and said, "Hi. My name's Katie Esh." Her vivid blue eyes sparkled like ripples of water on a hot summer day, and a small dimple was set in the middle of her chin. Allison thought Katie was the prettiest young woman she'd ever seen. Not plain and ordinary like her. That's what Aunt Catherine had always said about Allison, anyway.

"What's your name?" Katie asked, nudging Allison's arm again.

"Oh, I'm Allison Troyer, visiting from Pennsylvania."

"How long will you be here?"

"Until the end of August. I'm staying with my aunt and uncle, Mary and Ben King."

Katie leaned closer and whispered in Allison's ear, "Looks like the service is getting ready to start. We can talk later, jah?"

Allison nodded and sat up straight, thinking about the way Aunt Catherine expected her to behave in church. She remembered one time when she'd been sitting next to Sally and had been caught whispering. Aunt Catherine had marched up to them and plucked Allison right off the bench. Allison had spent the next three hours sitting beside Aunt Catherine, worried that she might receive a spanking if she moved wrong or did anything Aunt Catherine disapproved of.

Allison glanced over her shoulder at Aunt Mary, sitting a few rows behind. *I wonder what kind of mother she is to her children. Is she really kind and gentle, the way she appeared to be last night, or does she have a mean streak like Aunt Catherine?*

Aaron's mind drifted from the sermon Bishop John was preaching as he glanced at the women's side of the room and spotted Allison Troyer staring out the open barn door. Would she rather be outdoors, or was she bored with the service? As much as Aaron hated to admit it, Allison had his full attention. Maybe it was the fact that she'd mentioned yesterday how she liked the smell of leather. Aaron smiled to himself. *Or maybe it's because—*

Aaron felt a jab to his ribs, and he looked over at his brother Joseph and frowned. "What'd you poke me for?" he whispered.

"Church is over," Joseph said with a smirk. "You looked like you were off in some other world, so I figured I'd better bring you back to this one."

Aaron grunted. "Very funny."

A short time later, Aaron followed the men up to the house, where the common meal would be served. He'd no more than taken a seat when he felt another sharp jab to the ribs. He glanced to the left and saw Gabe sitting beside him. "What'd you prod me for?"

Gabe snickered. "I was wondering why you're making cow eyes at that new girl, Allison."

"I'm not!" Aaron bit off the end of a fingernail and was about to flick it over his shoulder onto the floor, when Gabe grabbed his hand.

"That's a nasty habit, and we're not outside, so you'd better not do that."

"You're right." Aaron slipped the sliver of fingernail into his pants pocket.

"Are you ever planning to quit that awful habit?" Gabe questioned.

"Maybe someday—if I feel like it."

"Falling in love might make you give up your crude ways."

Aaron elbowed his friend. "A lot you know; I'm not crude."

"Jah, well, I know a man with a crush when I see one."

"I don't have a crush on anyone. I barely know her."

"Who?"

"Allison Troyer. That's who we were talking about, right?"

Gabe put his finger in the small of Aaron's back. "Since you barely know her, why don't you remedy that by going over and talking to her? Or are you too much of a chicken?"

"I'm not scared of anything."

"Then prove it."

Joseph, sitting on the other side of Aaron, nodded his blond head in agreement. "I think it's about time you took an interest in some nice young woman."

"Just so you two will get off my back, I will go speak to Allison," Aaron said, his jaw tight. "But it's not because I have an interest in her." He hopped off the bench and strolled across the room, heading for the kitchen. He stopped a few feet from the table where Allison and Katie were serving a group of men. His heart hammered so hard he feared it might break through his chest, and he took in a couple of deep breaths in order to steady his nerves. He couldn't march right up to Allison and start yammering away. What would he say? What if she thought he was trying to make a play for her? Then again, he didn't want Gabe and Joseph to think he was a coward.

Aaron took a step back and bumped a table leg, jostling Bishop Frey's glass of water.

"Whoa there! What do you think you're doing,

boy?" the man asked as he blotted the table with his napkin.

"S-s-sorry, Bishop. I didn't realize you were behind me." Aaron glanced around. Everyone in the room seemed to be staring at him, including Allison.

Oh, great. She probably thinks I'm a real klutz. Aaron slunk away, knowing he would probably be in for more ribbing from Gabe. He figured a little teasing from his friend would be better than facing Allison and feeling more foolish than he already did. No, he wasn't about to start up a conversation with her now.

Allison watched from the sidelines as a group of young men got a baseball game going in the field behind the Kings' place. She longed to join them but figured, since she was new here, it would seem forward if she asked to be part of the game. Besides, none of the other young women had joined the fellows.

"What are you doing over here?" Katie asked, stepping up to Allison. "I figured you'd be up on the porch with some of the women, visiting and sipping iced tea."

Allison shook her head. "To tell you the truth, I'd like to play baseball, but since the next best thing to playing the game is watching, I decided to stand here by the fence and watch."

"If you'd rather play ball, why aren't you?"

Allison shrugged. "I wasn't invited."

"Me neither, but I'd play if I wanted to, invited or

not." Katie grinned. "Who do you think is the cutest fellow here today?"

"I . . . I haven't given it much thought."

Katie leaned closer to Allison. "Can you keep a secret?"

"Jah, sure."

"I think the cutest fellow here is Joseph Zook." Katie pointed across the field. "He's the one with curly blond hair. That's his brother Aaron with dark hair. They don't look much alike, because Joseph looks like his real daed, and Aaron takes after his mamm."

Katie rushed on. "There's going to be a young people's gathering tonight at the Kauffmans' place. Do you think you might attend?"

"I guess that all depends on whether Harvey's planning to go."

"I'm sure he will; he usually does."

"Tell me about your family," Allison said, changing the subject.

Katie smiled. "Let's see now. There's me; my younger sister, Mary Alice; and my older brother, Elam, still living at home, and I've got three other brothers who are married and out on their own. What about you, Allison?" she asked. "How many *kinner* are in your family?"

Allison opened her mouth to reply when the ball *whooshed* toward her. Instinctively, she reached up and caught it.

"Wow, that was *wunderbaar*!" her cousin Harvey

exclaimed. "Never knew a girl could catch a ball so well. And with only one hand."

An eager smile sprang to Allison's lips. She wondered if she should tell Harvey she was an expert ballplayer or let him think she had caught it by accident. If she had remembered to pack her new baseball glove when she'd left home, she'd probably be even more anxious to join their game.

"Allison wants to be part of your game," Katie spoke up. "She told me that she'd rather play ball than visit."

Harvey tipped his head and grinned at Allison. "Is that so?"

She nodded and handed him the ball. "I've been playing baseball with my brothers since I was a little girl."

"Maybe you'd like to be on Aaron Zook's team. He's one player short, and if you don't mind playing with a bunch of rowdy fellows, we'd be happy to have you."

Allison looked over at Katie. "Would you like to play, too?"

Katie shook her head. "You go ahead. I'll stand here and cheer you on."

Allison followed Harvey across the field to where Aaron stood. Harvey explained the situation.

Aaron's dark eyebrows drew together, making Allison wonder if he disapproved.

"You can play left field," he finally said.

For the next hour, Allison caught several fly balls,

hit three home runs, and chocked up more points for Aaron's team than any other player.

When the game ended, she headed toward Katie, but Aaron stepped in front of her. He swiped a grimy hand across his sweaty forehead. "A lot of women I know like to play ball, and they do okay, but I've never met anyone who could catch the way you did today."

She grinned at him. "I've always liked playing ball."

He shuffled his feet in the dirt. "I . . . uh . . . guess I'll go get myself something cold to drink."

Allison nodded. "I worked up quite a thirst out there, so maybe I'll do the same."

Aaron hesitated and stared at the ground. "Maybe I'll see you tonight at the young people's gathering."

"Jah, maybe so."

Chapter 4

I am glad you were willing to go with me tonight," Harvey said as he helped Allison into his open buggy. "It'll be a good chance for you to get to know some of the other young people in our district."

Allison nodded. "I did get acquainted with Katie Esh after church today, as well as some of the fellows who were involved in the ball game."

Harvey chuckled. "I still can't get over how well you played. I'll bet Aaron Zook was glad I suggested you be on his team."

"I don't know about that, but I did enjoy playing."

They rode in silence. The only sounds were the

steady *clippety-clop* of the horse's hooves and the *whoosh* of the wind whipping against their faces.

"Seemed like you and Katie Esh hit it off pretty well today," Harvey said, breaking the quiet.

Allison nodded. "Katie seems real nice."

"Several of the guys would agree with you on that. Some I know of have been interested in Katie ever since they were in school."

"I can understand that. Katie's very pretty." Allison stared down at her hands. Her friend back home was being courted by Peter, and her new friend here had a boyfriend, too. If only some young man would take an interest in her, she might not feel like such a misfit.

"Think you might get up the nerve to ask someone to ride home in your buggy tonight?" Joseph asked Aaron as the two of them entered the Kauffmans' barn.

Aaron shook his head.

"If you were to ask someone, who would it be?"

"I just said I wouldn't be asking anyone."

"You never said that; only shook your head."

"Same difference."

"But if you were to ask someone, who would it be?"

"That's my business, don't you think?"

Joseph pulled off his straw hat. "Aren't you the testy one tonight? I was only making sure you aren't interested in the same girl I am."

"I'm not interested in Katie Esh, so don't worry. You've got the green light to ask her yourself."

A wave of heat washed over Joseph's cheeks. Could his older brother read his mind? Aaron had always been able to stay one up on him when they were boys. Maybe things weren't so different now. "How'd you know I was interested in Katie?"

"It doesn't take a genius to see that you're smitten with her. You act like a lovesick *hund* every time she's around."

"I'm no puppy dog."

"But you are lovesick, right?"

Joseph wrinkled his nose. "If you're not willing to tell me who you'd like to take home tonight, I'm not willing to say how I feel about Katie."

"Suit yourself, because I'm not telling you a thing. Besides, I already know how you feel about Katie." Aaron sauntered off toward the refreshment table, leaving Joseph alone.

When Joseph glanced across the barn and saw Katie sitting on a bale of straw, he began rehearsing what he should say to her. *Should I come right out and ask if I can give her a ride home tonight, or would it be better if I dropped a couple of hints to see what she might be thinking?*

Drawing in a deep breath for added courage, he made his way to Katie's side. She looked up at him and smiled. "I'm glad to see you made it, Joseph. I saw Aaron over at the refreshment table, but I wasn't sure if you were here."

He took a seat beside her and decided to plunge ahead before he lost his nerve. "I . . . uh, came in my

46

own buggy tonight, and I was hoping—" A trickle of sweat rolled down Joseph's nose, and he reached up to wipe it away.

"You were hoping what?"

He licked his lips and swallowed hard.

"Do you need something to drink?"

"No, no. I'm just feeling a little nervous, is all."

"How come?"

You. You're the reason I've got a passel of butterflies tromping around in my stomach. Joseph drew in a quick breath and plastered a smile on his face. His mother had always said a friendly smile was the best remedy for a case of nerves. "I . . . uh . . . was wondering . . . "

Katie leaned a little closer to Joseph. "What were you wondering?"

"Would you be willing to ride home with me in my buggy tonight?"

Her eyes widened. "You want me to go to your house after the gathering?"

"No, no," he stammered. "I'd like to give you a ride home to your house. That is, if you're willing."

Katie's smile stretched from ear to ear. "Jah, Joseph. I'm more than willing."

Allison stepped into the Kauffmans' barn, and the first person she spotted was Aaron Zook. He stood next to the refreshment table, holding a paper cup in one hand and a cookie in the other. She was tempted to go over and talk to him but thought that would

47

seem too forward. Besides, Aaron could very well have a girlfriend, and Allison didn't want to do anything that might cause trouble between them if he did.

Glancing around the barn, she discovered Katie sitting on a bale of straw talking to Joseph Zook. Since they both had blond hair and blue eyes, they made quite a striking pair. Allison remembered Katie had mentioned earlier that she had her eye on Joseph. From the looks of the smile she saw on Joseph's face, she had a hunch he might be asking if he could give Katie a ride home.

Katie looked over at Allison just then and motioned her to come over. Allison hesitated until Joseph headed over to the refreshment table. Then she scurried over and took a seat on the bale of straw next to Katie.

"I'm glad you could make it tonight," Katie said.

Allison smiled. "Aunt Mary thought it would be good for me to come so I can get better acquainted with everyone."

Katie nodded and glanced over at Joseph. "Do you have a steady boyfriend back home?"

"Oh, no," Allison was quick to reply.

"Someday you will, I'm sure." Katie released a contented sigh. "Joseph Zook just asked if I'd like a ride home in his buggy tonight."

"What'd you say?"

"I said I'd be willing, of course." Katie nudged Allison's arm. "From the way some of the fellows are watching you, I'd say you might have your pick of whose buggy you get to ride home in."

Allison's eyebrows shot up. "What do you mean? I haven't noticed anyone staring at me."

"If you keep your eyes open, you will."

With a quick glance around the room, Allison scanned the faces of the young men present. Katie was right—one man was watching her. She hadn't seen him in church. The young man had shiny black hair worn a bit longer than any of the other fellows. When he caught her looking at him, he winked and lifted his hand.

Allison looked away. "Who is that guy leaning against the wall over there?" she asked Katie.

"Where?"

Allison nodded with her head and said quietly, "Over there by the back wall. The one with the hair black as coal."

"Oh, that's James Esh, my cousin. He's kind of wild, but I think he's harmless enough." Katie leaned closer to Allison. "Was he staring at you?"

"Jah. He winked at me."

Before Katie could respond, Joseph showed up with a plate of cookies and some pretzels, which he handed to Katie.

"Danki, Joseph." Katie scooted over, and he plunked down beside her.

Joseph glanced over at Allison and smiled. "I was impressed with how well you played ball today."

Allison smiled. "Danki."

"My brother Aaron wasn't too happy about being one player short at the beginning of the game, but after you joined, his team sure racked up the points."

"I was glad I could play. It was fun. We don't usually play ball after church in my district back home."

Just then, James showed up, carrying a plate of cookies. "Since we haven't been properly introduced, I thought I'd come over and say hello," he said, offering Allison a crooked grin.

"I'm Allison Troyer."

"And I'm—"

"My pushy cousin James," Katie cut in.

James's dark brows drew together as he scowled at her. "I can speak on my own behalf, you know." He squeezed onto the bale of straw beside Allison and handed her the cookies. "I thought you might be hungry."

Allison took one with chocolate frosting. "Danki."

Allison, James, Katie, and Joseph visited until the song leader called out the first song—"Mocking Bird Hill." James kept time to the music by tapping his finger on Allison's arm. His attention made her feel nervous, but she felt flattered, too.

When the singing ended, Allison decided to leave the stuffy barn and breathe some fresh air. Maybe she would join the group that had begun a game of volleyball.

"Hey, where are you going?" James called.

"Outside."

"Mind if I come with you?"

"No."

James joined Allison under a maple tree, where she stood staring up at the moonlit sky. "Sure is pretty tonight," he whispered against her ear. "Some of those stars are so bright they look like headlights in the sky."

Allison nodded. Being this close to James made her feel jittery as a june bug.

"Say, I was wondering if you'd be willing to let me take you home tonight."

Allison shivered even though the evening air was quite warm and muggy. Should she allow James to escort her back to Aunt Mary's? She'd only met him and didn't know anything about him other than the little bit Katie had shared. Still, if she accepted the ride, it would leave Cousin Harvey free to escort someone home without her tagging along.

"What's your answer?" James prompted.

"I . . . I guess it would be okay, but I need to speak with my cousin first."

"What for?"

"I can't take off without telling him. He'd probably be worried."

James pointed to a buggy parked near the end of the barn. "That's my rig—the one with the fancy silver trim. If Harvey's okay with me taking you home, then meet me over there."

Allison hurried off to look for her cousin. She found him talking to a young woman he introduced as Clara Weaver. From the affectionate looks the young couple gave each other, Allison figured Clara must be Harvey's girlfriend.

"Someone has asked to give me a ride home," Allison said to Harvey. "If you don't mind me going, then you won't have to bother taking me back home."

Harvey quirked an eyebrow. "Whose buggy are you riding in?"

"James Esh. He's Katie's cousin."

"I know who he is, and I'd rather you didn't ride in his buggy."

"Why not?"

Harvey leaned closer to Allison. "James is kind of wild; I'm not sure he can be trusted. I can't stop you from riding home in his buggy, but I don't think it's a good idea."

"He seems nice enough to me," Allison said. "Besides, I think I'm old enough to take care of myself."

Harvey shrugged. "Suit yourself. I'll see you at home then."

Aaron stood in the shadows watching James help Allison into his buggy. A feeling of frustration welled up in him. He'd spent most of the evening watching Allison and James as they sat together on a bale of straw, and now the fellow was obviously taking her home. He scuffed the toe of his boot in the dirt. *James isn't right for Allison. He's a big flirt, and he's way too wild.*

Aaron knew that James, who had recently turned twenty-one, was still going through his *rumschpringe*. The unruly fellow had a mind of his own and liked to show off with his fancy buggy and unmanageable horse.

He shouldn't be using that spirited gelding for a buggy horse, Aaron fumed. *And he shouldn't be escorting a woman home in a buggy pulled by that crazy critter.*

When James backed his buggy away from the barn, Aaron slunk back into the shadows and ambled toward his buggy. *Don't know why I care what Allison does. It's none of my business if she's interested in James or any other fellow.*

"I hope things are going well at the young people's gathering this evening," Mary said to Ben as the two of them sat at the kitchen table drinking lemonade.

"I'm sure everyone's having a good time." Ben reached across the table and patted her hand. "Remember how much fun we used to have when we attended young people's functions?"

Mary smiled at the memory of the evening when Ben had asked for the first time if he could give her a ride home in his buggy. She'd known from that moment that they would one day get married. "I wonder how Harvey will work things out if he wants to give some young woman a ride home tonight," she said.

"What do you mean?"

"Since he escorted Allison to the gathering, he'll have to bring her home."

Ben shrugged his broad shoulders. "Maybe Allison

will catch some young fellow's eye, and he'll ask to give her a ride home."

Mary took a sip of lemonade. "I hope it's someone nice and not one of those fellows like James Esh or Brian Stutzman who likes to show off."

"I'm sure if someone like that were to offer Allison a ride home, her answer would be no."

On the ride home, Harvey's words of warning echoed in Allison's head. She'd chosen to ignore her cousin's advice, not wishing to judge James without getting to know him. After all, it wasn't as if he was asking to court her. It was a ride home in his buggy—nothing more.

"You don't talk much, do you?" James asked, breaking into Allison's thoughts.

She shrugged. "I do when there's something to say."

He chuckled and reached for her hand. "A pretty girl like you doesn't need to say anything as far as I'm concerned."

She eased her hand away and tucked a wayward strand of hair back under her kapp. She wasn't used to receiving such compliments and wasn't sure how to respond. "Your horse is nice looking, and he trots very well," she said, for lack of anything better to say.

"As far as I'm concerned, he's one of the finest. He can get pretty feisty when he wants to, though."

"I've ridden bareback a time or two, though never on a spirited horse."

James glanced over at her, and his dark eyebrows drew together. "You like to ride horses?"

She nodded. *Does he think I'm a tomboy? Should I have kept that information to myself?*

"Besides owning a high-spirited horse, I also own a car," James said.

"You do?"

He nodded. "I was thinking maybe sometime you'd like to ride to Springfield with me, and we can do something fun. There's not much to do around here."

"Oh, I don't know."

"You haven't joined the church yet, have you?"

"No, I . . . I don't feel quite ready."

"That means you're still going through rumschpringe, so you ought to be able to go most anywhere with me." He reached across the seat and touched her arm. "Think about it, okay?"

Allison gave a quick nod. Being with James made her feel nervous, yet she felt an attraction to him.

They rode in silence. The only sounds were the steady *clop-clop* of the horse's hooves and the creaking of the crickets coming from the woods along the road. When they turned up the driveway leading to Aunt Mary and Uncle Ben's place, James pulled back on the reins. The horse and buggy came to a halt, and he slipped one arm around Allison's shoulders. "I'd really like to see you again. If you're not interested in going to Springfield, maybe we could go on a picnic sometime." He smiled.

Allison swallowed hard. "That sounds nice, but my

aunt mentioned last night that she'll need help with her garden this summer. I'll probably be kept pretty busy."

"You can't work every minute."

"That's true. I guess I'll just have to see how it goes."

James leaned toward her suddenly and bent his head. Before Allison knew what had happened, his lips touched hers with a kiss that took her breath away. Except for her father's occasional pecks on the cheek, she'd never been kissed and hadn't known quite what to expect.

He tickled her under the chin. "I hope to see you again, Allison."

No words would come, so Allison merely nodded and hopped down from the buggy. Then she sprinted up the driveway toward the house without looking back. Her heart pounded so hard, she feared it might explode. As she reached the porch, she heard James call to his horse, "Giddyup there, boy!"

A slight breezed swept under the eaves of the porch and pushed the mugginess away. "That was my first kiss," she murmured.

Chapter 5

Allison pulled the log-cabin-patterned quilt up over her bed and straightened the pillows. She picked up her faceless doll, placed it at the foot of the bed, and took a seat. Tears gathered in her eyes as she stroked the small kapp perched on the doll's head. Looking at it reminded her of home.

After the pleasant welcome Allison had received last Saturday, she thought she might do okay here. Yet now she found herself missing Papa, Peter, and Sally—everyone but Aunt Catherine. It was actually a relief to be out from under her aunt's scrutinizing eyes and sharp tongue.

Allison's thoughts shifted to the evening before and how James Esh had brought her home from the singing and then stolen a kiss. She was flattered by his attention and wondered if he'd offer to give her a ride home from the next young people's gathering. If he did, what should her response be? Despite the fact that she found James attractive and exciting, his boldness frightened her.

A vision of Aaron Zook flashed across Allison's mind—brunette hair, dark eyes, square jaw, and a shy-looking smile. It seemed odd that Aaron hadn't said more than a quick hello to her last night, since after church he'd asked if she'd be attending. Maybe he had only asked out of politeness.

Allison hadn't seen Aaron with any young woman last night, so if he had a girlfriend, she must not have been at the gathering.

A knock on the bedroom door startled Allison, and she jumped up. "Come in."

The door opened and Aunt Mary stepped into the room. "I was wondering if you were up yet."

"Jah, I'm up. I was just getting ready to do up my hair." Allison moved over to the small mirror hanging above her dresser. She picked up her comb, made a part down the middle of her hair, rolled it back on the sides, and secured it into a bun.

"Did you have fun at the young people's gathering last night?" Aunt Mary asked. "Since I was in bed when you got home, I didn't get the chance to ask."

"It was okay."

"When Harvey came downstairs this morning, he mentioned that James Esh gave you a ride home last night."

Allison nodded. She hoped the warmth she felt on her cheeks wouldn't let Aunt Mary know how embarrassed she felt over the kiss James had given her.

"In case you didn't know, James hasn't joined the church yet." Aunt Mary's brows furrowed. "You might watch yourself around James, because from what I've heard, he's kind of wild."

"I don't think James is really interested in me, but I'll be careful, Aunt Mary."

"I hope so, dear one." Aunt Mary moved over to the bed and picked up the faceless doll. "It looks like this poor thing is in need of repair."

Allison set her kapp on the back of her head. "According to my daed, my mamm made it for me when I was little. I don't remember that, but I've kept it because it reminds me that I had a mamm once."

Aunt Mary patted Allison's arm. "I'm sorry about that." She took a seat on the edge of the bed and placed the doll in her lap. "Is there a reason this poor thing is in such bad shape?"

"I . . . I don't know how to fix it." Allison sighed. "I

asked Aunt Catherine several times to repair the doll, but she said she wasn't much of a seamstress and was too busy to mess with something as unimportant as a faceless doll."

"Are you saying no one has ever taught you to sew?"

Allison nodded. "Whenever I tried on my own, I either managed to stick myself with the needle, or the thread never seemed to hold."

"Would you like to learn to use my treadle machine?"

Allison nibbled on the inside of her cheek. Truth be told, she'd never had a desire to sew.

"We could begin by repairing your faceless doll. Then later, when we have more time, I'd be happy to show you how to make a doll from scratch."

"Well, I—"

"I haven't made a faceless doll for some time, since most Amish children don't play with that kind of doll much anymore." Aunt Mary smiled. "I think it would be fun for you to make one, though. You might even want to sell some dolls at the farmers' market or in one of the gift shops in Seymour."

The thought of making some money appealed to Allison, but she wasn't sure she wanted to learn how to sew in order to accomplish that. *Of course,* she reminded herself, *the reason Papa sent me here is so I can learn to do more womanly things. If I'm ever to find a husband, I'll need to know how to sew, whether I like it or not.*

"Jah, okay," she finally said. "I'd be happy if you could show me how to use the sewing machine."

"Has the mail come yet?" Herman asked as he entered the kitchen after finishing his morning chores.

Catherine, who was sitting at the table, nodded and motioned to a stack of letters on the counter.

"Any word from Allison?"

"Not a thing."

Herman compressed his lips. "That's strange. I thought for sure there would be a letter from her by now."

"Your sister-in-law is probably keeping the girl too busy to write. She's supposed to be learning how to run a home, after all."

Herman noticed the bitter tone in his sister's voice. Was she jealous because Mary possessed home-making skills she didn't? Or could she be angry because having Allison gone meant she was stuck doing all the housework on her own?

"Is there any iced tea?" he asked.

Catherine shook her head. "I didn't make any cold tea today. Just some hot peppermint tea to soothe my stomach."

"What's wrong with your stomach? Are you feeling *grank*?"

"I don't think I'm sick; just a bit of indigestion is all." She shrugged. "It's probably those greasy sausage links I ate for breakfast. Never did care much for sausage."

"Then why'd you fix them?"

"That's what you and Peter said you wanted this morning."

In all the years Herman's sister had been living with them, he had never known her to cater to anyone's whims. Maybe she thought, with Allison gone and him missing her so much, she needed to be more agreeable.

"I'd better change out of these grubby clothes," he said. "I hope your stomach settles down soon."

Catherine grunted.

Herman stomped up the stairs, wondering why he'd bothered to say anything positive to Catherine. She seemed determined to spend the rest of her days finding fault and complaining about something or other. *Which is one of the reasons I sent Allison away for the summer. If I had the time, I'd take a vacation from that negative sister of mine myself!*

Aaron had just finished his chores in the barn and was about to head to the harness shop, when he spotted his collie crouched in the weeds near the garden. He moved closer to see if the dog had a mouse or some other critter cornered and discovered Rufus had a kitten between his paws. "Come here and leave that poor animal alone!"

The collie released a pathetic whimper and backed away slowly. Aaron figured the cat would take off like a flash, but it just lay there, still as could be.

"Rufus, if you killed Bessie's kitten, she'll have

your hide. Mine, too, for letting you run free." Aaron squatted in front of the tiny gray kitten and was relieved to see that it was still breathing. After a quick examination, he realized there were no teeth marks.

Aaron returned to the barn, placed the cat with its mother, and then tied Rufus up for the rest of the day.

When Aaron entered the harness shop a short time later, he found Paul at his workbench, assembling an enormous leather harness for a Belgian draft horse.

"How come you're late?" Paul asked.

"I caught Rufus with one of Bessie's kittens. I knew if I didn't get the critter away from him quickly it would soon be dead."

"You'd better keep that dog tied. At least until the kittens are big enough to fend for themselves."

"He's tied up now."

"That's good, because Bessie would have a conniption if something happened to one of her cats." Paul motioned to a tub sitting off to one side. "Better get started cleaning and oiling James Esh's saddle. He dropped it by on Friday afternoon while you were up at the house getting our lunches."

The mention of James's name set Aaron's teeth on edge. He'd never liked that fellow much. Ever since they were children, James had been a showoff and a bit of a rebel. Aaron hadn't liked the way James had looked at Allison last night at the young people's gathering, either. He especially didn't like seeing the two of them drive away in James's buggy after the gathering was over. *I hope he didn't try anything funny with Allison. If only I'd had the nerve to ask about giving her a ride myself.*

Aaron balled his fingers into tight fists. *What am I thinking? I'm not interested in a relationship with Allison. Courting leads to marriage, and I'm not getting married!*

"Aaron, did you hear what I said?"

Aaron whirled around. "Huh?"

Paul pointed to the tub. "The saddle needs to be cleaned."

"Jah, okay. I'll see that it gets done." Aaron set to work, but it was hard to concentrate when he kept thinking about Allison.

He shook his head in an attempt to get himself thinking straight. Why was he thinking about a woman who would be leaving in a few months—especially when he was dead set against love and marriage? *It's probably because she took an interest in the harness shop.*

Aaron and Paul worked in silence for the rest of the morning, interrupted only by an English customer who dropped off two broken bridles and a worn-out harness that needed to be replaced. By noon, Aaron had James's saddle finished, and he'd also done some work at the riveting machine on a new harness for Noah Hertzler.

"I think I'll go up to the house and see if your mamm's got lunch ready," Paul said as he headed for the door.

"Did you plan to bring the food back, or should we

63

close the shop and eat in Mom's kitchen today?" Aaron asked.

"I'll bring it back." Paul nodded toward the finished saddle. "James Esh said he'd be here around noon, and I don't want to miss him." The door closed behind him, but a few minutes later it opened again.

"Came to get my saddle," James announced as he stepped into the building. The straw hat he wore was shaped a little different than most Amish men's in their area, and it had a bright red band around the middle.

Anything to let everyone know he's going through his running-around years, Aaron thought. *I wonder if James will decide to jump the fence and go English.*

"Your saddle's ready and waiting," Aaron said, motioning to the workbench across the room.

James sauntered over to the saddle and leaned close, like he was scrutinizing the work Aaron had done. "Hmm . . . Guess it'll be good enough."

Aaron bit back an unkind retort and moved to Paul's desk. He reached into the metal basket and handed James his bill.

James squinted at the piece of paper. "This is pretty high for just a cleaning and oiling, wouldn't you say?"

Aaron shrugged. "I don't set the prices. If you've got a problem with the price, you'd best take it up with Paul."

"Paul, is it? Since when did you start callin' your daed Paul?"

64

Aaron shrugged. He didn't think he had to explain himself to James.

James glanced around the room. "Where is Paul, anyway?"

"He went up to the house to get our lunch. You can wait if you want to talk to him about the bill."

"Naw, I don't have any time to waste today." James reached into his pocket and pulled out a couple of large bills. He slapped the money down, then sauntered back to his saddle, which he easily hoisted onto his broad shoulders. He was almost to the door when he pivoted toward Aaron. "Did you know that I escorted that new girl from Pennsylvania home from the gathering last night? Allison Troyer, that's her name."

Aaron gritted his teeth. Did James have to brag about everything he did?

"Allison sure is cute," James said with a crooked grin. "Don't you think so?"

"I hadn't noticed." Aaron's fingers made a fist as he fought for control. He knew it would be wrong to provoke a fight, but at the moment, he felt like punching James in the nose.

Just then, the front door swung open and Paul stepped into the room, carrying a wicker basket. "How are you, James?"

"Doin' real good," James replied with a nod.

"I see you've got what you came for." Paul motioned to the saddle perched on James's shoulders.

"Jah. I'm headed home."

James made no mention of how much the cleaning and oiling had cost, and Aaron figured James had only made an issue of it just to see if he could get a rise out of him. The ornery fellow had a knack for irritating folks—especially Aaron.

"Well, I'd best be on my way. I might stop by the Kings' place sometime soon and see if their niece wants to go out with me." James had his back to Aaron, so Aaron couldn't see the fellow's face, but he had a feeling there was a wily-looking smile plastered there. "See you later, Paul. You, too, Aaron."

When the door shut behind James, Paul placed the basket on the desk in front of Aaron. "You ready to eat, son? There are a couple of roast beef sandwiches in here, as well as a carton of your mamm's tangy potato salad."

Aaron shook his head. "I'm not hungry."

"You need to eat something. Besides, your mamm worked hard making our lunches. She'd be real disappointed if you didn't eat yours."

"Oh, all right." It would be a shame to let a tasty roast beef sandwich go to waste on account of his dislike for James Esh.

"I just got around to checking for mail, and I discovered a letter in the box for you," Aunt Mary said as she entered the kitchen, where Allison was cutting slices of ham for their lunch.

"Is it from my daed?" Allison asked.

"No, it's from someone named Sally Mast." Aunt

66

Mary placed the mail on one end of the counter. "If you'd like to read it now, I'll take over making the sandwiches."

"Are you sure you wouldn't mind? Sally's my best friend, and I sure do miss her. I'd like to see what she has to say."

"I don't mind at all. Enjoy your letter, and feel free to answer it now, too." Aunt Mary moved over to the counter, took the knife from Allison, and started slicing the ham.

"Danki." Allison could hardly believe how agreeable Aunt Mary seemed to be. If Aunt Catherine had been getting the mail, she wouldn't have told Allison she had a letter until lunch had been served and the dishes had been washed and put away.

Allison thumbed through the mail until she located Sally's letter. Taking a seat at the table, she opened the envelope and silently read her friend's letter:

Dear Allison,

How are things in Missouri? Do you like it there? Have you made any new friends?

I miss you. We all do—your daed, Peter, and the rest of your family.

Allison grimaced. *Sally didn't mention anything about Aunt Catherine missing me. She's probably hoping I'll decide to stay here in Missouri and never come home.*

"Is everyone all right at home?" Aunt Mary asked.

"That frown you're wearing makes me think something might be wrong."

"Nothing's wrong," Allison said with a shake of her head. "Sally's letter says I'm missed."

"And I'm sure you're missing your family back home, too."

"Everyone but Aunt Catherine," Allison mumbled.

"What was that?"

"Oh, nothing. It wasn't important." Allison returned to the letter:

I probably shouldn't say anything just yet, but I think Peter's on the verge of asking me to marry him. If he does, I'll want you to be one of my attendants.

Write back soon and tell me all about Webster County. I want to know about everything you're doing.

Your best friend for always,
Sally

Allison was pleased to hear that Sally and Peter might be getting married soon, but she couldn't help feeling a pang of envy, wondering if she would ever become a bride. She moved over to the desk across the room and took out a writing tablet and a pen. Returning to the table, she wrote a letter to her friend:

Dear Sally,
It was good hearing from you. I'm glad things are going well for you and Peter. Be sure and let

me know when he asks you to marry him. I miss you a lot, but I'm making some new friends here, too, which helps me not to feel so homesick.

Things are so different from what I'm used to in Lancaster County. They drive only open buggies, which is fine during the warmer months, but I have to wonder how they manage during the cold winter months.

Aunt Mary is going to teach me to sew, but we'll have to see how that goes; I'll probably make a mess of things. I still prefer doing outdoor things better than household chores, but maybe I'll learn to like some domestic things, too.

A young man named James gave me a ride home from a young people's gathering awhile back. Don't tell anyone, but he gave me my first kiss. It wasn't quite what I expected, but it felt good to know he found me attractive enough to kiss. I've always felt so plain, and since I'm a tomboy, I didn't think anyone would ever want to kiss me.

"Lunch is about ready now," Aunt Mary said, touching Allison's shoulder.

Allison quickly folded the letter, slipped it into an envelope, and jumped up from the table. She would finish writing later.

Chapter 6

*K*eep your legs pumping while you hold the material just so," Aunt Mary said as she showed Allison how to use her treadle sewing machine.

It looked easy enough when Aunt Mary did it, but when Allison tried, things didn't go nearly so well. On her first attempt, she either pumped the treadle too fast or too slow. Then when she thought she had the hang of things, she pushed the hand wheel backwards and stitched right off the piece of cloth.

On Allison's next attempt, she stitched the end of her apron to the material. "I don't know how that happened," she muttered, pulling the thread from the scrap of fabric. "Makes me wonder if I'll ever get the hang of things."

"Try it again," Aunt Mary encouraged. "I'm sure you'll get it soon enough."

Allison pumped up and down with her feet as she guided the wheel with one hand and directed the cotton material with the other. When the thread snapped, so did her patience. "I'm no good at this!" She pushed her chair away from the machine and stood. "I'd rather do something else, if you don't mind."

Aunt Mary put her arm around Allison. "You'll catch on if you give it a chance. The more you practice, the better you'll get."

Allison shrugged. "Can it wait until later? It's such

a nice day. I wouldn't mind going fishing if there's someplace nearby— and if I can borrow someone's pole."

"There's a pond up the road that has some good bass in it. I'm sure Harvey wouldn't mind if you used his pole. But I don't think it's a good idea for you to go fishing alone."

"I'll be fine. I go fishing by myself a lot back home."

"Maybe so, but I'd feel better if you took one of your cousins with you," Aunt Mary insisted. "Dan's out in the garden pulling weeds with Sarah, but I'm sure he'd be happy to join you at the pond for a while."

Allison figured it wouldn't be so bad to have her ten-year-old cousin tag along. At least she'd have someone to talk to if the fish weren't biting. "That's fine with me," she said with a smile.

When Allison left the room, Mary took a seat in front of the sewing machine. *I can't believe a woman Allison's age doesn't know how to sew,* she thought as she picked up the piece of material Allison had been working on. *What kind of a woman is Herman's sister that she's never taught Allison to cook or sew?*

Mary remembered getting a letter from Allison's mother once, where she'd mentioned how unfriendly Catherine had been when they'd gone to visit Herman's family in Ohio. She'd said that Catherine had seemed distant and unhappy. Mary wondered what could have happened in Catherine's past that had left her with such a sour attitude. Whatever it was, it shouldn't have kept Catherine from teaching Allison the necessary skills for becoming a homemaker.

The back door opened with a bang, interrupting Mary's thoughts. She went to the kitchen, thinking maybe Allison had come back inside. Instead, she found her daughter Sarah.

"Hi, Mama." Sarah swiped at the perspiration on her forehead and sighed. "It's hot out in the garden, so I decided to come inside for somethin' cold to drink."

"Would you like iced tea or lemonade?" Mary asked.

"Water's fine and dandy." Sarah grimaced. "Dan left me alone to pull all the weeds while he took off for the pond with Allison. He sure doesn't care about helpin' me one iota."

"When Allison said she wanted to go fishing, I suggested that Dan go along," Mary explained. "I didn't think it would be a good idea for her to go traipsing off by herself when she doesn't know the area very well."

"Guess that makes sense."

"I suppose I should have asked if you wanted to go fishing, too."

Sarah wrinkled her freckled nose. "No way! I don't like fishin'!"

"Why not?"

Sarah held up one finger. "Too many bugs bite you." A second finger came up. "On a day like this, the sun's too hot to sit for hours waitin' and hopin' a fish might snag your line." She extended a third finger. "If you do catch any fish, you've gotta touch their slimy bodies!"

Mary chuckled. One young woman living in this house was certainly no tomboy!

Aaron rubbed at a kink in his lower back and glanced at the clock on the far wall. It was almost three thirty, and there hadn't been a single customer since noon. Paul had taken Mom, Grandpa, Grandma, and the girls into Springfield for the day, since both Grandpa and Grandma had doctor's appointments. Joseph, Zachary, and Davey were helping one of their neighbors in the fields. That left Aaron alone in the shop, which was just fine with him. But he was tired of working, and for the last several days he'd been itching to go fishing. Since things were slow, there would be no harm in heading to the pond. The folks had said they might go out for supper after their shopping and appointments were done, so Aaron was sure they wouldn't be back until late evening. That left him plenty of time.

He removed his work apron, hung it on a wall peg, turned off the gas lamps, and put the CLOSED sign in the front window. *Think I'll untie Rufus and take him along. The poor critter deserves some fun in the sun.*

Allison and Dan had been sitting on the grassy banks by the pond for nearly an hour without getting a single bite, and Allison's patience was beginning to wane.

"Are you sure there's any fish in here?" she asked her young cousin.

Dan's head bobbed up and down. "Oh, jah. Me and my daed have taken plenty of bass and catfish out of this here pond."

Allison sighed. "Maybe they're just not hungry today."

"We could move to a different spot."

"You mean cast our lines in over there?" Allison pointed to the other side of the pond.

Dan shook his blond head. "There's another pond about a mile down the road. Might be better fishin' over there."

Allison reeled in her line and stood. "I guess it's worth a try. Let's hop in the buggy, and you can show me the way."

When they arrived at the other pond, Allison noticed a lot more trees grew near the water than at the first pond. The trees offered plenty of shade, and it had turned into a hot, muggy day.

"Let's sit over there on a log," Dan suggested.

Allison followed as he led her to a place with several downed trees. She took a seat on one of the logs and lifted her face to the cloudless sky. She drew in a deep breath and closed her eyes, letting her imagination believe it was fall and a cool breeze was moving the stale air away. She could almost hear the rustling wind clicking the branches of the trees together. She could almost feel the crackle of leaves as she rubbed them between her fingers.

A sharp jab to the ribs halted Allison's musings, and her eyes snapped open.

"Hey, are ya gonna sit there with your eyes closed all day?" Dan pointed to her fishing pole. "Or did ya come here to fish?"

"I came here to fish, same as you." She baited her hook and had no more than thrown her line into the water when she heard loud barking.

"Great! Now all the fish will be scared away," Dan grumbled.

Allison glanced to her left and saw a young Amish man with a fishing pole step into the clearing. A collie romped beside him, barking and wagging its tail.

"Wouldn't ya know Aaron Zook would have to show up with that yappy dog of his?" Dan scowled. "Now we'll never catch any fish."

Allison shielded her eyes from the glare of the sun. Sure enough, Aaron seemed to be heading their way.

Aaron halted when he realized Allison and her cousin Dan were sitting on a log near the pond. He hadn't expected to run into anyone here—especially not her. With the exception of Aaron's mother, most of the women he knew didn't care much for fishing. Maybe Allison had only come along to keep Dan company.

Rufus's tail swished back and forth, and he let out a couple of excited barks. The next thing Aaron knew, the dog took off on a run, heading straight for Allison.

"Come back here, Rufus!" Aaron shouted. The collie kept running, and by the time Aaron caught up to him, the crazy mutt had his head lying in Allison's lap.

She stroked the critter behind its ears and smiled up at Aaron.

"Sorry about that," he panted. "Don't know what got into that mutt of mine. I told him to stop, but he seems to take pleasure in ignoring me."

"It's all right. I like dogs—at least the friendly ones."

Dan frowned and moved farther down the log. "Not me. Most dogs are loud and like to get underfoot." He pointed to his fishing pole. "And they scare away the fish with their stupid barking."

"Sorry," Aaron mumbled. "I'll try to make sure Rufus stays quiet."

"Let Allison keep pettin' him, and you won't have to worry about him barkin' or runnin' around," Dan said.

Aaron hunkered down beside the log. "You could be right about that. I've never seen my dog take to anyone so quickly."

"I've always wanted a dog," Allison said in a wistful tone. "But Aunt Catherine would never allow it."

"You've got no dogs at your place?" Dan's raised brows showed his obvious surprise.

"Nope. Just a few cats to keep the mice down." Allison stroked Rufus's other ear, and the dog burrowed his head deeper into her lap.

"Who's Aunt Catherine?" Aaron wanted to know.

"She's my daed's older sister. She came to live with us soon after my mamm was killed."

Aaron's forehead wrinkled. "Mind if I ask how your mamm died?"

"A car ran into her buggy." Allison frowned. "At least that's what I was told. I was only seven at the time and don't remember anything about the accident, even though I supposedly witnessed the whole thing."

"Sorry to hear that." Aaron started to bite off a fingernail but stopped himself in time. "When my real daed died, it was sure hard on my mamm."

"I can imagine. It was hard on my daed to lose my mamm, too. How'd your daed die?" Allison asked.

"He'd gone into town to pick up a stove he planned to give to my mamm," Aaron grimaced. He hated to think about this, much less talk about it, but he figured he ought to answer Allison's questions. "On the way home, the buggy my daed was driving got hit by a truck. The stove flew forward, killing him instantly. At least that's what my mamm was told when the sheriff came to tell her about the accident."

"That's *baremlich*," Allison said as her eyes widened.

"You're right; it was a terrible thing," Dan put in. "I can't imagine losin' either of my parents. I'd miss 'em something awful."

"Do you mind if we talk about something else?" Allison asked. She looked like she was on the verge of tears.

"Jah, sure," Aaron was quick to say. "What shall we talk about?"

77

• • •

Tears stung the back of Allison's eyes, and she tried to think of something to talk about besides death. The idea of dying scared her because she wasn't sure where her soul would go when it was time to leave this earth. Allison knew some folks felt confident that they would go to heaven, but she'd never understood how anyone could have that assurance. Did going to church every other Sunday guarantee that one would spend eternity with the Lord, or could there be more to it? Did following the church rules give one that confidence?

"I . . . uh . . . guess if I'm going to fish, I'd better see about getting my hook baited," she said, pushing Rufus away gently.

The dog whined and flopped on the ground beside Allison as she leaned over and picked up the jar of worms sitting by Dan's feet. "They sure are fat little things, aren't they?" She held up the glass container and wrinkled her nose.

"Would you like me to put one on your hook?" Aaron asked, taking a seat on the log next to her.

"Thanks anyway, but I've been baiting my own hooks since I was a young girl." Allison's cheeks warmed. She could have kicked herself for blurting that out. Aaron must think she was a real tomboy.

Dan grunted and shot her a look of impatience. "If you two are gonna keep on yammerin', then I'm movin' to the other side of the pond where it's quiet."

"No need to move; I'll quit talking." Allison baited

her hook and cast the line into the water. Aaron did the same.

They sat in silence, with only the sound of the breeze rustling the trees and Rufus's occasional snorts.

"Did you enjoy the young people's gathering last Sunday night?" Aaron asked suddenly.

"It was okay." Allison shifted on the log, almost bumping his arm. "Many of the songs were new to me, though."

"Not the same as you sing back home?"

"Just the hymns. The others were different."

Dan grunted again. "I thought you two weren't gonna talk anymore."

Aaron scowled at the boy. "We sat here for quite a spell without saying a word, and nobody had a nibble. Maybe a bit of chitchat will liven up the fish."

"Puh!" Dan stood and plunked down on a large boulder several feet away.

"He thinks he knows a lot for someone so young," Aaron muttered. "Reminds me of the way James Esh used to be when he was a boy." He looked at Allison pointedly. "Speaking of James, I understand that you rode home with him the other night."

She gave a quick nod and glanced at her cousin, who had lifted his face to the sun. *I hope Dan's not listening to this conversation. He might repeat it to someone outside the family.*

"Somebody should have warned you about James," Aaron continued.

"What do you mean?"

"He hasn't joined the church and is still in his rum-schpringe. I really have to wonder if he'll ever settle down."

Allison's forehead wrinkled. "Do you think he'll leave the faith and never come back?"

"Maybe so." Aaron released his grip on the pole and rubbed the bridge of his nose. "It's a shame the way some fellows like James get into all sorts of trouble during their running-around years."

"I take it you're not one of the rowdy ones?"

He shook his head. "I've never had the desire to do anything more than get involved in an occasional buggy race. For me, having fun means fishing, hunting, or playing ball."

"Same here," she blurted out. "I . . . I mean—"

"Hey, I've got a bite!" Dan hollered. He jumped off the rock and moved closer to the pond.

Allison cupped one hand around her mouth. "Be careful, Dan! You're getting awful close to the water."

The boy looked at her over his shoulder, but his line jerked hard. He lurched forward, and—*splash*—into the water he went!

Chapter 7

On the drive home from the pond, Allison's thoughts began wander. Until Dan had fallen into the water, she'd been having fun—even without catching any fish. It had felt nice to sit in the warm sun and get to know Aaron a little better. He didn't brag the way James did. If she had the opportunity to be with Aaron more, they might become friends. Of course, they could never be more than friends. Over the summer, there wouldn't be much chance of them developing a lasting relationship, even if she were to become a woman someone might want to marry.

"Are you mad at me, Allison?"

Dan's sudden question drove Allison's thoughts aside, and she turned to look at him. "Of course not. I know you didn't fall into the pond on purpose."

"That's for certain sure." Dan shivered beneath the quilt Allison had wrapped around his small frame. "That old catfish didn't wanna be caught, so he tried to take me into the water with him."

Allison laughed. "I think your foot slipped when the fish tugged on your line, and then you lost your balance."

Wrinkles formed in Dan's forehead. "Sure hope Mama won't be angry at me for gettin' my clothes all wet."

The boy's comment made Allison worry about her aunt's response. Would Aunt Mary be upset when she saw her waterlogged son? Would she blame Allison for the accident? Aunt Catherine certainly would have. She thought everything was Allison's fault. Even something as silly as Aunt Catherine stubbing her toe on the porch step a few years ago had been blamed on Allison. She'd been walking ahead of her aunt that day as they carried groceries into the house.

Aunt Catherine had said she wouldn't have stubbed her toe if Allison hadn't been dawdling.

Then there was the time Allison got her dress caught on the buggy wheel while climbing out. She'd landed in a mud puddle, and Aunt Catherine had been madder than a hornet. She would have spanked Allison for messing up her clothes if Papa hadn't stopped her, saying it was an accident and that Allison didn't deserve to be punished for something that wasn't her fault.

Pushing her thoughts aside and feeling the need to reassure her cousin, Allison reached across the buggy seat and patted Dan's knee. "I'll explain to your mamm about you falling in the pond."

"Danki."

Dan remained quiet for the rest of the ride, and Allison kept her focus on driving the buggy and making sure the horse cooperated with her commands. The shoulder of the road wasn't wide in this area, like it was in most places back home. Of course, there wasn't nearly as much traffic to deal with in Webster County.

When Allison guided the horse and buggy onto the Kings' property, she noticed a buggy parked out front and figured they must have company. *Good. If there's someone here visiting, Aunt Mary probably won't let on that she's mad when she finds out what happened to Dan.*

Dan clambered out of the buggy as soon as it came to a stop and hurried toward the house. Allison knew she should get the horse unhitched and into the barn right away, so she decided to let Dan tell his version of the pond mishap first. When she got to the house, she would explain things in more detail if necessary.

As Aaron traveled home from the pond, he thought about how much he'd enjoyed being with Allison. Even if they couldn't develop a lasting relationship, it would be nice to get to know her better while she was here for the summer. They'd begun a good visit this afternoon until Dan's little mishap had cut things short.

I wonder if Allison would enjoy working in the harness shop. Aaron slapped the side of his head, nearly knocking his straw hat off. *Don't get any dumb ideas. It would never work, even if she could stay here. I wouldn't be able to forget how things were for Mom when Dad died. I could never trust that it wouldn't happen to me.*

As Aaron turned onto his property, he noticed light shining through the harness shop windows. He'd thought he had shut off all the lanterns before he'd left.

He brought the horse to a stop in front of the building, hopped out of the buggy, and dashed inside. He discovered only one gas lamp lit—the one directly above Paul's desk.

Paul was seated in his oak chair, going over a stack of invoices. He squinted at Aaron. "Where have you been?"

Aaron shifted from one foot to the other, feeling like

a young boy caught doing something bad. "I went fishing this afternoon."

Paul's heavy eyebrows drew together as he fingered the edge of his full beard. "You went fishing when you should have been working?"

Aaron nodded. "There hadn't been any customers since noon, so I didn't think there'd be any harm in closing the shop a few hours early."

Paul pushed his chair aside and stood. "I left you in charge today because I thought I could trust you to take care of things in my absence." He motioned to the front door. "Then I come home and find the shop door is locked, the CLOSED sign's in the window, and you're nowhere to be found."

Aaron opened his mouth to defend himself, but Paul cut him off. "I know you're expecting to take over this shop someday, but your irresponsible actions don't give me any indication that you're close to being ready for something like that."

"I work plenty hard." Aaron pursed his lips. "I think I always do a good job, too."

"That's true, but you're often late to work, and sometimes you look for excuses to slack off. You can't coast along in life if you expect to support a wife and family someday."

"I don't think I'm coasting. Besides, I'm not planning to get married, so I won't have to worry about supporting a wife or a family."

"I've heard you say that before, Aaron. Would you care to explain?"

Aaron shook his head and started to walk away, but he halted and turned back around. "Say, how come you're home early from Springfield? I thought you were planning to eat supper out."

"Emma came down with a *bauchweh*."

"What's wrong with Emma? Has she got the flu?"

"I suppose she might, but more than likely her belly-ache's from eating too much candy earlier in the day. Our driver, Larry Porter, always has a bag of choco-lates he likes to hand out to the kinner." Paul grunted. "Emma ate way too much candy before either your mamm or I realized it."

"I remember once when Davey was a little guy and got into Mom's candy dish," Aaron said. "The little *schtinker* polished off every last piece. Mom said she didn't have the heart to give him a *bletsching* because suffering with an upset stomach was punishment enough."

"Sometimes the direct consequences of one's trans-gressions are worse than a spanking."

"I guess that's true." Aaron moved toward the door.

"Before you go up to the house, I'd like to say one more thing," Paul said.

Out of respect, Aaron halted. "What'd you want to say?"

"Just wanted you to know that I love you. That's the only reason I want to be sure you get your priorities straight."

Aaron nodded.

"Tell your mamm to ring the supper bell when it's time to eat."

"Jah, okay." Aaron opened the door and stepped outside. "I'm not a baby," he muttered under his breath, "and I wish he'd quit treating me like one."

Allison entered the house and was pleased to discover Katie Esh sitting at the kitchen table, talking with Aunt Mary. "I'm sorry about bringing Dan home soaking wet," Allison apologized.

"It's not the first time he's fallen into the pond, and it probably won't be the last." Aunt Mary smiled. "He's in the bathroom, taking a warm bath."

Allison looked down at the muddy footprints leading from the kitchen door to the hallway. "Since I'm the one who took Dan fishing, I'd better mop up the mess he left behind."

"Nonsense," her aunt said, pushing away from the table. "You sit with Katie and visit. I'll see to the floor."

Allison was amazed at her aunt's generosity. If this had happened in Aunt Catherine's kitchen, the woman would have been grumpier than an old goat.

Katie smiled and motioned to the chair beside her. "How about a glass of cold milk to go with the carrot cake I brought over?"

Allison glanced at Aunt Mary, who was at the sink, dampening the mop. "When are you planning to serve supper?"

"Not for an hour or so. Ben, Harvey, and Walter will

probably work in the fields until it's nearly dark, so feel free to eat some of Katie's cake."

A hunk of moist carrot cake did sound appealing, so Allison poured a glass of milk and helped herself to a slice of cake.

"I came by to visit with you, but your aunt said you and Dan had gone fishing. How'd it go?" Katie asked.

"Not so good. We didn't catch a single fish."

Katie snickered. "From the looks of Dan when he came through the door, I'd say the fish caught him."

Allison laughed, too. "Aaron and I rescued my waterlogged cousin before the fish could reel him in too far."

Katie's pale eyebrows lifted in obvious surprise. "Aaron Zook?"

"Jah."

"I didn't realize you were meeting him at the pond," Aunt Mary said.

"Oh, I wasn't," Allison was quick to say. "He and his collie showed up. It was shortly after they arrived that Dan fell in the water." She leaned closer to Katie. "Do you know if Aaron has a girlfriend?"

"Nope, he sure doesn't." Katie blinked a couple of times. "Why, are you interested in Aaron?"

"No, of course not. I barely know him." Allison quickly forked a piece of cake into her mouth. "*Umm* . . . This is sure good."

"I'm glad you like it."

"Next to chocolate, carrot's my favorite kind of cake."

"What kind of pie do you like?" Katie asked.

"Most any except for mincemeat."

Katie wrinkled her nose. "Me, neither. I never have understood why my mamm likes mincemeat pie so well."

Aunt Mary swished the mop past the table and stopped long enough to grab a sliver of cake. "My favorite pie is strawberry."

Allison's mouth watered at the mention of sweet, juicy strawberries, so ripe the juice ran down your chin.

As if she could read Allison's mind, Katie leaned over and said, "We've got a big strawberry patch. Why don't you plan to come over some Saturday toward the end of the month and help me pick some? They should be ripe by then."

"That sounds like fun."

Katie smiled. "In the meantime, let's set this Thursday evening aside, and the two of us can go on a picnic in the woods near my house. I'll furnish the meal," she quickly added.

Allison glanced at Aunt Mary, who had finished mopping and was now peeling potatoes. "Would that be all right with you?"

"I have no problem with it."

Allison smiled. She could hardly believe how agreeable her mother's twin sister seemed to be. She hated to keep comparing Aunt Mary to Aunt Catherine, but they were as different as winter and summer. What made the difference? What was the reason for Aunt Mary's sweet disposition?

Chapter 8

Allison sat at the kitchen table, reading the letter she'd just received from her father:

Dear Allison,

Except for that one letter you wrote soon after you arrived in Missouri, I haven't heard anything from you, and I'm wondering why. I'm anxious to hear how things are going and what it's like for you there.

We're getting along okay here. We went to Gerald and Norma's for supper the other night, and all your brothers were there except for Clarence and his family. They couldn't make it because Esther's been quite tired during this pregnancy.

A wave of homesickness washed over Allison. She'd always enjoyed spending time with her brothers, especially family dinners at one of their homes. All of her siblings except Peter were married, and from what Sally had said in her last letter, Allison figured it wouldn't be long before they were, too. Then she'd be the only one of her siblings not married.

Directing her focus back to the letter, Allison read on:

The weather has been hot and muggy. We could sure use a good rain. Peter and I are keeping busy as usual with the dairy, and Aunt Catherine stays busy with the household chores. We all miss you and hope you're having a good time. Write back soon.

Love,
Papa

Allison shook her head. "You might miss me, Papa, but I'm sure Aunt Catherine doesn't."

"What was that you were saying?" Aunt Mary asked as she stepped into the room.

Allison's cheeks warmed. "I was reading a letter from my daed that came in today's mail."

"How's my brother-in-law doing? I'll bet he's missing you already."

Allison nodded. "He says everyone misses me, but I don't think Aunt Catherine does."

Aunt Mary took a seat at the table. "What makes you think that?"

"Aunt Catherine has never shown much interest in me except to find fault. That's why I can't cook or sew very well."

"Still, that's no reason to believe she doesn't care about you."

Allison shrugged.

"Speaking of sewing, would you like to try to make a faceless doll after we've had lunch?" Aunt Mary asked.

"Do you think I'm ready for that?"

"You've been practicing at the machine nearly every

day this week, and you've been able to make several potholders." A wide smile spread across Aunt Mary's face. "I think you're ready to try making a doll."

"Okay."

Aunt Mary squeezed Allison's shoulder. "I'll leave you alone to answer your daed's letter, but I'll be back when it's time to start lunch."

"I probably should answer his letter right away," Allison agreed. "He seemed a little worried because I haven't written but one letter since I've been here."

Aunt Mary's forehead creased. "I guess that's my fault for keeping you so busy."

"It's not your fault. I've enjoyed staying busy." Allison smiled.

Aunt Mary motioned to the desk in the corner of the room. "There's a book of stamps, envelopes, and plenty of paper in there, so use whatever you need."

"Danki."

When Aunt Mary left the room, Allison hurried over to the desk. Maybe she would write Sally a letter after she finished writing Papa. She was anxious to let them both know how things had been going.

"I thought you were out in the fields," Aaron said when Joseph stepped into the harness shop.

"I was, but I'm here now."

"What happened? Did one of the mules' straps break?"

"Nope. I came to see Papa. Mom wanted me to tell him that she'll be taking Emma into Seymour to see the doctor."

Aaron frowned. "Is our little sister still feeling poorly?"

"Afraid so. That bellyache she's had for the last couple of days doesn't seem to be going away."

"I thought it was just the flu."

"If it is, it's lasting longer than most flu bugs do." Joseph glanced around the room. "Where is Papa, anyway?"

Aaron motioned toward the back of the shop. "Paul's in the supply room."

"I'll give him Mom's message. Then I need to get back to the house and grab something cold to drink for me, Zachary, and Davey." Joseph started to walk away but turned back around. "Say, I've been wondering about something."

"What's that?"

"Why have you started calling our daed by his first name?"

"Paul's not our real daed, Joseph. Have you forgotten that?"

"Of course not, but we've been calling him Papa ever since he married Mom."

Aaron shrugged.

Joseph's eyebrows drew together, and he took a step closer to Aaron. "What's Papa think of you calling him Paul?"

"He hasn't said anything, so he probably doesn't care." Aaron squinted at Joseph. "You were so little when our real daed died, you probably don't remember him."

"You're right, I don't, but what's that got to do with—"

"Paul's been our stepfather so long, you probably think of him as your real daed."

"That's right. He's always treated us like he's our real daed, too." Joseph nudged Aaron's arm. "Don't you think Paul acts like a real daed to us?"

"What I think is that he favors you and the younger kinner."

Joseph's mouth dropped open. "You're kidding, right?"

"No, I'm not."

"Well, if you think that, then your thinking is just plain *lecherich*." Joseph headed for the back room.

Aaron resumed work on the bridle he was making for Gabe. "A lot you know, Joseph," he mumbled under his breath. "My thinking is not ridiculous!"

When Joseph entered the supply room, he spotted his stepfather down on his knees, rummaging through a box of old harnesses.

"Joseph, what are you doing here?" Papa asked when Joseph cleared his throat.

"I came up to the house to get something and saw Mom hitching one of the horses to a buggy. She asked me to let you know she's taking Emma into Seymour to see the doctor. I guess whatever's been ailing her has gotten worse."

Papa's forehead wrinkled as he rose to his feet. "Emma's been feeling poorly ever since she ate too much candy the day we went to Springfield. If it's the flu, it's lasted a lot longer than normal."

"That's what Mom thinks, too, which is why she decided it was time to take Emma to see the doctor."

Papa rubbed his back. "Does she want me to go with her?"

Joseph shook his head. "I don't think so. She just asked if I'd let you know where she was going so you wouldn't worry."

"Danki for delivering the message." Papa moved toward the door leading to the main part of the shop. "I guess I should see how Aaron's doing, and you'd better get back out to the fields to check on your brothers."

"Jah. No telling what those two are up to." Joseph hesitated, wondering if he should say something about the conversation he'd just had with Aaron.

"Is there something else?" Papa asked.

"Uh, well . . . I've been wondering about something."

"What's that?"

"I was wondering how you feel about Aaron calling you Paul here of late."

Papa pulled his fingers through the ends of his beard. "To be perfectly honest, it kind of hurts."

"Then how come you let him get away with it?"

"Aaron's a grown man now, and there's not much I can do if he's made up his mind to call me Paul. After all, I'm not his real daed."

"Maybe not by blood, but you've been like a real

94

daed to us ever since you married Mom," Joseph was quick to say. "I think Aaron's being disrespectful by calling you Paul."

Papa shrugged as he gave his left earlobe a quick tug. "That may be, but I won't try to force Aaron to call me Papa. So unless he changes his mind, I've decided to just accept it and try to be Aaron's friend."

Joseph wanted to say more, but he figured his daed had made up his mind. And since it really wasn't his business, the best thing to do was to drop the subject and get on back to work.

"Is this the way the doll's hair is supposed to attach to its head?" Allison asked as she lifted a brown piece of material for her aunt's inspection.

Aunt Mary nodded. "You've got it pinned in exactly the right place. Now stitch that section of hair to the top of the head, and you'll be ready to put the rest of the body together."

Pumping her legs up and down and guiding the wheel of the treadle machine with one hand, Allison carefully sewed the hair in place.

"I thought I might go to the farmers' market this Saturday to sell some of my quilted pillows and our garden produce," Aunt Mary said. "If you finish with the doll by then, maybe you'd like to go along and try to sell it. That would give you an idea of whether there's a market for more."

Allison finished the seam and cut the thread before

she looked up. "I . . . I don't think I'm quite ready for anything like that yet."

Aunt Mary gave Allison's shoulder a gentle squeeze. "Maybe some other time—when you have more than one doll made."

"Maybe so. I'll have to wait and see how well my sewing goes."

"Are you ready to take a break? I thought a glass of your uncle Ben's homemade root beer might taste good about now."

"That does sound refreshing." Allison stood and arched her back. "I think after all that pumping on the treadle machine I worked up a thirst."

Aunt Mary chuckled. "Let's round up the kinner and have our snack out on the front porch. I'm sure they need a break from their garden chores, too."

A short time later, Allison, Aunt Mary, Sarah, and Dan sat in chairs on the front porch, enjoying tall glasses of root beer and some peanut butter cookies.

"This is real good." Dan made a slurping sound and swiped his tongue across his upper lip where some foamy root beer had gathered. "It would be even better if we had a batch of vanilla ice cream so we could make frosty floats."

"We'll see about making some homemade ice cream soon," his mother said.

"How about this Saturday night?" Sarah suggested. "We can invite Grandpa and Grandma King over. What do you think about that, Mama?"

"That sounds like a fine idea, but you and I will be

at the farmers' market all day Saturday. We could do it on Friday evening, though." Aunt Mary glanced over at Allison and smiled. "Maybe we can have an outdoor barbecue and invite some of our friends and family. It would be a nice way of giving everyone a chance to get to know you better."

"A barbecue sounds real nice," Allison said.

"Can we invite the Hiltys?" Sarah asked. "I'd like my friend Bessie to be here."

"Jah, maybe so. And we can ask Gabe and Melinda Swartz." Aunt Mary looked over at Allison. "Melinda's about your age, but she wasn't at our last preaching service because she was feeling sick." She eased out of her chair. "I'll pick up the ingredients we need for the ice cream sometime before Friday, but for now, I think I'd better see about making some corn bread and beans for supper."

Allison started to get up, but her aunt motioned her to sit back down. "Take your time and finish your root beer. When you're done, you can make the coleslaw while Sarah sets the table."

Chapter 9

Allison had never made coleslaw before, but she'd seen Aunt Catherine do it and figured it couldn't be that hard. Just chop up some cabbage, add a little mayonnaise, some vinegar, salt, and pepper. She watched with anticipation as Uncle Ben forked some of her coleslaw into his mouth. After the first bite, he puckered his lips and quickly reached for his glass of water. "Whew! How come there's so much vinegar in this?"

"I don't think there's that much." Aunt Mary spooned some onto her plate and took a bite. Her eyes widened, but she swallowed it down.

Dan grimaced when he ate some. "Papa's right. This stuff is awful!" He jumped up from the table, ran over to the garbage can, and spit out the coleslaw.

"Dan, you're being rude," Uncle Ben said sternly. "And I never said the coleslaw was awful."

Allison's face burned with embarrassment. She couldn't even make a simple thing like coleslaw without ruining it. "I-I'm so sorry," she stammered. "I should have asked how much vinegar to use."

"You mean *you* made the coleslaw?" Walter pointed at Allison as his eyebrows lifted high on his forehead.

She nodded and tears sprang to her eyes. "I thought it would be easy, but I . . . I guess I was wrong."

"What were you tryin' to do, make us all sick?" Walter wrapped his fingers around his throat and coughed several times.

"There's too much pepper in it, too," Sarah sputtered. She grabbed her glass of water and gulped half of it down.

"That will be enough about the coleslaw," Uncle Ben admonished. "I'm sure Allison didn't ruin it on purpose. Too much vinegar probably spilled from the bottle before she realized what had happened."

"I tried pouring some of that stuff onto a piece of cotton when I got a nosebleed a couple weeks ago,"

Harvey put in. "It ran out all over the counter."

Allison was sure everyone was just trying to make her feel better, but their comments hadn't helped. "No wonder Aunt Catherine never let me do much in the kitchen," she mumbled. "She was probably afraid I'd make everyone sick."

"I'm sure that's not true," Aunt Mary said kindly. "All you need is a little more practice. By the end of the summer, you'll probably be able to cook so well that your aunt Catherine will be happy to let you take over her kitchen when you return home."

"I doubt she'd let anyone take her place in the kitchen." Allison sniffed. "Besides, it's not just cooking I can't do well."

"With my *fraa* as your teacher," Uncle Ben said, looking over at Aunt Mary and giving her a wink, "I can almost guarantee that you'll be ready to get married and run a house of your own by the end of summer."

Sarah's head bobbed up and down. "Now we just need to find Allison a husband."

The telephone on Paul's desk rang sharply, and Aaron reached for it since Paul was outside talking to a customer. "Zook's Harness Shop," he said. At least Paul hadn't insisted on changing the name of their business to Hilty after he'd married Aaron's mother. He'd been the one to suggest they put a phone in the shop, too, since it wasn't allowed inside their home.

"Aaron, is that you?"

Aaron knew by the tone of his mother's voice that she was upset about something. "Jah, Mom, it's me. What's wrong?"

"Would you please put Paul on the phone?"

"He's outside talking to Noah Hertzler right now. Can I give him a message?"

"The doctor thinks Emma's problem is her appendix. He wants us to take her to the hospital right away."

Aaron gripped the receiver tightly. "If it bursts open, she could be in big trouble. Isn't that right?"

"I'm afraid so."

"Do you want Paul to hire a driver and pick you and Emma up in Seymour, or are you coming home first?"

"There's no time to waste. I've hired a driver in town, so please ask your daed to get a driver and meet us at the hospital in Springfield."

"Okay, Mom. I'll be praying for Emma."

"Danki."

Aaron hung up the phone and dashed outside to give Paul the news. "Mom just called. She wants you to hire a driver and meet her and Emma at the hospital in Springfield."

Deep lines formed in Paul's forehead. "Why are they going to the hospital?"

"The doctor thinks Emma's appendix is about to burst, so Mom hired a driver to take them to the hospital."

Paul's face blanched, and he turned to Noah. "Sorry, but I've got to go."

"Of course you do. We can talk some other time." Noah headed for his buggy, calling over his shoulder, "We'll be praying for Emma. Be sure to let us know how she's doing."

"We will." Paul nodded at Aaron. "Run back inside and phone one of our English neighbors to see if they can give me a ride to Springfield. I'll go up to the house and let your mamm's folks know what's happening. Bessie can help Grandma get supper going while your brothers finish helping the neighbor in his fields."

"What do you need me to do after I'm done making the phone call?" Aaron asked.

"Complete whatever you're working on in the harness shop." Paul gave his beard a couple of pulls. "Then maybe you should hang out there the rest of the evening so you can answer the phone. We'll call again to let you know how things are going at the hospital."

"Jah, okay. By the time you get back from the house, I should have a driver lined up for you." Aaron sent up a quick prayer and rushed back to the harness shop.

"Where's your aunt Catherine?" Herman asked when he found Peter in the kitchen, frying some eggs.

"She came out of her room long enough to say she wasn't feeling well; then she went back to bed."

Herman frowned. "She's been feeling poorly for several weeks, but she won't go to the doctor." He lifted his bedraggled straw hat from his head and hung it on a wall peg near the back door. "That woman is the most *glotzkeppich* person I know."

Peter nodded. "She can be pretty stubborn."

"If she doesn't get better soon, I might have to ask Allison to return home earlier than planned."

"How come?"

Herman motioned to the stove. "You have to ask?"

"I'm doing okay with breakfast." Peter handed Herman a plate of eggs.

"Jah, but who's going to clean up this mess?" Herman pointed to the broken egg shells and spilled juice on the counter.

Peter grimaced. "I see your point. It's one thing to fry up some eggs and bacon, but I don't really have the time to cook and clean. Not with all the other chores I have to do."

"Maybe I should make an appointment for Catherine to see the doctor," Herman said as he took a seat at the table.

Carrying a platter full of bacon, Peter took the seat opposite him. "You think she'd go if you did?"

"Probably not." Herman grunted. "Guess I'll wait a few more days. If she's not feeling better by the end of the week, I may take her to the doctor whether she likes it or not."

Aaron paced in front of Paul's desk, waiting for some word on his sister's condition. Paul had phoned shortly after he'd arrived at the hospital, saying the doctors had determined it was Emma's appendix and that she'd be going in for surgery soon. That had been several hours ago, and Aaron was getting worried.

At six o'clock Joseph had brought out a meatloaf sandwich, but that still sat on the desk, untouched. Aaron had no appetite. Not when his little sister's life could be in jeopardy. He'd tried to get some work done, but all he could do was pray and pace.

At nine o'clock the phone rang, and he grabbed the receiver. "Zook's Harness Shop." He didn't know why he was answering it that way. Nobody would be calling the shop at this time of night for anything related to business.

"Hi, Aaron, it's me. I wanted to let you know that Emma's out of surgery. She's in the recovery room."

"How'd it go, Mom?"

"The doctor said things went well, and Emma should recover fine."

"Had her appendix burst?"

"No, but it was getting close."

Aaron sighed. "I'm glad you got her there in time."

"So are we." There was a brief pause, and Aaron could hear his mother say something to Paul, but he couldn't make out the words. A few seconds later she said, "We've decided to stay here tonight. Could you make sure Grandma and Grandpa are okay and settled in at the *daadihaus*?"

"Sure, Mom. I'll head up to their house right now and check on them."

"Oh, and your *daed* said to open the shop without

him in the morning because we're not sure how long we'll be here."

Aaron gritted his teeth. He was tempted to remind Mom that Paul wasn't his daed . . . not his real one, anyway. "No problem," he said instead. "I can manage fine on my own."

"Danki, Aaron. I knew we could count on you."

"I'll be here bright and early tomorrow, so let me know if you need anything," he said. "I could hire a driver and send one of the brothers or close up the shop and come to the hospital myself."

"We'll let you know, son."

"Okay. Bye, Mom."

Aaron hung up the phone and sank onto the wooden stool behind the desk. *Thank You, Lord, for bringing Emma through her surgery. Now please heal her quickly.*

"I'm going out to the shop to see what's taking Aaron so long," Joseph said to his younger brother, Zachary, who sat on the front porch reading a book. "Since Bessie and Davey are both in bed, and we've checked on Grandma and Grandpa, I thought maybe you, me, and Aaron could play a game of Dutch Blitz while we wait for Mom and Papa to get home."

"Can we make a batch of popcorn and have some cold apple cider?" Zachary asked.

"Jah, sure. I don't see why not."

"I'll get the popcorn and popper out while you get Aaron."

"Okay. Be back soon." Joseph sprinted across the yard, singing a few lines from "Scattered Seed," one of his favorite songs from schooldays. *" 'In the furrows of life, scatter seed; small may be thy spirit field, but a goodly crop 'twill yield; sow the kindly word and deed, scatter seed!' "*

By the time Joseph reached the harness shop, he'd sung himself into a good frame of mind. Earlier, he'd been down in the dumps, worried that Emma's appendix might rupture and she might die. He'd been praying for his little sister all day and felt confident that his prayers would be answered and Emma would be okay.

A shaft of light illuminated the harness shop as Joseph opened the door. Aaron sat at their dad's desk, with his head in his hands.

"What's wrong, Aaron?" Joseph asked as he stepped into the building. "Have you got a *koppweh*?"

Aaron lifted his head. "No, I don't have a headache. I just got off the phone with Mom, and I was praying."

"How come you were praying? What did Mom have to say? How's Emma? Is she going to be all right? Did they have to do surgery?"

"Slow down with the questions." Aaron frowned. "I can only answer one at a time."

"You don't have to be so testy." Joseph pulled a wooden stool over to the desk and took a seat. "Why don't you start by telling me how Emma is doing?"

"She had surgery to remove her appendix."

"Had it ruptured?"

"No, but I guess it was getting real close." Aaron rubbed the bridge of his nose. "I hate to think of what would have happened if Mom hadn't gotten Emma to the hospital in time."

Joseph nodded. "Are Mom and Papa coming home soon?"

"Mom said they planned to spend the night with Emma, and they probably won't be home until sometime tomorrow. Paul wants me to open the shop in the morning." Aaron nodded toward the window. "Mom also said I should check on Grandma and Grandpa."

"It's already been done." Joseph smiled. "Davey and Bessie have gone to bed, so I thought it would be fun if you, me, and Zachary played a game of Dutch Blitz."

"You and Zachary go ahead if you want to," Aaron said with a shake of his head, "but I'm going to hang out here awhile and try to get some more work done."

Joseph's eyebrows shot up. "Are you kidding me? You've been out here all day."

"So what? There's a lot to be done—especially with Paul being gone most of the day."

Joseph winced at his brother's caustic tone.

"Guess I'll head back to the house," Joseph said, stepping down from his stool. No point in making an issue of Aaron's attitude. "If you change your mind about playing a game with me and Zachary, we'll be in the kitchen."

"I won't change my mind." Aaron grabbed a stack of invoices and thumbed quickly through them. "You and Zachary will probably be fast asleep by the time I come up to the house."

Joseph shrugged. He wondered if Aaron had decided to stay in the harness shop late because there was so much work to be done, or was he just being unsocial? Joseph turned and took one last look around the harness shop. When he was a boy, he used to feel a bit jealous whenever Aaron got to help out here. Now, he couldn't care less about working in the harness shop.

Chapter 10

I hope Bessie and her family can come to our barbecue Friday evening," Sarah said to Allison as they sat beside each other in one of Uncle Ben's open buggies. They were heading toward the Hiltys' place, and Allison was driving.

"Sure will be fun to have some homemade ice cream." Sarah smacked her lips. "I love ice cream!"

"Does your family make it often?" Allison asked.

"Oh, jah. During the summer we make it a lot. Doesn't your family make ice cream?"

"We do on occasion, but since most of my brothers are married, we don't make it as much as we did when they all lived at home."

Sarah wrinkled her nose. "The only part of ice cream makin' I don't like is the crankin'."

Allison grinned. "That can be hard, especially toward the end when the ice cream starts to freeze up."

They rode in companionable silence the rest of the way. As soon as Allison brought the buggy to a stop, Sarah jumped out and ran over to greet her friend Bessie, who sat under a tree in the front yard, playing with her dolls.

Allison tied the horse to the hitching rail near the barn and joined the girls on the lawn. She'd been tempted to drop by the harness shop to see Aaron but couldn't think of a good excuse to go there.

"I invited Bessie and her family to our barbecue on Friday evening, but Bessie's not sure if they can come," Sarah said.

"I'm sorry to hear that."

"It's not that we don't wanna come. My little sister Emma's in the hospital," Bessie explained. "Her appendix got sick, and she had to have it taken out."

"Will Emma be okay?" Allison remembered the day Peter's appendix had ruptured. He'd been thirteen years old at the time, and Papa had been afraid he might not make it. But after several days in the hospital, Peter had recovered nicely.

"I think Emma will be all right, but she's gonna be laid up at home for a while." Bessie turned to Sarah. "That means they probably won't be able to go over to your place on Friday."

"Say, I've got an idea," Sarah said to her friend. "Maybe one of your brothers can take you to the barbecue."

Bessie grabbed Sarah's hand. "Aaron's in the harness shop. Let's go see if he thinks he can go."

• • •

Struggling with an oversized piece of leather, Aaron looked up when the front door swooshed open. He was surprised to see Bessie step inside the harness shop with Sarah and Allison.

"Hey, Aaron. Look who's here," Bessie said.

"What brings you by the harness shop on this hot morning?" Aaron asked, looking at Allison.

"They came to invite us to a barbecue at their place on Friday evening," Bessie said before Allison could reply.

Aaron dropped the leather to his workbench and stepped forward. "Didn't you tell them about Emma?"

" 'Course I did."

"Even if our little sister comes home from the hospital by Friday, she won't be up to going to any barbecue."

"I realize that," Bessie said in an exasperated tone. "But that don't mean we can't go."

Aaron glanced at Allison, and she offered him a pleasant smile. "Would it be possible for you or one of your brothers to bring Bessie over?" she asked. "I think she's really looking forward to it."

"That's a nice idea," Aaron replied, "but somebody's got to stay here with Grandma and Grandpa Raber if Mom and Paul are still at the hospital with Emma."

Bessie's lower lip protruded. "I'm sure Grandpa and Grandma can manage on their own for a couple of hours."

Aaron contemplated the idea. Grandpa's arthritis had gotten so bad over the years that he could barely walk, and Grandma's bad back made it difficult for her to do much. While it was true that they could manage a few hours alone, he would feel better if someone were at home in case a need arose.

"I'll talk to Mom about it when she calls later today. If they don't mind you going, someone can probably drive you over to the Kings' place on Friday evening."

Bessie smiled and reached for Sarah's hand. "While you're here, would you like to go out to the barn and see the baby goat that was born a few days ago?"

"Sure!" Sarah turned to Allison. "Would ya like to come along?"

Allison shook her head. "You two go along. I'll visit with Aaron awhile."

Sarah and Bessie scampered out the door, and Allison moved toward the workbench where Aaron stood.

"Are you minding the shop on your own today?" she asked.

"Jah. Probably will be until Emma gets out of the hospital."

She leaned close to the piece of leather he'd been working on. "Is harness making hard work?"

"Sometimes, but I enjoy what I do." Aaron motioned to the leather. "It's a good feeling to make a bridle or harness."

"The harness shop back home repairs shoes, too," Allison said. "Do you do that?"

Aaron shook his head. "Paul thought about doing some shoe repair, but we get enough business with saddles, harnesses, and bridles. I doubt he'll ever do shoes."

Allison drew in a deep breath as she scanned the room. "I can't get over how nice it smells in here."

"You really think so?"

"I do. I think it would be fun to work in a place like this."

"You might not say that if you knew what all was involved."

"Why don't you show me?"

"All right." As Aaron gave Allison a tour of the shop, he demonstrated how he connected a breast strap to a huge, three-way snap that required some fancy looping, pointed out numerous tools they used, and showed her two oversized sewing machines run by an air compressor. He was surprised to see how much interest she took in everything.

"These are much bigger than the treadle sewing machine Aunt Mary uses." Allison smiled, and her cheeks turned a light shade of pink. "She's been teaching me how to sew, and I've learned to make a faceless doll."

"I'll bet that required some hand stitching, too."

She nodded. "Tiny snaps had to be sewn on the clothes."

"Nothing like the big ones we use here." He motioned to the riveting machine. "That's where we punch shiny rivets into our leather straps."

Allison followed as Aaron moved to the front of the store. "What were you working on when the girls and I first came in?"

"I was getting ready to cut some leather, but the thing's so long and heavy, I may need to wait until Paul's here and can help me with it."

Allison's eyes lit up like copper pennies. "I'd be happy to help."

"You wouldn't mind holding one end while I do the cutting?"

"Not at all."

Aaron handed one end of the leather to Allison, and she held it while he made the necessary cuts. They'd just finished when the shop door flew open, and Sarah rushed into the room. "The *gees* have all escaped! Bessie and I need your help gettin' them back in their pens!"

Aaron grimaced. How was he supposed to get any work done if he had to waste time chasing after a bunch of goats?

Allison smiled and said, "I'm sure Aaron has a lot of work to do here in the harness shop, but I'd be happy to help you round up the goats."

"That's okay. I can take the time to get those gees back where they belong." Aaron didn't want Allison to think he was willing to let the girls round up the goats on their own.

Allison placed her end of the leather onto the nearest workbench, and they headed out the door.

Out in the yard, they were greeted by a scene of total

chaos. Six goats frolicked on the grass, four goats raced up and down the driveway, and two more kicked up their heels on the porch. Aaron could only imagine how much damage those goats would do if they didn't get back in their pen quickly. The two on the porch needed to be corralled first, as one of the goats had jumped onto a chair and was nibbling away at the petunias dangling from a pot that hung from the porch ceiling.

"Bessie, why don't you and Sarah try to catch the goats in the yard, while I capture the ones on the porch?" Aaron called to his sister.

"Jah, okay!" Bessie hollered in response.

He glanced over at Allison. "If you'd like to join in, you can take your pick of whatever goat you want to chase."

With no hesitation, Allison headed for the porch. Aaron was right on her heels. By the time they reached their destination, both goats were standing on chairs, and Mom's pot of flowers was half eaten.

"Stupid gees! You're nothing but trouble," Aaron fumed. He lunged for one goat at the same time Allison did. The goat slipped between them and darted off the porch. *Smack!*—their heads came together.

"Ouch!" Allison pulled back like she'd been stung by a hornet.

"Yow!" Aaron did the same.

"Are you okay?" Allison asked, rubbing her fore-head.

He fingered the pulsating spot on his head and nodded. "I think I'll live. How about you?"

"I've got a little bump, but the skin's not broken."

Aaron fought the urge to touch the swollen red spot on Allison's forehead. "Sorry about that," he mumbled. "Guess I should have told you which goat I was going for."

"It's okay; no permanent damage has been done."

Pulling his gaze away from Allison, Aaron turned to see Sarah, Bessie, and eight frolicking goats leaping around the yard like a bunch of frogs. The goats that had been on the porch now joined the six in the yard, and the four that had been in the driveway were still slipping and sliding in the gravel.

"I guess I'd better see if my brothers can help out," he said.

Allison nodded. "We're going to need all the help we can get."

Chapter 11

I am glad you were free to go on a picnic with me this evening," Katie said to Allison as they rode in Katie's buggy toward one of the ponds off Highway C. "This will give us a chance to get to know each other better."

"Sorry we couldn't have left earlier, but Aunt Mary needed my help getting some things ready for tomorrow evening's barbecue."

"That's okay. I had plenty of chores to do at my

place today, too." Katie flicked the reins, and the horse broke into a trot. "I'm glad I got an invitation to your aunt and uncle's barbecue." She smiled. "You mentioned that the Hiltys were invited, so I'm hoping Joseph will be there."

"You've heard about little Emma's surgery, haven't you?"

Katie nodded. "It's a shame about her appendix."

"Sarah and I stopped by the harness shop yesterday to invite the family to the barbecue. That's when I heard about it. Aaron said maybe he or one of his brothers might bring Bessie over."

"If only one brother can come, I hope it will be Joseph," Katie said wistfully.

Allison chuckled. "I think you've got a one-track mind, and it leads to only one place."

"Where's that?"

"Joseph Zook."

Katie's face heated up. She cared for Joseph a lot, but she didn't feel she knew Allison well enough to discuss her deepest feelings. "Sure is a pretty evening," she said as they pulled onto the dirt road that led to the pond.

"Jah, it's real nice." Allison grinned. "Would you like to hear about my embarrassing experience while Sarah and I were at the Zooks' place?"

"Jah, sure. What happened?"

"The goats got out, and Aaron and I bumped heads trying to capture the same goat."

"Were either of you hurt?"

"We each got a bump, but it was nothing serious."

"Did you manage to get the goats okay?"

"Finally . . . after Aaron called his brothers to help."

"Joseph, too?"

"Jah. Joseph, Zachary, and Davey."

"It can be a real chore to get goats back in their pen," Katie said. "I can see why you'd need extra help."

"The breeze blowing against my face sure feels good," Allison said, changing the subject. "It's been so hot and muggy all week, and it makes it hard not to become cranky."

"Don't you have hot, humid weather in Lancaster County?"

"We do, but I've never gotten used to it." Allison drew in a deep breath and released it with a sigh. "On the really hot days of summer, I find myself envying the English with their air-conditioning."

"You'd never leave the Amish faith so you could have electricity, would you?"

"No, of course not," Allison said with a shake of her head.

"We're here!" Katie halted the horse. "Would you mind getting the picnic basket from the backseat while I tether Sandy to a tree?"

"Sure." Allison climbed down from the buggy and reached under the seat. She grasped the wicker basket with one hand and the quilt lying beside it with the other hand. As soon as Katie had the horse secured, they headed for the pond.

When they took seats on the quilt, they bowed for silent prayer. Then Katie opened the picnic basket and removed fried chicken, deviled eggs, dill pickles, and potato salad. She had also brought a thermos of iced tea, and for dessert, a pan of brownies with thick chocolate frosting.

"Everything looks so good," Allison said. "But there's so much food!"

Katie smiled. "Just eat what you can."

Allison reached for a piece of chicken and practically devoured it. "Umm . . . this is so good. I wish I could cook as well as you do."

Katie tipped her head and stared at Allison. "All the women I know can cook really well."

"Not me. Aunt Catherine has never allowed me to do much in the kitchen except dishes and mopping the floors. Whenever I would try to cook anything, she would scrutinize everything so much, I would get nervous and end up ruining it."

"How come she was so critical?"

Allison shrugged. "My aunt likes to be in charge. She's often said she can't be bothered with the messes I make in her kitchen."

"How does she expect you to learn the necessary things in order to run a house of your own someday?"

"I don't know, but Aunt Mary apparently doesn't think that way. She's been more than willing to teach me how to cook and sew." Allison wrinkled her nose. "I don't know if I'll ever learn, though. You should have tasted the awful coleslaw I made the other night.

I put in too much vinegar, and I'm sure from the things Walter said that he thought I was trying to make them all sick."

"I doubt anyone in your aunt's family would think such a thing." Katie reached for a deviled egg and was about to take a bite, when she heard voices nearby. She turned and spotted two young Amish men with fishing poles heading toward the pond. Her heart skipped a beat. It was Aaron and his brother, Joseph.

She jumped up and ran over to them. "Allison and I are having a picnic supper. There's still plenty of food left if you'd like to join us."

Aaron glanced over at Allison, then back to Katie. "Thanks anyway, but we've already had our supper," he said before Joseph could respond. "Fact is, my bruder and I just came here to do a little fishing, so don't let us bother you."

"It won't be a bother," Katie insisted.

"See, Aaron, they don't mind us joining them. Besides, I think I could eat a little something," Joseph put in.

Aaron thumped his younger brother on the back. "You must have a hollow leg."

Joseph shrugged, leaned his fishing pole against a tree, and joined Katie on the quilt.

Allison waited anxiously to see what Aaron would do and was pleased when he followed Katie and Joseph.

"Did you bring your fishing pole along?" Aaron

asked Allison as he took a seat on the edge of the quilt near her.

She shook her head. "Katie and I just came to eat and visit."

"Then we showed up and ruined your picnic." Joseph winked at Katie, and she swatted him playfully on the arm.

A stab of jealousy pierced Allison's heart. Katie and Joseph obviously cared for each other, and Allison longed to have someone look at her the way Joseph looked at Katie, with love and respect.

"How's your little sister doing?" Katie asked Aaron. "Is she still in the hospital?"

He nodded. "She's doing well and will probably be home soon."

"I'm glad she's going to be okay," Allison spoke up. "Me, too."

"Will either one of you be at the barbecue Allison's aunt and uncle are having tomorrow evening?" Katie asked.

"I thought I might go," they said at the same time.

Joseph grinned at Katie. "You'll be there, too, I hope." She nodded. "Definitely."

"Glad to hear it," Joseph said as he helped himself to some potato salad and chicken.

Katie extended the container of chicken to Aaron. "How about you? Wouldn't you like to try a piece?"

He shook his head. "I'm still full from supper."

"Who's watching things at home while you and Joseph are here?" Allison asked.

"Paul came home from Springfield and left Mom to stay with Emma," Aaron replied. "Since I've been taking care of things in Paul's absence, he said Joseph and I could go fishing for a few hours this evening."

"That was nice of him," Katie said.

They continued to visit while Joseph ate. When the food was put away, the men invited the women to join them at the pond.

Aaron squatted beside Allison and extended his pole. "Would you like to fish awhile?"

She smiled and eagerly reached for it but pulled her hand back in time. "I'd better just watch."

"How come? You fished the other day and even baited your own hook."

"That's true, but if my aunt Catherine had seen me do that, she wouldn't have approved."

"Why not?"

"She thinks fishing isn't very ladylike."

"That's lecherich. My mamm likes to fish, and she's a lady. Of course, she doesn't go fishing as often as she used to now that my grandma and grandpa need her help so much more."

"Don't you have other family to help with their care?" Allison asked.

"My brothers and I try to help out as much as we can, just like we've been doing while Emma's in the hospital." Aaron wedged his pole between his knees, leaned back on his elbows, and lifted his face toward the sky. "Ever wonder what heaven is like?"

"Sometimes." Allison thought about heaven a lot,

wondering whether she would ever get there. Even though she'd attended church since she was a baby, she'd never felt as if she knew God in a personal way. For that matter, Allison didn't think God knew her, either. She envied people like Aunt Mary, who read her Bible every day and seemed to walk closely with the Lord. She often wondered how her mother had felt about spiritual things when she was alive.

"I know there's supposed to be streets of gold in heaven," Aaron said, "but I'm hoping there will be fishing holes, too."

Allison smiled and was about to reply, when Aaron leaned forward and hollered, "Hey! I've got a bite!"

She watched with envy as he gripped his pole and started playing the fish. "I think it's a big one!" he hollered.

"Don't fall in the water like my cousin Dan did."

"I won't; don't worry." Aaron moved closer to the edge of the pond, reeling in his catch a little at a time. Soon a nice-sized bass lay at his feet, and he knelt beside it with a satisfied smile.

Allison knew it would sound silly, but she almost offered to remove the hook. She caught herself before the words popped out. She glanced over at Katie, who sat beside Joseph with a contented smile. Katie didn't seem the least bit interested in fishing, but she could cook, and if that's what a man wanted in a wife, then Allison would need to learn to do the same.

Aaron extended the pole toward Allison. "Now it's your turn."

"What?"

"I know you like to fish, so quit trying to fool me and fish."

Allison drew in a deep breath, savoring the musty aroma of the pond and the fishy smell of the bass he'd landed. Oh, how she longed to grip that fishing pole and throw the line into the water. It would feel so satisfying to snag a big old bass or tasty catfish. "I'll just watch," she mumbled.

"Okay, suit yourself." Aaron cast out his line once more, and they sat in silence.

Allison could hardly contain herself when Aaron reeled in another bass, followed by a couple of plump catfish. Her fingers itched to grab hold of the fishing pole and cast her line into the water.

"Hey, Joseph," Aaron called to his brother, "I'll bet you can't top the size of my last fish!"

"I'm not tryin' to," Joseph shot back. "I've got three nice catfish, and I'm not a bit worried about their size."

Aaron chuckled. "All my brother worries about is trying to make an impression on Katie Esh." His face sobered. "Speaking of the Esh family . . . Katie's cousin James isn't coming to your barbecue tomorrow night, is he?"

"I don't know who all my aunt and uncle have invited."

"It would be just my luck if James was there." Aaron bit off the end of a fingernail and spit it onto the ground.

Allison wrinkled her nose. "Do you have to do that? I think it's *ekelhaft*."

Aaron examined his hands and frowned. "You're right. It is a disgusting habit, but I do it whenever I'm nervous or upset."

"Would you be upset if James came to the barbecue?"

"Guess I would, but it's not my decision who comes."

Allison wasn't sure what Aaron had against James, but she didn't think it was her place to ask.

Chapter 12

Allison didn't know why, but thinking about the barbecue that would begin in less than an hour made her feel jittery as a june bug. Could it be because she was excited about seeing Aaron again? Or maybe she was worried over who else might be in attendance.

If James shows up, how should I act around him? Allison asked herself as she sliced tomatoes. *I don't want to hurt his feelings, but I'm really not interested in having him court me.* She grunted. "Guess I'll have to cross that bridge when I come to it."

"What was that?"

Allison whirled around. She'd thought she was alone in the kitchen. Aunt Mary had gone outside to see if Uncle Ben had the barbecue lit. Sarah and Dan were supposed to be setting the picnic tables. Walter was outside somewhere, too. She'd certainly never expected Harvey to come into the kitchen. But here he was, looking at her like she'd taken leave of her senses.

"I . . . uh . . . was talking to myself," she mumbled, quickly turning back to cutting the tomatoes.

He chuckled. "No need to look so flustered. We all talk to ourselves sometimes."

Allison smiled. She still couldn't get over how easy-going this family seemed to be. If Aunt Catherine had caught Allison talking to herself, she would have made an issue of it.

"I came in to get the hamburger buns," Harvey said, moving toward the ample-sized bread box.

"Have any of the guests arrived yet?" Allison asked.

"Not that I know of, but I'm sure they'll be here soon."

"And you don't know who all is coming?"

"Nope. Just heard that Mom and Dad had invited the Hiltys, Eshes, Swartzes, and Hertzlers."

"Which Eshes?"

Harvey shrugged. "I'm not sure."

"So you don't know whether James was invited?"

"Nope."

Allison went to the refrigerator and removed a jar of pickles. "I guess we'll know soon enough."

Harvey stared at her in a strange way. "You're not interested in James, I hope."

"Why do you ask?"

"Well, I know he brought you home the night of the last young people's gathering, and Clara said she saw

James in Seymour one day and that he'd mentioned that he might ask you out."

Allison shook her head. "He hasn't."

"That's good to hear." Harvey started across the room. "Oh, Mom said to tell you to bring out the stuff you're cutting up as soon as you're done."

"I will." Allison turned back to her chore as Harvey went out the back door. *Now if I can just relax and have a good time. It's plain silly for me to get all worked up over who's coming and who's not.*

Aaron clucked to his horse to get him moving faster, then glanced over at Joseph, who sat on the seat beside him. Bessie was in the back of the buggy and had been practicing her yodeling ever since they'd left home. Earlier today, she'd mentioned that Gabe's wife, Melinda, had been teaching her some special yodeling techniques. Aaron figured Bessie had a long way to go before she could yodel half as well as Melinda.

His thoughts shifted gears. He was glad Emma had come home from the hospital today and that Mom and Paul hadn't minded him and Joseph escorting Bessie to the barbecue. It meant he would see Allison again, and that thought pleased him more than he cared to admit. He'd never met anyone like her before. If he weren't so set against marriage, he might even want to court her. Since Allison would be returning to Pennsylvania at the end of summer, what harm could there be in them doing a few things together? Surely she wouldn't have any expectations of love or romance.

Aaron gripped the reins tighter. *I wonder if James will be at the barbecue tonight.*

"You're awfully quiet," Joseph said, breaking into Aaron's thoughts.

"It's kind of hard to talk with Bessie in the backseat, cackling away."

"You're right." Joseph glanced over his shoulder. "Our little sister seems determined to master the art of yodeling."

Aaron nodded. "She'll need a lot more practice."

"Melinda started yodeling when she was a girl, and she sure does it well. In time, Bessie will get the hang of it."

"Maybe so."

"I don't know about you, but I'm sure looking forward to the barbecue and all that good food." Joseph gave his stomach a couple of pats.

"More than likely what you're really looking forward to is spending time with Katie."

"Jah, that, too."

"You're not thinking of marrying the girl, are you?"

Joseph's ears turned pink. "Uh . . . I'd sure like to, but—"

"Maybe someday, when you're both a little older?"

Joseph nodded. "I'll probably need to find myself a better job before then."

"You're not happy working part-time at the Christmas tree farm and working the fields for our neighbors when you can?"

"Not really. I don't think I'd want to spend the rest

of my life flagging trees, pulling weeds, or traipsing through the dusty fields behind a pair of stubborn mules."

"Noah Hertzler has worked at Osborn's Christmas Tree Farm for several years, and he seems happy enough. Maybe Hank Osborn will hire you full-time."

"Jah, well, one man's pleasure is another man's pain. I'm not really looking to work there full-time."

"You hate it that much?"

"I don't hate it. Just don't like it well enough to keep doing it forever." Joseph looked over at Aaron. "I need something that provides more of a challenge—the way your work in the harness shop does."

Aaron frowned. "You've never shown any interest in working in the harness shop before."

Joseph bumped Aaron's arm. "I'd just like to find something that's more of a challenge for me."

"The harness shop can be challenge, all right." Aaron drew in a breath and released it quickly. He hoped Joseph didn't want to work at the harness shop. If he did, Paul might decide to turn the shop over to him when he was ready to retire, and not give it to Aaron, the way his real dad had wanted. Of course, there was always Zachary and Davey to consider. One of them might want in on their real dad's shop. If that proved to be the case, where would it leave Aaron? "Maybe you should consider carpentry or painting. There's always a need for that," he said.

"Naw. Those jobs don't interest me, either."

"Maybe you could go to work on a dairy farm.

That's what Allison's daed does for a living. He runs the farm with one of his sons."

Joseph shook his head. "I don't think so. Cows are too smelly for my taste."

"Oddle-lei-de-tee! Oddle-lei-de-tee!" Bessie's shrill voice grew louder and louder, until Aaron thought he would scream.

"Would you quiet down back there? I can hardly think, and all that howling is giving me a headache!"

Bessie finally quieted, but Aaron figured it was only because she was afraid he might head back home if she didn't.

A short time later, they pulled onto the Kings' property, and Aaron parked the buggy near the barn. "I'll get the horse put in the corral and join you and Bessie up at the house," he said.

"Jah, okay." Joseph grabbed Bessie's hand, and they sprinted across the yard.

Allison stepped onto the back porch in time to see Bessie and Joseph enter the yard. She felt a keen sense of disappointment when she realized Aaron wasn't with them. She'd hoped he would come to the barbecue but figured he must have responsibilities that had kept him at home.

At least Katie will be happy this evening, since Joseph is here, Allison thought. *Guess I shouldn't be so envious, but it's hard to see Katie and Joseph all smiles when they're together.*

Determined to be pleasant, Allison stepped forward

and greeted her guests. "Sarah's in the house helping Aunt Mary make some lemonade. I'm sure she'll be glad to see you," she said, smiling at Bessie.

"I'll go inside and help 'em." Bessie bounded away, and Allison turned to Joseph. "You and Bessie are the first to arrive, but I'm sure Katie and her family will be here shortly."

Joseph grinned. "I hope so."

Allison motioned to the barbecue grill across the lawn. "Uncle Ben's got the chicken cooking, and he'll be doing up some burgers, too. We should be able to eat soon, I expect."

"It sure smells good." Joseph sniffed the air. "Guess I'll wander over there and say hello."

When he sauntered off, Allison moved over to the picnic tables and spotted Aaron coming out of the barn. Her heart did a little flip-flop, and she drew in a quick breath to steady her nerves.

"When Bessie and Joseph showed up without you, I didn't think you'd come," she said when Aaron walked into the yard.

"I put my horse in the corral, then stopped off at the barn to talk to Harvey and Walter. They were checking on the new horse their daed recently bought."

Allison smiled. "Jah, I know."

Aaron shifted from one foot to the other as he glanced around, kind of nervous-like. "Where is everyone? Are we the only ones here?"

"You, Joseph, and Bessie are the first to arrive, but I'm sure the others will be along soon."

Aaron took a seat on one of the picnic benches, and Allison sat across from him. Feeling a bit nervous and shy all of a sudden, she fiddled with the napkin in front of her.

Aaron cleared his throat. "Uh, I was wondering . . ."

"Jah?"

"Do you think you might be free to—"

A buggy rumbled into the yard and a deep male voice hollered, "Whoa there! Hold up, you crazy critter!"

Allison's mouth dropped open when she saw James Esh in his fancy buggy, with his unruly horse trotting at full speed straight for the barn.

Chapter 13

As James's horse and buggy thundered into the barn, everyone in the yard took off on a run.

"That crazy fellow is going to hurt himself if he keeps pulling stunts like that," Aaron mumbled as he sprinted along beside Joseph.

"Jah," Joseph agreed. "He had no call to be running his horse like that. I'm sure he could have gotten the animal stopped in time if he'd had a mind to."

"The way James raced into the barn, his horse could have been injured," Uncle Ben added.

"I hope James isn't hurt," Allison said breathlessly.

It would serve him right if he did get hurt. Aaron bit back the words on his tongue and drew in a sharp breath. His attitude wasn't right; he really didn't want to see anyone hurt, no matter how irritating they could be.

By the time they reached the barn, James, who appeared to be unharmed, was backing his horse and buggy out the door. "Get back, everyone!" he shouted. "I'm comin' through!"

When James had maneuvered the buggy out of the barn, Allison stepped up to him and asked, "Are you all right? Is your horse okay?"

"I'm fine, and my horse wasn't hurt. I was just trying to give everyone a little thrill for the day."

"You could have picked a better way to do it," Aaron said, stepping up to James. "Someone could have been trampled by that crazy horse of yours."

James leveled Aaron with a piercing look. "You think so?"

Aaron nodded.

James glanced over at Allison and smiled. "I told you my horse was a spirited one."

Allison stood silently, a peculiar expression on her face. Was she impressed with James's brazen behavior? Did she find him exciting?

Just then, two more buggies rolled into the yard—the Eshes and Hiltys had arrived.

"Why are we all standing here?" James asked. "Let's head over to the picnic tables and eat ourselves full!"

As Allison moved over to one of the picnic tables, she thought about how foolish James had been to run his horse into the barn like that. He'd said he'd been trying to give them a thrill, but she figured he was probably showing off, the way her brother Peter did when he was trying to impress Sally. *Could James have been trying to impress me?* she wondered. She thought about how he'd kissed her the night he'd given her a ride home from the young people's gathering. Maybe James didn't mind her tomboy ways. Maybe he accepted her as she was.

Allison grimaced. *But James hasn't joined the church, so it's not likely that he's ready to settle down. Besides, I'll be going home in a few months, so there wouldn't be much point in starting a relationship with James or anyone else, even if they are interested in me.*

She glanced over at Aaron, who had taken a seat at the picnic table across from her. Truth be told, it was Aaron she wished would take an interest in her, not James. But that was about as unlikely as Aunt Catherine saying she missed Allison and begging her to come home. Aaron had given no indication that he was interested in her in a romantic way.

"Sure is a nice night, isn't it?" James asked, plopping onto the bench beside Allison.

"Jah." Allison glanced at Gabe and Melinda Swartz, who sat across from Aaron. They looked happy and content. Katie and Joseph were all smiles, too. Allison couldn't help but envy the two couples who were obviously in love.

"Maybe you young people would like to play a

game of croquet after we're done eating," Aunt Mary suggested, smiling at Allison. "Later, after everyone feels hungry again, we'll start cranking the homemade ice cream."

"Croquet sounds like fun," Katie spoke up. She turned to Joseph. "Don't you think so?"

He nodded with an eager expression. "I've always enjoyed battin' the ball around."

Katie jabbed Joseph in the ribs. "It's not baseball we'll be playing, silly. We're supposed to hit the ball through the metal wickets, using a mallet."

Joseph jiggled his eyebrows. "I knew that."

Allison felt James's warm breath on her neck as he leaned over and whispered, "Why don't you and me take a walk down the road while the others play croquet? We can get to know each other better if we're alone."

The back of Allison's neck heated up. What would everyone think if she went off with James? What if he tried to kiss her again? "I'd really like to join the game," she replied. "If you don't want to play, maybe you can find something else to do until the ice cream is made."

"I can't think of anything I'd rather do than spend time with you," James said, offering her a crooked grin. "So if it means hitting a ball through some silly wicket, then that's what I'll do."

Aaron pushed a spoonful of macaroni salad around on his plate as irritation welled in his soul. He didn't like seeing James sitting beside Allison, whispering in her ear like she was his girlfriend. Couldn't she see what that pushy fellow was up to? Didn't she realize all James wanted was a summer romance with no strings attached?

Aaron clenched his fists. *If I'd come in my own buggy, and Joseph and Bessie had a way home, I'd head out now so I wouldn't have to watch James carry on like a lovesick cow.*

"You're not eating much." Gabe leaned across the table and pointed at Aaron's plate. "If you're gonna beat me at croquet, then you'd better do something to build up your strength, don't you think?"

Aaron shrugged. He was in no mood for Gabe's ribbing. Truth was he wasn't sure he wanted to get in on the game.

"You look like you're sucking on a bunch of tart cherries," Gabe said. "Is something bothering you?"

"I'm just not hungry."

"I'll bet he's saving room for that homemade ice cream." Melinda reached for the dish of deviled eggs and took two.

Gabe looked over at his wife and smiled. "Now that Melinda's eating for two, she takes second helpings of everything."

Melinda needled him in the ribs with her elbow. "That's not so, and you know it."

Aaron's mouth fell open. "I—I didn't know you two were expecting a *boppli*."

Melinda nodded, and Gabe's smile widened. "The

baby should be born in October. I'm hoping for a boy to help me in the woodworking shop."

"Congratulations."

"Danki," Melinda said. "I'm really looking forward to being a *mudder*."

Aaron grabbed his glass of iced tea and took a big drink. He would never know what it was like to have a loving wife and a baby of his own.

The young women teamed up to play the first round of croquet against the men. Aunt Mary sat on the side-lines, visiting with Katie's mother, Doris, while the children played a game of tag. Uncle Ben and Katie's father, Amos, had taken a walk to the barn.

Allison went first, since she was the guest of honor. Then it was Katie's turn, followed by Melinda, Sarah, and Katie's fifteen-year-old sister, Mary Alice. Next, the young men took turns.

"It sure is obvious that the fellows are trying to win this game," Melinda said to Allison when Gabe hit his ball through the middle wicket, leaving everyone else two wickets behind.

"I guess it doesn't matter who wins as long as everyone has fun." Allison wouldn't have admitted it, but she'd intentionally not played as well as she would have at home. She was trying to act like a woman and not a tomboy.

"I didn't get much chance to visit with you at the last preaching service," Melinda said to Allison. "But I understand you're from Pennsylvania."

Allison nodded and took aim with her mallet. She gave the ball a light tap, but it missed the wicket by several inches.

"How long will you be in Webster County?" Melinda asked as Katie took her turn.

"Just until the end of summer."

"Do you like animals?" came the next question from Gabe's pretty, blond-haired wife.

"Some. I like dogs, although I've never had one as a pet."

"Really?"

"My aunt Catherine doesn't care much for pets," Allison explained.

"You'll have to go over to Melinda and Gabe's sometime," Katie said after she'd taken her turn. "Melinda's got more pets than you'll see at the zoo."

Allison's interest was piqued. She couldn't imagine having that many pets.

"I have an animal shelter where I care for orphaned animals or those that have been hurt and need a place to stay while they're recuperating," Melinda explained. "Gabe's a woodworker, and he's built lots of cages for me to keep my animals in."

"Is that so?"

Melinda nodded as Katie explained, "Melinda used to work at the veterinary clinic in Seymour, so Dr. Franklin sends all his orphaned patients to her once he's done all he can for them."

"There must never be a dull moment at your place," Allison said.

"That's for sure. I think my folks were glad when I married Gabe and they no longer had to put up with all my animals and the crazy stunts they pulled." Melinda giggled. "Now it's Gabe's job to help me round up any runaway critters."

Allison thought the idea of having a safe haven for animals was wonderful. She figured Gabe must be a caring husband to have built cages for Melinda, not to mention him being willing to run after a bunch of stray animals.

"All right," Sarah shouted, interrupting the conversation, "let's see if anyone can catch up with me now!"

Allison scanned the yard and was surprised to see her cousin's red ball lying a few feet from the final set of wickets. Apparently Sarah had made it through the previous four without Allison realizing it.

The women stood on the edge of the grass while the men took their turns, each with a determined look on his face. Aaron swung his mallet, and his ball ended up right next to Sarah's.

"This is gonna be a close game," Harvey shouted. "It's your turn, Allison, so do your best!"

Allison lined up her mallet, pulled both arms back, and let loose with a swing that sent the ball sailing through the air. Aaron was on his way to the sidelines when—*whack!*—her ball hit him square in the knee.

Aaron crumpled to the ground with a muffled groan.

Allison gasped and rushed forward, but James caught her hand. "Don't worry about him; he's probably faking it."

"These balls are awfully hard, and I'm sure it hurts real bad," she said. By this time everyone had gathered around Aaron, and Allison couldn't see how he was doing.

"Aw, he'll be okay," James insisted. "A little ice on his knee and he'll be just fine."

Allison wasn't convinced. She had smacked her ball with a lot of force—enough to knock Aaron down. She pulled her hand free and started to move away, but James grabbed her elbow and said, "Say, Allison, did you know there's to be another young people's gathering next Sunday night?"

She shook her head, wondering why he'd brought the gathering up now. Didn't James care that Aaron had been hurt?

"How would you like to take another ride home in my buggy after the get-together on Sunday night?" James asked.

Allison opened her mouth to respond, but before she could get a word out, Aaron limped through the crowd and announced, "That won't be possible because Allison's riding home with me!" Before Allison could respond, he turned and hobbled off toward the house.

"Can I have a word with you?" Allison asked as she stepped onto the porch.

Dropping into a chair near the door, Aaron merely nodded.

"Is your leg okay?"

"It'll be fine. I think it's just badly bruised."

"I'm really sorry. I didn't realize I had hit the ball so hard or that you were standing in line with where the ball would head."

"No problem. It's not like you did it on purpose or anything." Aaron looked up at her. "If it had been James's ball that clobbered me, I'd have figured he did it intentionally."

"Speaking of James, I was wondering why you told him you'd be taking me home from the young people's gathering next week." Allison moistened her lips with the tip of her tongue. "I'm curious about whether you meant it or not."

"Of course I meant it. Wouldn't have said it if I didn't."

"Do you mind if I ask why?"

He shrugged. "Just didn't want to see you with James. He's trouble with a capital *T*."

"You don't have to protect me from James," Allison said. "I'm perfectly capable of making my own decisions and speaking on my own behalf."

Aaron stared at her. "Are you saying you'd prefer to ride home with James on Sunday night?"

"I-I'm not saying that at all," she stammered, her face turning a light shade of red.

Aaron rubbed the sore spot on his knee. "So, do you want a ride home after the gathering or not?"

Allison looked a bit hesitant, but finally nodded. "Jah, okay." She moved toward the door. "I'll go inside and get you some ice."

"Danki."

Allison stepped into the house, and Aaron grimaced, wondering why he felt so befuddled whenever he was in Allison's presence.

Chapter 14

*E*ven though the barbecue at her aunt and uncle's had been over a week ago, Allison's mind was still in a jumble over what had transpired during the game of croquet. Aaron's announcement that he'd be taking her home after the young people's gathering had taken her completely by surprise. As she sat in the Kauffmans' barn during the gathering, she wondered if Aaron had extended the invitation only to irritate James, or if he'd been trying to protect her from James's flirtatious ways. Aaron obviously didn't care much for James, but she wasn't sure why. Was there some kind of a rift going on between them, or maybe a clash of personalities?

"Allison, did you hear what I said?"

Allison jumped at the sound of a woman's voice. Katie stood beside her holding two glasses of root beer.

"I was deep in thought and didn't hear you," Allison said.

"I thought maybe you would have fallen asleep." Katie handed one of the glasses to Allison. "Here's some cold root beer for you."

"Danki." Allison reached for the glass and took a sip. The frothy soda pop tasted sweet, and the coolness felt good on her parched lips. It was another warm evening, and summer was only beginning. She hated to think what the weather would be like by August.

"I'm surprised you're not sitting with Joseph," Allison commented as Katie took a seat beside her.

"Joseph isn't here yet, but Aaron showed up awhile ago. I figured you might be with him." Katie gave her a knowing look. "Since he's taking you home tonight, I thought you would probably spend at least part of the evening together."

Allison shook her head. "Truth be told, I'm not sure Aaron really wants to take me home."

"Are you kidding? Last week during our game of croquet he made it clear that was his intention."

"That's true, but I'm not convinced he made the announcement because he enjoys being with me."

"What makes you say that?"

"He acts so moody and sometimes kind of distant whenever I'm around."

"Aaron does tend to be a bit temperamental, but he has many good qualities, too."

"Such as?"

"Let's see . . . He's kind, dependable, and he works at the harness shop. Aaron's nothing like my lazy cousin James." Katie smiled. "I think Aaron will make a good husband and father someday. He just needs to find the right woman."

Ever since Aaron had arrived at the young people's gathering, he'd hung around the refreshment table, trying to work up the nerve to take a plate of food over to Allison. A few minutes ago, he'd seen Katie head over to the bale of straw where Allison sat, but he didn't feel right about interrupting their conversation. Besides, he didn't want to give anyone the impression that he and Allison were a courting couple. It was bad enough that he'd foolishly announced that he'd be taking her home tonight. He'd already taken too much ribbing about that from Gabe, who seemed to take pleasure in telling Aaron how great life was now that he was married to Melinda and they were expecting a baby.

Aaron glanced across the room and saw James swagger into the barn. His straw hat was tipped way back on his head, he had a red bandanna tied around his neck, and he wore a pair of blue jeans with holes in the knees. *Anything to draw attention to himself.*

After a quick survey of the room, James headed toward Allison and Katie. Aaron clenched his fists and waited to see what would happen. Sure enough, James marched right up to Allison, bent over, and whispered something in her ear.

Aaron grabbed a handful of pretzels and inched his way closer to the bale of straw Allison and Katie shared.

Suddenly Katie stood, said something to Allison, and headed for the barn door. That's when Aaron noticed Joseph had arrived. Apparently Katie cared more about being with his brother than she did about protecting Allison from her overconfident cousin.

Katie had been gone only a few seconds when James plunked down next to Allison.

Aaron halted and leaned against the wall. He was close enough now that he could hear what James said to Allison.

"I was wondering if I could give you a ride home again tonight," James said.

Allison shook her head. "I'm riding home with Aaron."

"I think you'd enjoy riding home with me more."

"I really can't."

"Come on, Allison; I won't take no for an answer."

That did it! With no thought of the consequences, Aaron marched over, seized James by the collar, and pulled him to his feet. "I believe you're sitting in my seat!"

Aaron didn't know who was more surprised—James, whose face had turned red as a ripe tomato; Allison, whose eyes were huge as saucers; or himself, because he'd never done anything quite so bold.

"Don't get yourself in a snit," James snarled. "I wasn't sayin' anything to Allison that she didn't want to hear."

Aaron held his arms tightly against his sides. It was all he could do to keep from punching James in the nose. "You're nothing but trouble, and if I ever catch you bothering Allison again, I'll—"

"You'll what? Put my lights out?" James glared at Aaron like he was daring him to land the first punch.

"You know I won't fight you," Aaron mumbled. "But I can make trouble in other ways if you don't back off."

James stepped forward so that he was nose to nose with Aaron. "What are you gonna do—run to the bishop or one of the other ministers and tell 'em what a bad fellow I am?"

Aaron glanced around the room, feeling as if all eyes were on him. Sure enough, everyone within earshot was watching them.

"Why don't you leave now, James?" Aaron said through clenched teeth. "Knowing the kind of things you usually do for entertainment, I'm sure an evening of singing and games would only bore you."

James looked over at Allison. "Do you want me to go?"

She stared at her hands, folded in her lap, and nodded slowly. "Jah, it might be best."

"Okay, but only for you, Allison." He threw Aaron an icy stare. "This ain't the end of it, ya know."

As James walked away, Allison sat, too numb to say a word. What was wrong with James for talking to Aaron like that? And why had Aaron gotten so defensive? Surely he couldn't be jealous of James.

"That was some scene you had going on with James there, brother," Joseph said, stepping up to Aaron. "If I hadn't known better, I'd have thought you were going to start a fight with him."

"That fellow can be so cocky sometimes. I wish he would have stayed home tonight." Aaron's face had turned cherry red, and his voice quavered.

"James has always been a bit overbearing, but he's

gotten worse in the last few years," Katie said as she joined the group.

"Why do you think that is?" Joseph questioned.

Katie shrugged. "I'm not sure, but I suppose it might have something to do with the fact that James's daed turned his wheel shop over to James's older brother Dennis a few years ago."

"Why would that make James act so brazen?" Allison asked.

"Because James thought the blacksmith shop should belong to him." Katie slowly shook her head. "Some folks do strange things out of jealousy."

Aaron cleared his throat real loud. "Are we just going to stand around here all night talking about James, or should we get something to eat?"

Joseph thumped Aaron on the back. "You're right; all this speculating about James is getting us nowhere. Let's head over to the refreshment table."

Katie smiled at Joseph. "I brought a plate of brownies tonight."

He licked his lips. "Umm . . . can't wait."

The couple hurried off, and Allison and Aaron followed.

"I don't know about you, but I can't wait for summer to be over," Peter said to Herman as the two of them strolled toward the barn to begin their nightly milking process.

"What's the matter? Can't stand the hot, muggy weather?"

Peter shook his head. "It's not that. I'm just anxious for Allison to return."

"I didn't think you would miss your sister so much—especially since you've been spending so much time with Sally lately." Herman needled Peter in the ribs with his elbow.

"Jah, well, I'm hoping Aunt Catherine will be a little nicer once Allison returns home. I think she misses her, Dad."

"I've noticed that she's been crankier than normal lately, but I'm not sure it's because she misses Allison."

Peter stopped walking and turned to face Herman. "What do you think's the reason for her sour mood?"

"Even though she tries to hide it, I think that pain in her stomach that she complains about may have gotten worse."

"Has she seen the doctor yet?"

Herman shook his head. "Stubborn woman still refuses to go."

"Would it help if I asked Sally's mamm, Dorothy, to speak to Aunt Catherine? She's got an easygoing way about her, and maybe she could convince Aunt Catherine to see the doctor."

Herman smiled and thumped Peter on the back. "That's the best idea you've had in weeks."

Peter turned on the diesel engine for their milking machine. "I'll talk to Dorothy about it when I go over to see Sally later this week."

Chapter 15

$\mathcal{A}$llison climbed into Aaron's buggy and settled herself on the passenger's side. Even though she'd been with Aaron a few times, she'd never felt as nervous as she did right now. She glanced at him as he stepped in and took the seat beside her. Their gazes met, and the moment seemed awkward. Was Aaron nervous, too? Would this be the only time he would offer her a ride home, or might he repeat the invitation?

Aaron gave Allison a brief smile and picked up the reins. "Mind if I trot the horse once we get on the main road?"

She shook her head. "I don't mind at all. The breezy air might help cool us off."

"It has been a hot day," Aaron agreed. "We could use a good rain to lower the temperature some."

They pulled onto Highway C, and the buggy picked up speed when Aaron gave his horse the signal to trot.

"Ah, that feels better," Allison said as the air lifted the strings of her kapp.

Aaron pointed to his trotting horse. "I think he's enjoying it, too."

Allison smiled. "How's your sister Emma doing since she came home from the hospital?"

"She's doing real well. We're all thankful they got her to the hospital before her appendix burst."

"That was a good thing. My youngest brother's

appendix burst when he was a teenager. He was pretty sick for a spell."

"I guess the infection spreads quickly when someone's appendix bursts."

"That's what I understand."

"Do you miss Pennsylvania much?" Aaron asked, changing the subject.

"I miss Papa and my brothers." Allison figured it would be best not to mention that she didn't miss Aunt Catherine. Aaron might think she didn't appreciate her aunt stepping in to help after her mother had died.

"It won't be long before summer will be over, and then you'll be on your way home," Aaron said.

"I hope I'm ready to go by August."

Aaron tipped his head and quirked an eyebrow.

"If I can't sew or cook well enough, it'll be hard to go home and face my daed. The only reason he sent me here was so Aunt Mary could teach me how to be a woman."

Aaron's cheeks turned red and he looked away. "I'd say you're already a woman."

Allison felt the heat of a blush stain her cheeks as well. She might look like a woman on the outside, but she had a long way to go before she would be ready to take on the responsibility of becoming a wife. Even if she did manage to accomplish that task, she would need to find a man who'd be willing to marry her.

"Why would you have to come all this way so you could learn to cook and sew?" he asked. "Isn't there someone in your family who could have taught you the necessary skills?"

"My aunt Catherine, but she hasn't taught me much."

"How come?"

"I'm not really sure, but she acts like she doesn't want me in her kitchen."

"I guess some women are territorial when it comes to their kitchen."

Allison nodded. "Only thing is, it's not really *her* kitchen. She wouldn't even be living with us if my mamm hadn't died."

Aaron's forehead wrinkled. "I've been wondering something."

"What's that?"

"It's about James Esh."

"What about him?"

"As I'm sure you know, James hasn't been baptized or joined the church. Even though he's in his twenties, he's still running wild like some kid who's *ab im kopp*."

Allison felt a surge of guilt. She hadn't been baptized or joined the church yet, either. Did that mean she, too, was crazy? Her reluctance to join the church, however, wasn't because she was going through rumschpringe and wanted to experience things the modern world had to offer. It had more to do with her lack of faith in God. The truth was Allison didn't think it would be right for anyone to join the church when they felt so empty and faceless inside. Maybe James felt as faceless as she did and had acted wild and arrogant in order to hide behind his feelings.

They rode in silence the rest of the way home, and Allison was glad Aaron had dropped the subject of James. It made her uncomfortable to think about the way James had carried on at the gathering tonight. It had also convinced her that James wouldn't be a good choice for a boyfriend, even if there was a certain charm about him.

When they pulled into Uncle Ben's driveway, Aaron stopped the buggy and came around to help Allison down. She had planned to step out on her own, but before she could make a move, he put his hands around her waist and lifted her out of the buggy as if she weighed no more than a feather. He held her like that for several seconds, and Allison's heart pounded so hard it echoed in her ears.

"I heard that your uncle's going to rebuild his barn soon," Aaron said as he set Allison on the ground and took a step back.

Allison nodded. "I believe Uncle Ben plans to start sometime in the next few weeks."

"I imagine there'll be a work frolic then."

"Probably so."

"Most of the men in our community will be there to help." Aaron removed his straw hat and fanned his face with the brim. "Whew! Sure can't believe how hot it still is, even with the sun almost down."

"It will be hard to sleep tonight," she said, turning toward the house. "Maybe I'll sleep outside on the porch where it's not so stifling."

"You like sleeping outdoors?" Aaron asked as he strode up the path beside her.

"I do. My friend Sally and I used to sleep on her front porch when we were younger. It was great fun to listen to the music of the crickets while we lay awake visiting and watching for shooting stars."

Aaron leaned on the porch railing as Allison moved toward the door.

Should I invite him in for a glass of cold milk and some cookies? No, he might think I'm being too forward. Allison reached for the doorknob. "I appreciate the ride home, Aaron. Danki."

"You're welcome. Maybe we can do it again sometime."

"I'd like that."

Aaron shuffled his feet across the wooden planks. "Well, *gut nacht* then."

"Good night, Aaron." Allison shut the door and hurried up the stairs to her room, anxious to write Sally a letter.

As Aaron drove away, a vision of the moon shining down on Allison's pretty face stuck in his mind. He was attracted to her; there was no denying it. Would it be a mistake if he tried to pursue a relationship with her?

Aaron halted his thoughts when another horse and buggy passed him and the driver shouted, "Can't that old nag of yours go any faster than that? That poor critter must be half dead."

James. Aaron gritted his teeth and gripped the reins as he fought to keep from hollering something mean in return. It would only give James the satisfaction of knowing he'd been able to get Aaron riled.

Aaron kept his horse going at a steady pace as he watched James's buggy disappear over the next hill. He was probably in a hurry to get someplace, but it sure couldn't have been home, since James lived in the opposite direction.

He's probably heading for Seymour, Aaron thought. *Probably plans to hang out there until the wee hours of the morning.* He clicked his tongue to get his horse moving up the hill. *It's not my problem what James does or how he spends his time. I've got my own life to worry about.*

When Aaron descended the hill, he was surprised to see James's buggy pulled off to the shoulder of the road. "Guess you must have struck out with Allison, since you're headed for home so soon, huh?" James called.

Aaron ground his teeth together and kept going. *I won't give that ornery fellow the satisfaction of goading me into an argument.*

"That Allison, she's really something, isn't she?" James hollered as Aaron's rig went past.

Keep going. Don't look back. Don't give him what he wants. He's not worth it.

"Giddyup there, boy!" James whipped his horse and buggy past Aaron again. This time James just laughed and kept on going.

Aaron held his horse steady and felt relieved when he came to his driveway. At least he didn't have to put up with James's antagonizing anymore.

"Weren't you surprised when Aaron spoke up to my cousin like that tonight?" Katie asked Joseph as they headed down the road in his open buggy.

"I sure was," he said with a nod. "I didn't know my bruder could be so feisty."

"I think it's because he likes Allison."

Joseph looked over at Katie and raised his eyebrows. "What makes you think that?"

Katie gently nudged him in the ribs. "Think about it. Aaron did ask to give Allison a ride home tonight."

"True, but I believe he may have only asked her in order to get a rise out of James."

"Why would he do that?"

"Aaron and James have never gotten along well. From the time we were kinner, James has always thought he was stronger, smarter, and better looking than Aaron." Joseph grunted. "Of course, that arrogant fellow thinks he's better than anyone."

Katie sighed. "I hate to say it, but I have to agree. Ever since James and I were kinner he's been a show-off."

"Enough about James now." Joseph reached for her hand. "Let's talk about us, shall we?"

"What about us?"

"I love you, Katie," Joseph whispered against her ear. "Have ever since we were kinner."

Katie shivered as Joseph's warm breath tickled her neck. "I . . . I love you, too."

"Really?"

"I wouldn't have said so if I didn't."

"Enough to marry me?"

Katie's jaw dropped. She'd thought Joseph might have strong feelings for her, but she'd never expected a proposal of marriage—not so soon, anyway.

"You look surprised. Didn't you figure if I was declaring my love for you that a proposal would be next?"

She moistened her lips with the tip of her tongue. "Well, I—"

"What's wrong? Don't you want to marry me?"

"It's not that." She paused and drew in a quick breath.

"What's the problem?"

"The thing is . . . " How could she say this without hurting Joseph's feelings?

"The thing is what?"

"Well, we're so young, and—"

"We both know what we want, and we love each other. I don't see why our age should matter."

"Do you think our folks will agree with that?"

A light danced in Joseph's eyes as he looked at Katie. "When we tell 'em how much we love each other, I'm sure they'll understand and give us their blessing. After all, they were young and in love once, too."

She nodded. "I guess that's true."

"If our folks have no objections, will you agree to be my wife?"

She leaned her head against his shoulder. "Jah, Joseph. I'd be honored to marry you."

Chapter 16

Throughout the next several weeks, Allison kept busy helping her aunt and cousins in the garden, practicing her cooking skills, and making potholders and faceless dolls. Yet despite her busy days, thoughts of Aaron occupied her mind. She kept comparing him to James, wondering if Aaron might be right for her. She knew from the things James had said that he was interested in her. She wasn't sure about Aaron, though. Did he enjoy her company as much as she did his? It had seemed so when he'd brought her home from the last young people's gathering, but she didn't want to get her hopes up.

"Your sewing abilities have improved," Aunt Mary commented as she stepped up to the treadle machine where Allison worked on a dark green dress for a faceless doll.

Allison looked up and smiled. "I'd never be able to sew a straight seam if you hadn't been willing to work with me."

Aunt Mary placed a gentle hand on Allison's shoulder. "You've been a good student."

"Do you think I'm ready to sell some of these at the

farmers' market?" Allison motioned to the two dolls lying on the end of the sewing table.

"I believe so. Sarah and I plan to take some fresh produce to the market this Saturday. Would you like to share our table?"

"I think I would." Allison picked up one of the dolls and studied its faceless form. Every time she looked at one of these dolls, it reminded her that she felt faceless and would continue to feel that way until she figured out some way to get closer to God.

As though sensing Allison's troubled spirit, Aunt Mary pulled a chair over and sat down. "Is something bothering you? You look kind of sad today."

Tears welled in Allison's eyes, and she blinked, trying to dispel them. "Being with you and your family has made me realize there's something absent in my life."

"Are you missing your mamm? Is that the problem?"

"I don't remember her well enough to miss her, but I do miss *having* a mother."

"That's understandable. You've had your aunt Catherine through most of your growing-up years, and now you have me." Aunt Mary patted Allison's hand affectionately. "I'm here for you whenever you need anything or just want to talk. I hope you won't be too shy to ask."

Allison's throat clogged, making it difficult for her to speak. There were so many things she wanted to say—questions she wished to ask, things she would never feel comfortable discussing with Aunt Catherine. "I-I've never said this to anyone before," she began shakily, "but I feel faceless, just like these dolls."

"I'm afraid I don't understand. Why would you feel faceless?"

"I—I don't know God personally, the way you seem to." Allison swallowed hard. "Sometimes I feel so empty inside, like I'm all alone. It's as if my life has no real purpose."

"We're never alone, Allison. God is always there if we just look for Him. Jeremiah 29:13 says: 'And ye shall seek me, and find me, when ye shall search for me with all your heart.'"

Allison pursed her lips. "How can I seek God when I don't feel as if He knows me?"

"Jeremiah 1:5 says: 'Before I formed thee in the belly I knew thee; and before thou camest forth out of the womb I sanctified thee.'" Aunt Mary smiled. "Isn't it wonderful to know that God knew us even before we were born?"

Allison could only nod in reply, wondering why no one had ever told her this before. Had she not been listening during the times she'd been in church?

"God not only knew us before we were born," Aunt Mary went on to say, "but He loved us so much that He sent Jesus to die for our sins. By Christ's blood, God made a way for us to get to heaven. All we need to do is ask Him to forgive our sins and yield our lives to Him."

Allison had heard some of those things in church. She knew that Jesus was God's Son and had come to earth as a baby. When He grew up and became a man, He traveled around the country, teaching, preaching, and healing people of their diseases. Some men were jealous and plotted to have Jesus killed. She also knew the Bible made it clear that Jesus had died on a cross and was raised to life after three days. What she hadn't realized was that He had done it for the sins of the world—hers included.

She swallowed and drew in a shaky breath. "I . . . I sin every time I think or say something bad about Aunt Catherine. Even my anger toward God for taking my mamm away is a sin. He must be disappointed in me."

Aunt Mary shook her head. "God loves you, Allison. You're His child, and He wants you to come to Him." She took Allison's hand and gently squeezed her fingers. "Would you like to pray and ask God to forgive your sins? Would you like to invite Jesus into your heart right now?"

A shuddering sob escaped Allison's lips. "Jah, I surely would."

When Aaron's mother stepped into the harness shop, he looked up from the riveting machine. A strand of brown hair had come loose from her bun, and dark circles shadowed her eyes. She looked tired. Probably had spent another night helping Grandma Raber take care of Grandpa, whose arthritis seemed to be getting worse all the time.

"What brings you to the harness shop?" he asked. "Paul's not here. He went to town for some supplies."

"I know he did." Aaron's mother moved closer. "I was supposed to go over to Leah Swartz's this morning to work on a quilt with her and a couple other women. But since neither Grandma nor Grandpa are feeling well, I didn't want to leave Bessie alone to care for them and Emma, too."

"But Emma's doing better, isn't she?" Aaron knew his mother didn't get away much anymore, and he figured it would do her good to spend the day with Gabe's mother and whoever else would attend the quilting bee.

"Jah, but Emma still tires easily, and I don't want her overdoing."

"Can't you take her with you?"

"I don't think she's up to a whole day out yet." Mom glanced around the room. "Since you have no customers at the moment, I was hoping you'd be free to run over to Leah's and let her know I won't be coming after all."

Aaron chewed on the inside of his cheek as he contemplated his mother's request. "Paul won't like it if he gets back from Seymour and finds the shop closed."

Mom pursed her lips. "I wish you'd quit calling him *Paul*. Ever since he and I got married, you've been calling him *Papa*. Why the change now?"

"Just doesn't feel right to be calling him *Papa* anymore. Especially since he's not my real *daed*."

"But he's been like a real daed to you, Aaron. I think it's rude and unkind of you to call him by his first name."

Aaron shrugged. "He doesn't seem to mind."

"Maybe he does and he's just not saying so."

"Can't we talk about something else?"

She nodded. "Let's get back to our discussion about you delivering my message to Leah."

"Can't you send Davey or Zachary?"

"I could, but they aren't home. Zachary's helping Joseph at the tree farm today, and Davey went fishing with Samuel Esh."

The mention of the name *Esh* set Aaron's teeth on edge. Samuel was James's younger brother, and Aaron was concerned that the boy might follow in his unruly brother's footsteps. "Might not be a good idea for Davey to hang around Samuel," he said.

Mom's dark eyebrows drew together. "Why would you say something like that?"

"Samuel's brother James is nothing but trouble. If Samuel goes down the same path, he could lead Davey astray."

"For a boy of only fourteen, your youngest brother has a good head on his shoulders. I don't think he would be easily swayed, even if Samuel were to suggest they do something wrong."

"I hope you're right, but no one, not even my level-headed little bruder, is exempt from trouble if it comes knocking at the right moment." Aaron felt so upset over the thought of Davey hanging around Samuel that he was tempted to chomp off the end of a fingernail. Instead, he reached for another hunk of leather and positioned it under the riveter.

Mom frowned. "You seem distressed, and I have a feeling it goes deeper than your concern for Davey."

"Maybe so."

"Would you like to talk about it?"

He shrugged.

"Does it involve Allison Troyer?"

"What?" Aaron nearly dropped the piece of leather, but he rescued it before it hit the floor. "Why would you think that?"

Mom pulled a wooden stool over to the machine and took a seat. "I heard that you escorted Allison home from the last young people's gathering."

"Joseph's a *blappermaul*," Aaron grumbled. "He ought to keep quiet about things that are none of his business."

"Your brother did mention what happened at the gathering, but that's no reason for you to call him a blabbermouth." She touched Aaron's shoulder. "You've been acting strange ever since Allison arrived in Webster County."

Aaron grunted.

"Are you planning to court Allison?"

"No way!" Aaron wasn't about to admit that the thought of courting Allison had crossed his mind.

"She seems like a nice girl, and since you've never had a steady girlfriend—"

"There wouldn't be much point in me courting Allison."

"Why not?"

"She'll be leaving at the end of summer."

"Maybe she will decide to stay."

He shrugged. "Even if she were to stay, I can't court her."

"Why not?"

"She might expect me to marry her someday." He shook his head. "I'm never getting married. Plain and simple."

Mom clucked her tongue. "You've been saying that ever since you were little, but I figured once you found the right girl you'd decide to settle down and start a family of your own."

"Nope."

"Mind if I ask why?"

Aaron did mind. He didn't want to talk about the one thing that had troubled him ever since his real dad had been killed. But he knew if he didn't offer some sort of explanation, Mom would keep plying him with questions.

"I . . . uh . . . haven't found anyone who'd be willing to work in the harness shop with me," he mumbled.

"There's a lot more to marriage than working side by side on harnesses." Mom's lips compressed. "Paul and I still have a good marriage, and I'm not helping in the shop anymore."

Aaron tried to focus on the piece of leather he'd been punching holes in, but it was hard to concentrate when Mom sat beside him, saying things he'd rather not hear.

"Does the idea of marriage scare you, Aaron? Is that why you're shying from it?"

He looked up and met his mother's penetrating gaze. Did she know what he was thinking? Could she sense his fear?

"Aaron, please share your thoughts with me."

His mouth went dry, and he swallowed a couple of times. "I . . . I'm scared of falling in love, getting married, and having my wife snatched away from me the way Dad was from you!"

Mom's mouth dropped open. "Oh, Aaron, I'm sorry we've never talked about this before. I can see by your pained expression that you're deeply disturbed."

Aaron was about to respond, but she rushed on. "Life is full of disappointments, but we have to take some risks. None of us can predict the future, for only God knows what's to come."

"If you had known Dad's buggy would be hit by a car and that you'd be left to raise four boys on your own, would you have married him?"

She nodded as tears filled her dark eyes. "I wouldn't give up a single moment of the time I had with your daed."

"You really mean that?"

"I do. And look how God has blessed me, despite my loss. I found a wonderful husband in Paul, and now besides my four terrific sons, I have two sweet daughters. As much as it hurt when I lost your daed, I've had the joy and privilege of finding love again."

"I . . . I see what you mean." Aaron gulped in a quick

breath. "But how can I pursue a relationship with Allison when she's going home at the end of summer?"

"If you're meant to be together, then the distance between here and Pennsylvania won't keep you apart." Mom squeezed Aaron's shoulder. "As I said before, Allison might decide to remain here, or you may decide to relocate there. It's something you need to pray about, don't you think?"

Aaron nodded. Was it possible that he could set his fears aside and find the same kind of happiness Mom had found? Was Allison the woman he might find it with?

The minute Herman entered the house he knew his sister was in a foul mood. She stood in the middle of the room, holding a mop in one hand and wearing a frown on her face that could have stopped the clock on the kitchen wall from ticking.

"I hope you wiped your feet before you entered the house," Catherine growled. "Because if you didn't, then you can turn right around and head back outside." She pointed to the muddy boot prints marring the floor. "When Peter came in awhile ago, that's what he left behind."

Herman's face heated up. He was tempted to tell Catherine that she could get more bees with honey than vinegar but decided it was best to keep his tongue. "I'll be right back," he mumbled as he went out the door.

A few seconds later he returned, having left his boots on the back porch. "I came in to see if there's any coffee brewing," he said.

She gave a curt nod toward the stove. "Help yourself."

Herman tiptoed around the spot she was mopping and removed a mug from the cupboard. Then he poured himself some coffee, added a teaspoon of sugar, and took a drink. "Ugh! This coffee is way too strong! How many scoops did you put in?"

"If you don't like the way I brew coffee, then you ought to start making it yourself!"

He poured the rest of the coffee down the sink. "Guess maybe I'll do that from now on."

Catherine kept mopping. He could tell from the determined set of her jaw that she had no more to say on the subject.

"I thought after Allison left that there'd be less work for me to do, but I find instead that there's more," Catherine grumbled.

"Why would there be more?"

"Because you and Peter never wipe your feet or pick up after yourselves."

"I forget sometimes, but I'll try to do better."

"I shouldn't be expected to do all this work by myself, you know."

"Do you want me to ask Allison to come home?"

She shook her head. "She wasn't a lot of help anyway."

"Maybe that's because you didn't let her do much of anything."

Catherine opened her mouth to reply, but only a groan came out, and she doubled over.

Herman dashed across the room. "What's wrong? Have you got a crick in your back?"

She gritted her teeth and placed both hands against her stomach. "It's not my back; the pain's in my stomach."

He pulled out a chair and helped her over to the table. "I think it's time you see the doctor, don't you?"

She nodded slowly, as a deep frown marred her forehead. "I was planning to anyway. Sally's mamm came over the other day, and she talked me into making an appointment."

"Have you done that?"

"Not yet."

"How come?"

"Just haven't gotten around to it."

"Do you want me to make the appointment for you?"

"No, I'll do it today."

Herman breathed a sigh of relief. If Catherine got in to see the doctor, they would soon know the cause of her pain. He just prayed it was nothing serious.

Chapter 17

Allison had just placed her faceless dolls on the table she and Aunt Mary had set up at the farmers' market when she caught sight of Aaron heading her way. Her heart lurched. Would he be as happy to see her as she was to see him?

"I didn't know you were going to be here today," he said, stopping in front of the table and leaning on the edge of it.

"I didn't expect to see you, either. I figured you'd be working at the harness shop."

"I usually do work on Saturdays, but Paul said I could have the day off." Aaron grinned. "I can't figure out why, but lately he's been nicer to me."

"Maybe he appreciates all the hard work you did at the shop while he and your mamm were in Springfield during your sister's hospital stay."

"That could be." He glanced around. "Are you here alone?"

She shook her head. "Aunt Mary and Sarah are getting some produce and baked goods from the buggy. I'll be sharing this table with them."

Aaron picked up one of Allison's dolls. "Looks like you've been hard at work. This is real nice."

"It took me awhile, but I think I'm finally getting a feel for the treadle machine."

He nodded and placed the doll back on the table. "I would say so."

"Are you planning to sell anything today, or did you just come to look around?"

"Actually, I came to see Gabe. He's supposed to be selling some of his wooden items here today. Melinda will probably sell her drawings and maybe some of her grandpa's homemade jam."

"I didn't know Melinda was an artist," Allison said with interest. "With all her animals to care for, plus keeping house and cooking for a husband, I wonder how she finds the time to draw."

"Melinda makes time to do whatever she feels is important."

"Maybe she won't be able to do so much once the boppli is born."

Aaron chuckled. "Knowing Melinda, she'll try to do everything she's doing now, and then some."

"Aunt Mary's like that," Allison said. "She keeps busy all the time and is good at everything she does."

Aaron motioned to the faceless dolls. "Looks to me like you're able to do lots of things, too."

Allison shook her head. "I'm good at baseball, fishing, and most outdoor chores; but my sewing skills are just average, and I still can't cook very well." She grimaced. "You should have tasted the buttermilk biscuits I made the other night. They were chewy like leather."

He snickered. "I doubt they were that bad."

"Let's just say nobody had seconds."

"Speaking of food, how would you like to go across the street with me at noon and have a juicy burger at the fast-food restaurant?"

"I'd like that." Allison couldn't get over how relaxed Aaron seemed to be. All the times she'd been with him before, he'd seemed kind of nervous and hesitant, like he might be holding back from something. The way he looked at her now made her feel like he really wanted to be with her.

"Guess I'll head over to Gabe's table now," he said. "I'll be back to pick you up for lunch a little before noon."

"I'll be right here."

As Aaron headed across the parking lot, he thought about his conversation with Allison. He couldn't get over how contented she looked this morning. He wondered if something had happened since he'd last seen her. Maybe she was just excited about being at the farmers' market and trying to sell some of her dolls.

Aaron spotted Gabe and Melinda's table on the other side of the open field. He jogged over to it and tapped his friend on the shoulder. "How's it going?"

Gabe nodded at his wife. "Why don't you ask her? She's the one who's selling everything this morning."

Melinda smiled. "Most people have been buying Grandpa's rhubarb-strawberry jam, but I have sold a couple of my drawings."

"At least you've got people coming over to your table," Aaron said.

"How come you're not working today?" Gabe asked.

"Paul gave me the day off, and since I knew you were planning to be at the market, I figured I'd come by and see you."

"Anything in particular you wanted to see me about?"

Aaron placed his hands on the table and leaned

closer to Gabe. "I was wondering if I could hire you to do a job for me."

Gabe's eyebrows lifted. "What kind of job?"

"I need a dog run built for Rufus. He's not happy being tied up all the time, and if I let him run free, he chases Bessie's kittens."

"A dog on the loose can be a problem," Gabe agreed.

"You're right," Melinda put in. "Remember when Gabe built a dog run for my brother's dog? Jericho was chasing my animals all over the place, and he kept breaking free from his chain."

Aaron nodded. "Gabe did a good job, which is why I want him to build a run for Rufus. I'll pay whatever it costs."

"Sorry, but you can't hire me," Gabe said.

"How come? Are you too busy at your shop?"

"You're my good friend, Aaron. I'll gladly build the dog run as a favor, with no money involved."

"That's real nice of you. I'll pay for all the supplies, of course."

"Sounds fine. When do you want me to start?"

"Whenever you have the time. There's no rush, but the sooner I get Rufus in his own run, the sooner Bessie will quit bugging me."

Gabe chuckled. "I'll come over and talk about where the run should be built some evening after work. How's that sound?"

"Sounds fine to me." Aaron rubbed his clean-shaven chin. "Say, I've got an idea. Why don't you and

Melinda join Allison and me for some fishing at Rabers' pond one night next week? If you drop by my place before we go, I can show you where I was thinking the dog run could be built."

"I think that would be fun," Melinda said. "I love going to the pond, where there's so much wildlife. It will give me a chance to get to know Allison better, too."

Aaron smiled. "I still need to ask Allison, but I'm hoping she'll say yes."

Allison sat in a booth at the restaurant, with Aaron in the seat across from her. They both had double cheeseburgers and an order of fries. This felt like a real date, and she couldn't seem to calm her racing heart. Was it her imagination, or did the look of admiration on Aaron's face mean he was beginning to care for her? Maybe he didn't mind that she was a tomboy. She hoped that was the case. And she hoped . . . . What was she hoping for—that she could stay in Webster County and be courted by Aaron? After that first young people's gathering when James had brought her home and then stolen a kiss, she'd thought he might ask to court her. She was glad he hadn't. She'd been so flattered by his attention, she might have said yes. After hearing all the negative things others had said about James, she knew he wasn't the sort of fellow she would want to court her.

It's strange, she thought. *James hasn't been around lately.* The last time Allison had seen him was at their preaching service a few weeks ago, but she hadn't had a chance to speak with him, and he'd hightailed it out of there as soon as the service was over.

Allison bit into another fry and tried to imagine what it would be like if she and Aaron were married. *Would he be willing to teach me how to work in the harness shop? I'll never find out if Aaron and I can have a future together if I go back to Pennsylvania at the end of summer. If Aaron asked me to stay, I'd write Papa a letter and see what he thought of the idea.*

"There's something about you that looks different today," Aaron said, breaking into Allison's thoughts.

She smiled. "Actually, I am different, and for the first time in my life, I feel carefree and happy."

"In what way?"

"I accepted Jesus as my Savior last week."

His forehead wrinkled. "You've never done that before?"

She shook her head. "I'd heard some of our ministers talk about how Jesus had been crucified on the cross, but until Aunt Mary explained things to me, I didn't realize He had died for my sins."

"I suppose there might be some in our community who don't understand about having a personal relationship with Christ," Aaron said. "But my mamm started reading the Bible to me, my brothers, and sisters as soon as we were old enough to comprehend things. I confessed my sins when I was fifteen and joined the church by the time I was eighteen." He reached for his glass of root beer. "Of course, that doesn't mean I'm the perfect Christian. I've had my share of problems along the way."

"I doubt there's anyone in this world who hasn't had problems," Allison said. "But with God's help, I feel like I'll be able to deal with anything that comes my way."

He smiled. "That's where Bible reading and prayer come in. I'm trying to remember to do both every day."

"Me, too. As Aunt Mary says, 'It's the only way to stay close to God.'" She blotted her lips with the paper napkin. "I used to feel like the dolls I make—faceless and without a purpose. Now that I know God in a personal way, I think my purpose in life is to share His love through my actions as well as my words."

It seemed as though Aaron wanted to say something more, but they were interrupted when Gabe and Melinda walked up to their table.

"It looks like you two are about done eating," Gabe said, thumping Aaron on the shoulder.

"Just about."

"Mind if we join you?"

Aaron looked over at Allison as if he was waiting for her approval. When she nodded and slid over, he said, "Sure, have a seat."

Melinda slipped in beside Allison, and Gabe plunked down next to Aaron. "What'd Allison say about going fishing?" he asked, reaching over and grabbing one of Aaron's fries.

Aaron's ears turned red. "I . . . uh . . . haven't asked her yet."

"The fellows want to take us fishing some evening this week," Melinda said before either Aaron or Gabe could explain. "I hope you can go, because I'd like the chance to get better acquainted with you."

"I plan to take my canoe along," Aaron said quickly. "Haven't had the chance to use it yet this summer."

Allison smiled. "That sounds like fun. Jah, I'd like to go."

"Mama, there's something I need to talk to you about," Katie said as she and her mother stood at their kitchen counter, rolling out pie dough.

"What's that, daughter?"

Katie moistened her lips with the tip of her tongue, wondering how best she could say what was on her mind. "Well, uh—"

"Raus mitt," her mother said. "If there's something on your mind, then just out with it."

Katie drew in a quick breath to steady her nerves and plunged ahead. "The other night, when Joseph brought me home from the young people's gathering . . . "

"Joseph Zook?"

"Jah."

"I didn't realize he'd brought you home."

Katie nodded. "It's not the first time, either."

Mama's eyebrows lifted. "It's not?"

"No. We've . . . uh . . . been kind of courting here of late, and—"

"I see."

"And the thing is . . . " Katie paused for another quick breath. "The other night Joseph asked if I would marry him, and I said—"

"I hope you said no!"

Katie swallowed a couple of times. "I love him, Mama, and he loves me."

Mama dropped the rolling pin and placed both hands on her hips. "Joseph Zook is a nice enough boy, and I have no problem with him courting you, but you're both too young to be thinking about marriage right now."

"But, Mama, I know several others who've gotten married when they were eighteen, and—"

Mama shook her head forcibly. "Besides the fact that you're both too young, Joseph only has a part-time job working at the Osborns' tree farm. How does he expect to support a wife and kinner when he's not working full-time?"

The tears Katie had been trying to hold back stung like wildfire. She knew her mother was right about Joseph needing a full-time job, but she didn't know what could be done about it. "Maybe I could speak to Joseph about finding a better job," she murmured. "If he did find one, then would you give us your blessing?"

"We'll have to see about that." Mama grabbed the rolling pin and pushed the pie dough back and forth really hard. She was obviously upset. Katie wondered if she should have brought up the subject of marrying Joseph at all.

She gripped her rolling pin tightly. *The next time Joseph and I are alone together, I'll see if he's willing to look for a better job.*

Chapter 18

*E*xcitement welled in Allison's soul as Aaron and Gabe lifted the canoe from the back of the larger market wagon he'd driven to the pond. It would be fun to sit in the boat and fish in the deepest part of the pond rather than trying to do it from shore.

"Sure is a beautiful evening," Melinda commented.

Allison nodded.

Melinda spread a quilt on the ground and motioned Allison to come over. "Let's have a seat so we can visit while the men put the canoe in the water and get our fishing gear ready to use."

Allison dropped to the quilt, and Melinda did the same.

"Oh, look, there's a little squirrel over by that tree," Melinda said excitedly.

"You really like animals, don't you?"

"Jah, almost as much as I think Aaron likes you." Melinda winked at Allison.

"What?"

"I've seen the way he looks at you. Gabe told me that Aaron's decided to give up the nasty habit of biting his nails." Melinda grinned. "A change like that could only come about for one reason. He wants to impress someone. I'm guessing it's you."

The back of Allison's neck radiated with heat, and she knew it wasn't from the warmth of the evening sun. "Has Aaron told Gabe he has an interest in me?"

Melinda shrugged. "I don't know about that, but I do know Aaron has never shown much interest in any woman until you came along."

Allison shifted on the quilt, tucking her legs under her long blue dress. "Even if Aaron does care for me, I'll be leaving at the end of summer."

"You can always write to each other."

"I suppose, but it would be hard to develop a lasting relationship with me living in Pennsylvania and him living here."

"I guess that depends on how you feel about Aaron," Melinda said.

Allison felt the warmth on her neck spread quickly to her face. "I'd like to come by your place sometime and see all those animals you care for," she said, quickly changing the subject.

"I'd like that." Melinda grinned. "How about next Monday morning? Would you be free to come over then?"

Allison nodded. "Sounds good to me."

"Who's ready for the first canoe ride?" Gabe called, interrupting their conversation.

Allison shielded her eyes from the sun filtering through the trees and realized that the canoe was already in the water.

"Why don't you go ahead?" Melinda suggested. "I'd

like to draw awhile, and Gabe can fish from shore while he keeps me company."

Since Allison had come to realize that Aaron didn't think it was unladylike for her to fish, she didn't need any coaxing. She scrambled to her feet and started for the pond.

"Wait a minute!" Melinda called. She rushed over to Allison and handed her a couple of large safety pins.

"What are these for?"

"To pin your skirt between your legs."

Allison tipped her head in question. "Why would I want to do that?"

"In case the canoe tips over and you end up going for a swim you hadn't planned on." Melinda smiled. "My aunt Susie, who recently got married and moved to an Amish community in Montana, showed me how to do that when we were young girls."

"I don't plan on moving around much in the canoe, so I doubt it will tip over."

"Even so, it never hurts to be prepared."

Allison shrugged and took the pins. She bent over and attached them to the inside of her dress, laughing as she did so.

Melinda snickered. "It's real fashionable, don't you think?"

"Jah, sure." Allison wondered what Aaron would think of her getup, but she decided not to worry about it and just try to have fun. She trotted off toward the pond, and when she reached the canoe, she took hold of Aaron's hand and stepped carefully in.

Aaron's gaze went to her safety-pinned skirt, but he never said a word. He just grabbed a paddle, hollered for Gabe to let go of the canoe, and propelled them toward the middle of the pond.

It had been hard for Aaron not to laugh when Allison got into the canoe with her dress pinned between her knees, but he wasn't about to say anything. She might take it wrong, and he didn't want to ruin their evening together.

When they reached the middle of the pond, they baited their hooks, cast their lines into the water, and sat in companionable silence. It was peaceful with the ripple of water lapping the sides of the canoe and the warble of birds serenading them from the nearby trees.

I could get used to being with Allison, Aaron thought as she leaned her head back and closed her eyes. *Can I really set my fears about marriage aside and try to build a relationship with her? I want to. I've never wanted anything so much or felt this happy being with anyone before. But she'll be leaving for Pennsylvania in a few months, and then what?*

Aaron cleared his throat, and Allison's eyes popped open. "What's wrong? Have you got a nibble?" she asked, glancing at the end of his pole.

"No. I wanted to ask you something."

"What is it?"

"I was wondering . . . ." Aaron fought the temptation to bite off a fingernail. Why did he feel so tongue-tied when all he wanted to do was ask her a simple question?

"What were you wondering?"

He drew in a deep breath for added courage. "I enjoy your company and would like to court you, Allison. I was hoping you might consider staying here longer instead of leaving in August like you'd planned."

Allison's eyes glowed with a look of happiness. "To tell you the truth, I had been thinking about writing my daed and asking if he would mind if I stayed here longer."

"You'd really consider doing that?"

"Jah. And I'm pleased that you want to court me, because I enjoy being with you." She smiled sweetly, and Aaron knew he wanted to kiss her.

He leaned toward her, and when the canoe rocked gently, he grabbed both sides, hoping to hold it steady. It finally settled, and he inched forward until his lips were inches from hers. He felt relief when Allison made no move to resist. Maybe she wanted the kiss as much as he did.

Aaron extended his arms and reached for Allison, but before he could get his hands around her waist, the boat rocked harder. He tried to steady it, but there wasn't time. In one quick movement, the canoe flipped over. *Splash!*—they plunged into the chilly water.

Aaron kicked his way to the top and panicked when saw no sign of Allison. He dove under, taking in a nose full of water, frantically searching for Allison. Where was she? Why hadn't she surfaced when he did? Could she have hit her head on a rock and been knocked unconscious? No, the water level was too deep in the middle of the pond. It wasn't likely that she could have gone under that far.

The water in the pond was murky, and Aaron couldn't see much at all. He surfaced again and gulped in a breath of air. Treading water, he scanned the area around the canoe, which was turned upside down and bobbing like a cork. "Allison! Where are you?"

He heard Melinda's terrified shouts from shore, and then water splashing. Aaron was relieved to see Gabe swimming toward him. "I can't find Allison! You've got to help me find her!"

Gabe had just reached the canoe when one side of it lifted, and Allison popped her head out. "What's all the yelling about?"

"Thank the Lord you're okay," Aaron hollered as relief flooded his soul. "I was afraid you had drowned."

She shook her head. "I had all the air I needed under the canoe."

"Do you know how to swim?" Gabe asked.

"Of course I do. I'm able to tread water, too."

Aaron held the edge of the canoe while Allison swam out. "Let's get this thing turned over," he called to Gabe.

Gabe grabbed hold, and they lifted it together. A few seconds later, the canoe was in an upright position.

"We'll hold it steady while you climb in," Aaron instructed, nodding at Allison.

"I might be safer out here," she said in a teasing voice. "Besides, the cool water feels kind of good."

"You'd better do as Aaron says," Gabe put in, "or we'll be here all day arguing with him."

"Okay, but please don't let go of the canoe. I've already had one drink of pond water, and it's all I need for the day."

Gabe steadied the canoe with both hands, while Aaron held on with one hand. The other hand he used to give Allison a boost. When she was safely inside, he handed her the paddle, which he'd found floating nearby. "Do you think you can row this slowly back to shore?" he asked.

"I'm sure I can, but what about you? And what about our fishing gear?"

Aaron glanced at the shadowy water. "I'm afraid it's at the bottom of the pond, but that's not important. I'm just relieved that you're all right."

"I'm glad you're okay, too."

"Gabe and I will swim alongside of you. I don't want to chance tipping the canoe again by me trying to climb in."

Allison looked like she might argue the point, but Gabe intervened once more. "Aaron's right. You'll do better on your own. We're both good swimmers; we can help steady the boat if you run into a problem."

"Okay." Allison grabbed the paddle and soon had the canoe gliding along.

Aaron was exhausted when they finally got to dry land, but he was thankful the accident had happened while they were in a small pond and not a larger body of water. He and Gabe steadied the canoe as Allison climbed out.

Melinda came running, eyes wide and mouth open. "That was so scary! I'm glad everyone's okay."

"Just sopping wet." Allison grabbed the edge of her dress and wrung out the excess water. "I must look a mess."

Aaron gazed at her as affection welled in his chest. Any other woman would have probably cried or complained about her plight, but not Allison. Her dress was completely soaked, and her hair had come loose from its bun, spilling from her white kapp, which hung down her back by the narrow strips of material tied under her chin. Yet she had been able to laugh about it. At that moment, Aaron knew he had fallen hopelessly in love with Allison Troyer.

Allison shivered as a chill ran through her body, but she didn't utter a word of complaint. Aaron had almost kissed her, and if the canoe hadn't capsized, she was sure he would have.

Melinda draped a quilt around Allison's shoulders. "I think we should go, Gabe," she said, glancing at her husband. "The three of you need to get out of those wet clothes."

"I'll be okay if I sit in the sun awhile," Allison argued.

"What sun?" Aaron pointed to the clouds overhead. "Looks like our sun is gone, and rain might be on the way."

"We can't get any wetter than we are," Gabe said with a chuckle.

"Except for me," Melinda reminded.

Gabe shook his head, sending a spray of water all over her navy blue dress. "Now everyone's wet."

Melinda planted both hands on her ever-widening hips and scowled at him, but Allison could see by the twinkle in Melinda's eyes that she wasn't really upset by her husband's antics. "Just for that, I'm going to yodel all the way home," Melinda announced.

"Go ahead. I'm not Grandpa Stutzman; I like it whenever you yodel."

"Well, see if you like this." Melinda cupped her hands around her mouth and let loose with a terrible shriek. "Oh-lee-oh-lee-oh-lee-de-tee!" She held the last note and made it go so high that Gabe covered his ears. Allison and Aaron did the same.

"Enough already! I'm sorry I got water on your dress," Gabe apologized.

Allison laughed, and Aaron reached for her hand. "Now that's true love, wouldn't you say?"

She gazed at his handsome face, still dripping with pond water. *What I'm feeling for you—that's true love.*

Chapter 19

*O*n Saturday morning, Allison awoke to hammers pounding against wood and the deep murmur of men's voices. She climbed out of bed, rushed over to the window, and pulled the dark curtain aside. There were at least a dozen men in the yard, moving back and forth from the barn to the plywood-covered sawhorses where all their supplies were laid out. She'd almost forgotten this was the day they'd be tearing down Uncle Ben's rickety old barn. If everything went well, construction on the new barn would begin next week.

Allison thought about the previous night's discussion with Aunt Mary and Uncle Ben about the possibility of her staying with them longer than originally planned. She was pleased when they'd said they would be happy to have her stay as long as she wanted. After that, Allison had hurried to her room and written a letter to her father, asking if he would mind if she stayed awhile longer. She hoped he would have no objections.

Pulling her thoughts back to the present, Allison hurried to get washed and dressed. She knew Aunt Mary would need her more than ever today, as it would be the women's job to feed the men and see that they had plenty of water and snacks to sustain them throughout the day.

Allison entered the kitchen and found Aunt Mary and Sarah bustling around. "Sorry I'm late," she apologized. "Until I woke up to all that pounding, I'd forgotten the men would begin tearing down the old barn today."

Aunt Mary smiled. "That's all right. You're here now, and we can certainly use another pair of hands."

"What would you like me to do?"

"The menfolk have had their breakfast already, so after you eat, you can make a batch of gingerbread."

Allison wished she could do something that had nothing to do with food, but she nodded agreeably and headed for the refrigerator to get some milk.

"Want me to see if the mail's here yet?" Sarah asked her mother.

"That would be fine." Aunt Mary nodded at some envelopes lying on the table. "If the mailman hasn't come yet, please put those bills in the box for him to pick up."

Sarah grabbed the mail off the table and was almost to the door when Allison remembered the letter she'd written to her father.

"I've got a letter that needs to go out," she said. "Would you wait a minute while I run upstairs and get it?"

"Sure."

"Did you write your daed a letter?" Aunt Mary asked.

"Jah. I asked him if he'd mind if I stay on here longer, and I told him you said it would be okay."

Her aunt smiled. "I hope he agrees."

Allison nodded. "Me, too."

As Aaron pulled his buggy into the Kings' yard, he noticed Gabe's rig in front of him. They both pulled up to the hitching rail near the corral and unhooked their horses from the buggies.

"I was going to start work on Rufus's dog run

186

today," Gabe said. "But I figured I was needed here more, tearing down the barn."

"That's okay. Rufus has waited this long, so a little longer won't matter." Aaron led his horse to the corral, and Gabe followed.

"From the looks of all the men milling around, I'd say every Amish shop in Webster County must be closed for the day," Gabe commented.

Aaron nodded. "Paul didn't think twice about closing the harness shop so we could both come here to work. He should be along shortly and so should my brothers."

Gabe pointed across the yard. "I think my daed's here already."

"Guess we'd better go see what jobs we're needed to do."

Sometime later, while Aaron was hauling a stack of wood from the old barn to the pile across the yard, he spotted Allison heading that way. She smiled and waved, but since his hands were full, he could only nod and smile in response.

"I was wondering if you'd be here today," she said when she caught up to him.

"Wouldn't have missed it." He grinned at her. "I've been looking forward to seeing how you look in dry clothes."

Allison's cheeks turned crimson. "I did look pretty awful in those sopping clothes after our dunking in the pond, didn't I?"

He dropped the wood to the growing pile and

chuckled. "Guess I didn't look so good myself."

"I wrote a letter to my daed last night," Allison said, changing the subject. "I asked if he would mind if I stayed here longer."

"How much longer are you thinking?"

"As long as Aunt Mary and Uncle Ben are willing to put up with me."

Aaron moved closer to her. "I'm glad to hear that. I hope your daed says you can stay indefinitely."

"We'll have to see about that." Allison motioned to what remained of the barn. "I wish I could help the menfolk tear the wood off the walls instead of serving them cold drinks and meals."

He chuckled and shook his head. "Why would someone as pretty as you want to get her hands all dirty?"

She thumped his arm playfully. "Are you teasing me?"

"Jah, I sure am." The truth was, Aaron was impressed with Allison's willingness to help the men, and if he had his way, she'd be working alongside of him today. He was fairly certain Allison's uncle would never go for that. Except for Paul, most men he knew thought a woman's place was in the kitchen.

Allison released a sigh. "I suppose I should get back inside. I've got two loaves of gingerbread baking, and if I'm not careful, they'll be overdone."

"I'll look forward to sampling a piece," Aaron said as he moved toward the work site. Suddenly he turned back around. "Say, how would you like to go over to

Katie Esh's place and pick strawberries with me one evening next week? Katie's mamm told my mamm that the berries are coming to an end. If we don't get them soon, they'll be gone."

"I'd like that. Katie had mentioned that idea to me several weeks ago, but I haven't been over there yet." Allison smiled. "I made plans to visit Melinda and see the animals she's taking care of on Monday morning, but I think the rest of my week is fairly free."

"I have a hunch you'll like seeing all her critters." Aaron reached under his straw hat and scratched the side of his head. "Guess I'd better ask Joseph to join us for the strawberry picking. He and Katie have begun courting, and this could be like a double date."

"That sounds good to me." Allison flashed him another smile and headed for the house.

Aaron started toward the old barn as he hummed a song the young people sometimes sang at their singings. He thought about the words and how they related to the way he felt about Allison. *"Every minute of the day I'm thinkin' 'bout you; and without you, life is just a crazy dream. Every breath I take I'm hopin' that you're hopin' that I'm hopin' you'll stay here with me."*

As Joseph headed to the work site, he spotted Katie coming around the corner of the house, and his heart skipped a beat. He loved her so much and wished they could be married this fall. But if he didn't find a better job soon, he saw no way he could adequately support a wife, much less any children they might be blessed with.

"I was hoping you'd be here today," she said breathlessly.

"I wouldn't have missed it for anything." He smiled. "It's not just the work that brought me here, either."

Katie's cheeks turned pink, and tears gathered in the corners of her eyes.

Joseph felt immediate concern. "What's wrong?"

"I—I talked to mamm the other night—about us wanting to get married."

Joseph's spine went rigid. The tears he saw in Katie's eyes probably meant things hadn't gone so well. "What'd your mamm say?"

"Besides the fact that she thinks we're too young, she doesn't feel that you're making enough money working at your part-time job to support a wife and family."

"What about your daed? What'd he have to say about this?"

Katie's chin quivered. "I talked to him this morning, and he agreed with Mama."

Joseph groaned. "As much as I hate to say this, I think your folks are right."

"Have you changed your mind about marrying me?"

"Of course not, but until I'm able to find a full-time job that pays a decent wage, I know I won't be ready for marriage."

Katie's gaze dropped to the ground. "I see."

"I hope it won't be long until I can find the right job, and as soon as I do, I'll speak to my folks about us getting married, and you can talk to yours again." He reached for her hand. "Doesn't that make sense to you?"

She lifted her gaze to meet his, and a few tears spilled over onto her cheeks. "Jah, it does."

Joseph motioned to the place where the old barn was being torn down. "In the meantime, I'd better get busy. If I don't, my daed will probably come looking for me."

She smiled shakily. "I'd best get into the kitchen and find out what I need to do as well."

"See you later, Katie." As Joseph walked away, he determined in his heart that he would find a full-time job as soon as possible.

When Herman entered the living room and found Catherine sprawled on the sofa, he felt immediate concern. "Are you hurting again, or just tired?" he asked, moving to stand beside her.

She stared up at him with a pinched expression. "I've just been lying here, thinking."

"About what?"

"About the appointment I had with the doctor earlier this week." Her eyelids fluttered. "What if this pain I've been having is something serious? What if—"

"Didn't you tell me the doctor said he didn't think it was serious?"

She nodded. "He thinks I've got irritable bowel syndrome, and that a change in my diet and some medication might help. Of course, he'll know more after I have some tests run and he gets the results."

Herman took a seat in the chair across from her. "We'll just have to pray it's nothing serious."

"Humph! A lot of good prayer has ever done me."

Herman was about to respond, when Peter stepped into the room. "Papa, are you coming back to the barn? I think Bossy's about to deliver her calf."

"I'd better go, Catherine," Herman said, rising to his feet. "We can talk more about this later."

Chapter 20

When Allison pulled her horse and buggy into the Swartzes' driveway on Monday morning, she was surprised to see so many empty animal cages stacked along the side of the barn. From what she'd heard about Melinda's animal shelter, she figured all the cages would be full.

She spotted Melinda coming out of the house and waved to her.

Melinda hurried out to meet Allison, just as Allison hitched the horse to the hitching rail.

"Wie geht's?" Allison asked.

"I'm doing well. How about you?"

"Real good." Allison smiled. "Guess what?"

"What?"

"I think I may be staying in Webster County longer than originally planned."

"That's wunderbaar." Melinda led the way as Allison took her horse to the corral. "How much longer will you be staying?"

"I'm not sure. Maybe indefinitely if my daed agrees to it."

"It would be nice if you could stay, but won't you miss your family back home?"

"I will miss my papa and my brothers, and of course my friend Sally Mast. But I've got family here, too, and I've made several new friends. I was really home-sick when I first came here, but now I want to stay." Allison smiled. "Besides, I can go home for visits, and maybe Papa and my brothers can come visit here, too."

Melinda gave Allison a knowing look. "Does this decision to stay have anything to do with Aaron Zook?"

Allison's face heated up as she stared at the toes of her sneakers. "Jah."

"I thought so." Melinda squcezed Allison's shoulder. "You're in love with him, aren't you?"

"I do care for Aaron," Allison admitted, "but—but I'm not sure—"

Before Allison could finish her sentence, a ball of white fur darted in front of her and raced for the barn.

"There goes my cat, Snow," Melinda said with a laugh. "She's either after a mouse or is trying to get away from some other critter."

"Have you had the cat long, or is she one of your newer pets?"

"Oh, I've had Snow since my nineteenth birthday. She's kept things livened up for me ever since." Melinda motioned to the barn. "She's got a litter of kittens that are little characters, too."

Allison's interest was piqued. "Can I see them?"

"Jah, sure." Melinda led the way to the barn.

When Allison stepped inside, she spotted several kittens sleeping in a pile of straw. "They're so cute," she said, kneeling next to them.

Melinda dropped down beside her. "Would you like one?"

"You mean it?"

"Of course. I need to find good homes for them, and I'm guessing by the look on your face that you might like to have one."

"I've never had a pet before, and if Aunt Mary and Uncle Ben don't object, I'd love to have a kitten." Allison picked a gray and white one out of the litter and held it against her chest.

"I can't believe you've never had a pet of your own!"

"We've had a few barn cats to keep the mice down, but Aunt Catherine wouldn't allow me or my brothers to make pets out of them."

Melinda frowned. "That's a shame. I make pets out of almost any animal that comes into my care." She rose to her feet. "Speaking of which, would you like me to show you the rest of my menagerie?"

Allison nodded. That was, after all, why she'd come to see Melinda.

• • •

Herman fiddled with the edge of his straw hat as he waited for Catherine's doctor to give them the results of her tests. The solemn expression on the doctor's face indicated the news wasn't good.

"I'm sorry to have to tell you this, Catherine," Dr. Rawlings said, placing both hands on his desk, "but the results of your tests reveal that you have colon cancer, and it appears to be spreading."

Herman drew in a sharp breath, but Catherine just sat with a stoic expression.

"There are a couple of treatment options," the doctor said. "I'd like to go over them with you now."

"How long have I got to live?" Catherine's blunt question jolted Herman to the core.

"That all depends on how well your body responds to the treatment plan," Dr. Rawlings replied. "We'll want to start with surgery, and then add chemo, and maybe—"

"Can you guarantee that surgery, chemo, or anything else you have on that list of yours will make me well again?"

He shook his head. "There are no guarantees, but—"

"Then forget about the treatment plan."

The doctor blinked a couple of times. "What?"

"If there are no guarantees, then I'm not putting myself through any kind of treatment that will probably make me feel worse than I do now."

Herman placed his hand on Catherine's arm. "Think

about what you're saying. Without treatment, you'll die."

"Humph! Seems to me like I'm going to die anyway."

"But if the treatment will extend your life, then—"

"*If* is a little word, and it sounds like my chances are little or none." Catherine compressed her lips, the way she always did when she was trying to make a point. "It's my life, and I'll live and die the way I choose."

"You should listen to your brother," the doctor put in. "I'm sure he's got your best interest at heart."

"Puh!" She waved a hand. "The only thing he's thinking about is who's going to look after his house and cook his meals once I'm dead and gone."

Herman's mouth dropped open. "That's not true, Catherine."

Dr. Rawlings looked at her steadily. "I'd like you to give serious consideration to what I've said."

She stalked out of the room.

"I'll talk to her," Herman said to the doctor. "See if I can't make her listen to reason."

The doctor nodded. "If your sister changes her mind, have her call my office for another appointment."

By the time Herman left the doctor's office, Catherine was already heading down the hall. "Wait up!" he called. "We need to talk about this."

She whirled around, her eyes flashing and her lips set in a determined line. "You're not going to talk me into going under the knife or taking any kind of treatment."

"But, Catherine . . . "

She shook her head vigorously. "And whatever you do, I don't want you telling Allison about this or bringing her home early on account of me. Is that clear?"

"I won't say anything now," he promised, "but if the time comes that I feel she's needed, I'll bring her home."

"She won't be needed." Catherine turned and rushed out the door.

"I'm glad we're finally getting to do this," Katie said as Allison climbed down from her uncle's buggy.

"Me, too. I love ripe, juicy strawberries, and Aunt Mary said if I bring enough home she'll teach me to make a strawberry pie."

"I'm sure there'll be plenty for that." Katie pointed to the garden, where clusters of fat strawberries grew in abundance. "I was surprised to see you drive in alone. I figured Aaron and Joseph would stop by your aunt and uncle's place on the way over and give you a ride."

Allison shook her head. "When I saw Aaron on Sunday, I told him I would drive myself, since I knew he'd be working at the harness shop until suppertime and Joseph would be doing the same at the Christmas tree farm." She glanced at the road in front of the Eshes' place. "I hope they get here soon."

Katie nodded and her cheeks turned pink. "I always

look forward to spending time with Joseph, and I hope—" Her voice trailed off.

"What do you hope?"

"Oh, nothing." Katie shielded her eyes from the evening sun filtering through the trees. "We don't have to wait until the fellows arrive to start picking. I can run into the house and get some containers right now."

"That's fine with me," Allison replied. "The sooner I get started, the more berries I'll have to take home to Aunt Mary."

Katie nodded and hurried off.

Allison strolled around the edge of the garden, breathing in the pungent aroma of dill weed and feasting her eyes on the colorful vegetables growing among a few scattered weeds. All kinds of produce would soon be ready for harvest—long skinny pole beans, leafy green carrot tops, an abundance of plump tomatoes, and several kinds of squash.

She bent down and plucked a fat, red berry off the vine, then popped it into her mouth. "Umm . . . this is wunderbaar." She swished the juice around on her tongue, savoring the succulent sweetness and allowing it to trickle down her throat.

When Allison heard the screen door slam shut, she glanced up at the house. Katie stepped onto the back porch, holding two plastic containers. When she reached the berry patch, she handed one to Allison. "I see someone's been sampling the goods already; there's berry juice on your chin."

Allison rubbed the spot Katie had pointed to and laughed. "I'm guilty."

"Shall we start picking?"

"Sure." Allison knelt at the end of the first row, and Katie took the next row over.

"Maybe we can get our containers filled before Aaron and Joseph show up," Katie said.

Allison plucked off several berries and placed them in her container, being careful not to crush any. "Guess what?" she asked.

"What?"

"I went to visit Melinda Swartz Monday morning, and she gave me one of her cat's kittens."

"That was nice. I take it your aunt and uncle were okay with you bringing it home?"

Allison nodded. "They didn't have a problem with it at all."

"What'd you name the kitten?" Katie asked.

"Since it followed me around the whole time I was visiting Melinda, I decided to call it Shadow."

Katie smiled. "That sounds like an appropriate name."

They worked in silence for a time; then Allison said, "I haven't seen your cousin James lately. He wasn't at church last week, and he didn't come to help tear down Uncle Ben's barn on Saturday." James had been on Allison's mind ever since she'd made things right with God. He seemed angry and brash, thinking only of himself. Since God could change anyone's heart, and she knew it wasn't His will that any should perish, she hoped James might find the same peace in his heart as she'd found by accepting Jesus as her Savior.

"James doesn't care much for church these days, and he doesn't worry about helping anyone." Katie wrinkled her nose. "He probably drove that fancy car of his to Springfield for the day so he could have some fun."

"Maybe James is away on a trip or something. That might be why he hasn't been around."

"Could be. You never know what that fellow might be up to. It makes me sick to say this, but I wouldn't be surprised if he doesn't decide to jump the fence."

"You mean, 'go English'?"

Katie nodded.

Allison looked up when she heard horse's hooves clomping against the pavement. She hoped it was Aaron and Joseph. Sure enough, Aaron's buggy slowed. They were just turning up the driveway.

"They're here!" Katie scrambled to her feet and rushed over to the hitching rail near her father's barn. Allison followed, her heart hammering with excitement. She hoped what she felt for Aaron wasn't just a silly crush. She hoped she hadn't misinterpreted his feelings for her.

"Sorry we're late," Aaron apologized as he and Joseph jumped down from the buggy. "Paul and I had a harness that needed to be fixed while the customer waited, and that made us late for supper."

"It's okay. You're here now." Katie gave Joseph a deep-dimpled smile.

"Would you rather I hitch my horse to the rail or put him in the corral?" Aaron asked her.

"Whatever you want is fine. My daed's still out in the fields with my brother Elam, so none of the work-horses are in the corral yet."

"We'll meet you in the garden when we get the horse unhitched," Joseph said.

Aaron waved his brother aside. "You go on ahead. I don't need any help."

"Let's go then." Joseph reached for Katie's hand, and Allison followed as the happy couple hurried toward the berry patch.

Soon Katie and Joseph were on their knees together, and Allison returned to the spot where she'd been working. Rhythmically, she picked one berry after another, but her thoughts were on Aaron. She glanced up every once in a while, wondering what was taking him so long.

Several minutes later, Aaron finally showed up. His straw hat was tipped way back on his head, and his face was red and sweaty.

"What happened?" she asked as he knelt beside her. "You look like you've been running."

"Something spooked my horse, and he pulled away from me. I had to chase him down before I could get him into the corral."

Since the barn was out of sight of the garden, Allison hadn't heard or seen the incident, but she imagined it must have looked pretty funny. She held back the laughter bubbling in her throat and pointed to her half-full bucket of berries. "You can help fill mine if you want. When it's full, we can get another container for you to take home."

"Sounds good." Aaron wiped his forehead with his shirtsleeve and started picking.

During the next hour, they cleaned out most of the ripe berries. When they were done, they sat in wicker chairs on the back porch, drinking cold milk and eating the brownies Katie's mother had made.

As the sun began to set, Allison stood and smoothed the wrinkles in her dress. "Guess I'd better be going. Uncle Ben and Aunt Mary will worry if I'm out after dark."

Aaron jumped up. "I've got an idea. Why don't I drive you home in your buggy, and Joseph can take our rig?"

"How will you get home once you've dropped me off?" she questioned.

Aaron rubbed the bridge of his nose as he contemplated the problem.

"I know how we can make it work," Joseph spoke up. "I'll stay and visit with Katie awhile, and that'll give you a chance to take Allison home. When I'm ready to head out, I'll swing by the Kings' place and pick you up."

"That's fine by me." Aaron glanced at Allison. "Are you okay with it?"

She nodded. "Of course."

The breeze hitting Allison's face as they traveled in the buggy helped her cool off, but when Aaron guided the horse to a wide spot alongside the road and slipped his arm across her shoulders, her face heated up.

He grinned at her. "I hope you don't mind that I stopped, but it's hard to talk with the wind in our faces and the horse snorting the way he does. It's not very romantic, either."

Allison smiled. "I don't mind stopping."

"I really enjoy being with you," Aaron said, leaning closer. He smelled good, like ripe strawberries and fresh wind.

She opened her mouth to reply, but his lips touched hers before she could get a word out. The kiss was gentle yet firm, and Allison slipped her hands around Aaron's neck as she leaned into him, enjoying the pleasant moment they shared.

The *clomp-clomp* of horse's hooves, followed by a horn honking, broke the spell, and she reluctantly pulled away. "I think a buggy and a car must be coming."

Aaron nodded and reached for her hand. "Just sit tight and let 'em pass."

As the two vehicles drew closer, Allison's mouth dropped open. The horse was trotting fast in one lane, and the car, going the same way, sped along in the other lane.

"That car is attempting to pass, but the *mupsich* fellow in the buggy is trying to race him," Aaron said with a shake of his head.

Allison sat, too stunned to say a word. She could hardly believe the buggy driver would try to keep up with a car. It really did make him look stupid.

"I should have known. That's James Esh in his fancy rig," Aaron mumbled. "He hasn't got a lick of sense."

The buggy raced past them so quickly, Allison felt a chilly breeze. Suddenly, the horse whinnied, reared up, and swerved into the side of the car.

Chapter 21

Allison gasped as she watched James's buggy careen into the car, bounce away, swerve back and forth, and finally flip over on its side. The panicked horse broke free and tore off down the road, and James flew out of the buggy, landing in the ditch.

The car screeched to a stop, the Englisher jumped out, and Allison and Aaron hopped down from the buggy. "I didn't hit that fellow on purpose," the middle-aged man said in a trembling voice. "He was trying to keep me from passing and kept swerving all over the road." He raked shaky fingers through his thinning brown hair and winced as his gaze came to rest on James, who lay motionless in a twisted position.

From where Allison stood, she couldn't see the extent of James's injuries. As the man and Aaron rushed over to him, she could only stand, too dazed to move. She saw the English man bend down and touch the side of James's neck; then he reached into his shirt pocket and pulled out a cell phone. Aaron's lips moved, but she wasn't able to make out his words.

Taking short, quick breaths, Allison leaned against

her buggy. Her heart pounded wildly as a vision from the past threatened to suffocate her . . .

"Mama!" Allison gasped as she watched a car slam into her mother's buggy, thrusting it to the middle of the road before it toppled on its side with a sickening clatter.

"Mama! Mama!" Allison rushed into the road, but someone—maybe the English man who'd driven the car—pushed her aside. She swallowed against the bitter taste of fear in her mouth. "Oh, Mama, please don't die. You've got to be all right!"

Allison struggled to bring her thoughts back to the present and had to lean over and place both hands on her knees in order to slow the rate of her heartbeat. "I remember," she murmured. "I remember seeing Mama's accident on that hot summer day when she pulled out of our driveway."

She glanced over at James and saw that the lower part of his body had been covered with a quilt. Aaron must have taken it from the back of the buggy without her realizing it.

When Aaron and the English man joined Allison, she noticed that Aaron stood in such a way that her view of James was blocked. She wondered if Aaron was trying to shield her from seeing the extent of James's injuries.

"Is. . . is he dead?" Allison's voice was little more

than a gravelly croak, and the moisture on her cheeks dribbled all the way to her chin.

"There's a faint pulse, but it doesn't look good," the English man answered before Aaron could reply. "I've called 911 on my cell phone, and an ambulance is on its way."

"I . . . I need to see James. There's something I must tell him." Allison stepped around Aaron, but he grabbed her arm.

"He doesn't seem to be conscious, and there's really nothing we can do but wait for help to arrive."

"Shouldn't we get him up off the ground?"

"That's not a good idea," the English man said with a shake of his head. "He's likely got internal injuries, and from the looks of his left leg, I'd say he has at least one broken bone."

Allison swallowed around the lump in her throat. "I have to talk to James."

Aaron shook his head. "You don't want to go over there, believe me. He's been seriously injured, and—"

"And it's not a pretty sight," the Englisher interrupted. "You'd better listen and wait in the buggy."

"No, I won't! I can't!" Allison pulled away from Aaron's grasp.

"Then let me go with you," he offered.

"I'd rather do this alone." Without waiting for Aaron's reply, she rushed over to James and knelt beside his mangled body. Her heart lurched at the sight of his head, twisted awkwardly to one side and covered in blood. His left leg was bent at an odd, distorted angle, and his arms were scraped and bleeding.

"James. Can you hear me?"

There was no response—no indication that he was even alive.

Heavenly Father, Allison prayed, *help me get through to him. Please don't let it be too late for James.* With her eyes closed, Allison quoted Jeremiah 29:13, the same verse that Aunt Mary had shared with her. " 'And ye shall seek me, and find me, when ye shall search for me with all your heart.' "

Allison heard a muffled moan, and her eyes popped open. James's eyes were barely slits, but at least they were open. She hoped he could see her.

"James, have you ever asked God to forgive your sins? Have you accepted Jesus as your personal Savior?" she whispered, leaning close to his ear.

His only response was another weak moan.

She laid a gentle hand on James's chest. It was the only place on his body where there was no blood showing. "If you can hear me, James, blink your eyes once."

His eyelids closed then opened slowly again.

"I'm going to pray with you now. If you believe the words I say, then repeat them in your mind."

James closed his eyes, but the slight rise and fall of his chest let Allison know he was still breathing.

"Dear Lord," she prayed, "I know I'm a sinner, and I ask Your forgiveness for the wrongs I have done. I believe Jesus died for my sins, and that His blood saves me now."

When Allison finished the prayer, James opened his eyes and blinked once. Had she gotten through to him? Had he sought forgiveness for his sins and yielded his life to the Lord?

Sirens blared in the distance, but Allison felt a strange sense of peace. She had done all she could for the man who lay before her. James's life was in God's hands.

As Herman sat on a bale of straw inside his barn, confusing thoughts swirled in his brain like a raging tornado. Catherine had cancer but refused any kind of treatment. Short of a miracle, she was going to die. She didn't want Allison to come home.

He let his head fall forward into his open palms. *Why, God? Why? I know Catherine hasn't been the best sister or even such a good aunt to my kinner. But she's always seen that we had meals on the table and kept the house clean, organized, and running smoothly so I could be about my dairy business. Even though my sister and I don't always see eye to eye on things, I don't want her to die.*

"Papa, what's wrong?"

Herman jumped at the sound of Peter's voice. He looked up and slowly shook his head. "I took your aunt Catherine to see the doctor again today. He gave us some bad news."

"What kind of bad news?"

"Your aunt's got colon cancer."

Peter's face blanched. "Ach, no!"

"The doctor says it's spreading to other parts of her body." Herman's voice shook with emotion. "The worst of it is she refuses to take any kind of treatment."

"But that's lecherich! Even if treatment won't cure her cancer, I'm sure it can give her more time."

Herman nodded. "That's what I believe, too. Even though we both think your aunt's decision is ridiculous, unless we can get her to change her mind, I'm afraid we'll have to abide by her wishes."

Peter sank to the bale of straw beside Herman. "Does anyone else in the family know about this yet?"

"So far, just you and me." Herman released a shuddering sigh. "I'll tell your brothers and their wives about it sometime this week, but I'm not sure what to do about Allison."

"What do you mean?"

"My stubborn sister doesn't want Allison to know."

"Why not?"

Herman shrugged. "I don't know. She wouldn't say; just insisted I not tell Allison or ask that she come home."

"Isn't Aunt Catherine going to need some help? I mean, with her not feeling well, and—"

"There'll come a time when she won't be able to do much at all. I'm hoping that won't happen until after Allison returns home."

"So you're not going to tell her about Aunt Catherine's diagnosis?"

Herman shook his head. "Not yet, but I will when it becomes necessary."

"I guess all we can do right now is pray," Peter said. "Pray that Aunt Catherine comes to her senses and agrees to take whatever treatment the doctor thinks she should have."

Herman nodded. "Prayer is all we have right now."

As Aaron watched Allison kneeling beside James's wounded body, a pang of jealousy crept into his soul. Only moments ago, she and Aaron had been kissing. Now she was at James's side, whispering in his ear.

I feel bad for the poor fellow and hate being a witness to such a terrible accident. Even though I've never cared much for James, I find no pleasure in him getting hurt or possibly dying. Aaron hoped James's injuries weren't life threatening and had even been praying on his behalf. Yet he couldn't set his feelings of rejection aside as he witnessed Allison bent over James. She obviously had strong feelings for the man.

Aaron gritted his teeth. *If it were me lying there hurt, would she care so much?* He was tempted to move closer so he could hear what she was saying, but that might make things worse. If Allison did love James, she would probably see Aaron's coming over as interference. She needed this time to express her feelings and possibly say her last good-byes. No, Aaron would not disturb their time together, no matter how much he wanted to know what was being said.

Blaring sirens drove his thoughts aside, and he felt relief when the ambulance and a police car approached the scene of the accident. Two paramedics rushed over to James, while a policeman headed for the English man, waiting beside his car.

Aaron stepped forward, knowing he'd been a witness to the crash and needed to tell the police everything he'd seen.

Just before Aaron approached the uniformed officer, he glanced over his shoulder. The paramedics had lifted James onto a stretcher, and Allison followed as they headed for the ambulance. Was she planning to go with them to the hospital?

Aaron squeezed his eyes shut. *Lord, please be with James, and if Allison's in love with James, then give me the strength to let her go.*

Chapter 22

Allison drew in a deep breath and tried to steady her nerves. Today was the day the men in the community had originally planned to build Uncle Ben's new barn. Instead, they stood at the cemetery, saying good-bye to James Esh. The barn raising would have to wait another week or so.

Allison was confident that James had heard the prayer she'd offered on his behalf, but she grieved for his family. It didn't seem right that a young man in the prime of his life had been killed in such a senseless, tragic accident.

She pitied Clarence and Vera Esh. James was the only one of their children who had never been baptized and joined the Amish church. Allison hoped for the chance to speak with James's parents later on and explain how she'd been able to pray with their son. It might offer some measure of comfort if they knew James had been given the opportunity to make things right with God before he died.

Allison glanced at her friend Katie, who stood with her folks next to James's family. Katie's eyes were downcast, as were the rest of the family's. Vera Esh leaned her head on her husband's shoulder and trembled with obvious grief.

Allison felt moisture on her cheek and realized that she, too, was crying. She knew it was partly in sympathy for James's family, but she also grieved for her mother's passing. It had been hard to witness James's tragic accident, and remembering the crash that had taken her mother's life was nearly Allison's undoing. Even now, as she tried to focus on the verses of scripture Bishop Frey quoted, she could picture Mama lying in the road after being tossed from her buggy when the car had smashed into it. There'd been no chance for good-byes, no opportunity to touch her dear mama one last time. Allison's brothers Ezra and Gerald had insisted that she and Peter go up to the house while Papa waited with Mama until the ambulance arrived. Peter went willingly, but Allison remembered sobbing and begging to stay. Ezra had threatened to carry her if she didn't cooperate, so Allison had remained in the house all afternoon, waiting for some word on her mother's condition. Papa and her other brothers, Darin and Milton, hadn't returned from the hospital until that evening, bringing the grim news that Mama had passed away. That's when Allison's world had fallen apart, and then her memory of the accident had completely shut down.

With a determination to leave the past behind, Allison's gaze went to Aaron, standing between Joseph and Zachary, looking very somber. Allison hoped Aaron would look her way so she could offer a nod of encouragement, but the one time he glanced in her direction, he frowned and looked quickly away.

Ever since the evening of James's accident, Aaron had seemed distant toward Allison, and she didn't know why. She hadn't been allowed to accompany James to the hospital, since she wasn't a family member. Also, the police had wanted to ask her about the things she had witnessed. So Allison, Aaron, and the English man who'd driven the vehicle that collided with James's buggy had taken seats in the police car to answer questions, while James had been rushed to Springfield. It wasn't until the following morning that Allison learned James had died en route to the hospital.

Allison hadn't realized at first that Aaron was acting differently toward her. He'd only said a few words and seemed almost as if he were in daze when she'd joined him in the police car for questioning. She'd thought he was upset over witnessing the horrible crash. But then Joseph showed up, and Aaron suggested his brother take Allison home while he drove over to James's house to tell his parents what had happened. Later, when Aaron came back to Uncle Ben and Aunt Mary's to pick up Joseph, Allison had hoped they could talk. However, Aaron had said he and his brother needed to get home, and they'd left in a hurry. Aaron didn't come around the rest of the week.

Allison squeezed her eyes shut as a silent prayer floated through her mind. *What's gone wrong between Aaron and me? Lord, please give me the opportunity to speak with Aaron today. If it's Your will for us to be a couple, then make things right between us again.*

Another thought popped into Allison's mind. Maybe Aaron wasn't upset with her at all. He might be grieving over James's death and feeling guilty for the unkind words he'd said about James when he was alive. Not that those things weren't true. Allison had seen for herself how wild James was, and she'd never doubted anything Aaron had said. Still, she knew it wasn't right to talk about someone behind his back. If Aaron felt guilty, that might be the reason for his distant attitude. She prayed that was all there was to it and hoped she would have a chance to speak with Aaron after the funeral dinner. If there was any possibility of them having a permanent relationship, they needed to clear the air.

Aaron tried to concentrate on the words of Bishop Frey, who stood at the head of James's casket. But it was hard not to think about Allison and how their relationship had crumbled on the night of James's death. Aaron had thought they were drawing closer and that she might be falling in love with him. But when he'd seen her reaction to the accident, heard the panic in her voice when she insisted on seeing James, and watched her bend over James's body as though she was his girlfriend, he'd been hit with the realization that Allison had deep feelings for James.

Aaron clenched his fingers as he held his hands rigidly at his sides. *That's what I get for allowing myself to fall in love with her. It was stupid to think Allison might become my wife someday. I wish I'd never gone anywhere with her now.* He swallowed around the lump in his throat as a sense of despair crept into his soul, pushing cracks of doubt that threatened his confidence and caused the notion that he'd finally found the perfect woman for him to crumble. *From now on, I'm going to concentrate on my work and forget about Allison loving me, for it's obviously not meant to be. Even if Allison chose to be with me now, I'd be her second choice.*

Aaron turned his thoughts to the harness shop. He'd had a disagreement with his stepfather yesterday morning. Paul had said Aaron was careless and sometimes seemed lazy. Aaron had become angry and reminded Paul that he wasn't his real father and didn't have the right to tell him what to do.

I shouldn't have lost my temper like that, Aaron berated himself. *Paul's a good man, and I know he loves my mamm. I'm sure he cares about everyone in the family—including me. I should have apologized right away, and I'll need to do that when we get home.*

Life's too short to allow hard feelings to come between family members.

Aaron pulled his thoughts aside and concentrated on the bishop's final words. It wasn't right that he'd let his mind wander during the graveside service. No matter how much of a scoundrel James Esh had been, he'd passed from this world into the next and deserved everyone's respect during the last phase of his funeral.

Allison kept busy during the funeral dinner, which was held at Clarence and Vera Esh's house. She helped the women serve the meal and clean up afterward, and was pleased to see that all the strawberry pies she and Aunt Mary had made had been eaten. By the time the last dish was put away, some people had already headed for home. Allison hoped Aaron and his family were not among those that had gone already.

Allison stepped onto the front porch and scanned the yard. Some of the older men sat in chairs under a leafy maple tree, a group of children played nearby, and several women had gathered in another area to visit. There was no sign of Aaron or anyone from his family, though. Maybe he was in the barn.

Allison headed that way, kicking up dust with each step she took. It had been a humid, hot summer, and they needed rain. Inside the barn, she spotted Joseph and Katie sitting on a bale of straw next to Gabe and Melinda. She hurried over and tapped Joseph on the shoulder. "Is Aaron still here? I need to speak with him."

Joseph shook his head. "Sorry, but he left when our folks did. Grandpa and Grandma Raber were tired and needed to get home. I guess Aaron didn't feel like hanging around because he followed them in his buggy. Emma, Bessie, and Zachary rode with him. Davey and I are the only ones from our family still here."

Allison felt a keen sense of disappointment. "I plan to take some of my faceless dolls to the gift shop at the bed-and-breakfast in Seymour on Monday morning," she said. "Maybe I'll drop by the harness shop and speak to him on my way into town."

"I'm sure Aaron will be glad to see you," Joseph replied.

Allison nodded, but she wasn't so sure he would be pleased to see her. She was prepared to exit the barn when Katie said, "How's Shadow doing?"

"Fine. He seems right at home in Uncle Ben's barn."

"That's probably because there are plenty of mice for him to chase," Gabe said with a snicker.

"Won't you sit and visit awhile?" Melinda asked, patting the bale of straw.

"I'd better not," Allison replied. "Aunt Mary and the rest of the family will be ready to leave soon, and I don't want to keep them waiting."

"Gabe and I would like to get together with you and Aaron and go fishing again." Melinda rubbed her protruding stomach and glanced over at Katie. "Maybe you and Joseph can join us."

Katie and Joseph nodded, but Allison shrugged and said, "I'll have to wait and see. Right now I need to speak with Clarence and Vera Esh."

Joseph watched Katie out of the corner of his eye. He sensed that she wanted to speak with him alone, but Melinda seemed to be monopolizing the conversation.

"You should have seen how excited Allison was when I gave her that kitten," Melinda said with an enthusiastic nod. "She said she'd never had a pet before."

"She could have taken her pick of any critter at our place." Gabe nudged Melinda with his elbow. "Why didn't you pawn a few other animals off on Allison that day?"

She nudged him right back. "Very funny."

Katie cleared her throat. "I don't mean to be rude, but I need some fresh air, so I think I'll head outside and take a walk."

"That's fine," Melinda said. "We'll just sit here and visit with Joseph awhile."

Joseph jumped to his feet. "Actually, I think I could use a bit of fresh air, too."

Gabe gave him a knowing smile. "You go right ahead."

Joseph followed Katie to the barn door, and when they stepped outside, he turned to her and said, "Should we take a walk down by the creek?"

"That'd be nice," she said with a nod. "Hopefully no one else is there right now."

They walked in silence until the water came into view, and Joseph was relieved to see that there wasn't a soul in sight. He motioned to a nearby log. "Should we take a seat?"

Katie sat down and released a sigh. "This has been such a trying day. I still can't get over the pitiful look on my aunt Vera's face during the graveside services."

Joseph nodded. "Losing a loved one is never easy, but I think it's especially hard for parents to lose a child."

She shuddered, and when she looked at Joseph, tears glistened in her eyes. "I can't imagine how it would be if I ever lost you."

"I wouldn't want to lose you, either." He reached for her hand. "I've been doing a lot of thinking in the past few days, and I've made a decision."

"What's that?"

"If the main reason your folks don't want you to marry me is because I don't have a good job, then I'm going to ask my daed if he'll hire me at the harness shop."

Katie's brows lifted high on her forehead. "But Aaron's worked there for several years. I thought the shop was supposed to be his someday. Isn't that what you told me once?"

"That's true," he agreed, "but Papa's got lots of work right now, so I'm sure he could use another pair of hands. And as far as who gets the shop—"

Joseph halted his words when his younger brother,

Davey, and Melinda's brother Isaiah showed up on the scene.

"What are you two doin' down here at the creek?" Davey asked.

"We're talking. What's it look like?"

Davey snickered. Isaiah did the same.

"Knock it off." Joseph hoped his little brother wasn't going to say or do something to embarrass him in front of Katie.

Isaiah picked up a flat rock and pitched it into the creek. "Sure is hot today. Makes me wish I could go swimmin' in this old creek."

"I don't suppose it would hurt if we went wading." Davey dropped to the ground and removed his shoes and socks. Then he rolled his pant legs up to the knees and plodded into the water.

Isaiah followed suit.

Joseph looked over at Katie and rolled his eyes.

"I guess I'd better get back to the house," she said, rising to her feet. "I should see how Aunt Vera and Uncle Clarence are doing."

"Jah, okay."

As Joseph and Katie walked away, he leaned close to her ear and whispered, "I'll be talking to my daed sometime this week, and I'll let you know what he has to say about me working for him."

Allison spotted James's folks standing under a maple tree, talking to one of their church ministers. She waited patiently until the minister moved away, then she hurried over to Vera and Clarence.

"Hello, Allison," Vera said. "I heard you were with our son when he died, and I was hoping for the chance to talk to you."

Allison nodded. "I'm not sure if James understood everything I said, but I did get the chance to speak with him before the ambulance came."

"Vera and I had hoped our son would settle down and marry a nice Amish woman from our community," Clarence spoke up. "We'd have even been happy if he'd found an Amish woman from outside this community." He slowly shook his head. "It's so hard for us to accept his death."

Vera's hands trembled as she dabbed at the corners of her eyes with a handkerchief. "My biggest fear is that James didn't make it to heaven."

Allison gave Vera's arm a gentle squeeze. "I can't say for sure what was in James's heart when he died, but I had the chance to pray with him. When I asked if he wanted to seek forgiveness for his sins, he blinked twice."

"What are you saying?" Clarence asked.

"I'm saying that when I prayed the prayer of forgiveness out loud, I think James repeated it in his mind."

Tears welled in Vera's eyes and ran down her cheeks. "Danki, Allison. I'm glad you were there for James in his last moments, and I'm thankful you cared enough to offer that prayer on his behalf."

Allison swallowed around the lump in her throat. She wished she could have prayed with her mother before she'd died. Deep in her heart, she felt confident that Mama had known Jesus personally and made it to heaven. She had such a sweet spirit; she had to know Jesus.

Chapter 23

"Aunt Mary, could I speak with you a minute?" Allison asked before she headed out after breakfast the following morning.

"Of course." Aunt Mary dried her hands on a towel and turned to face Allison. "What did you wish to say?"

"I wanted you to know that I remembered my mamm's accident."

"You did?"

"Jah. The day I witnessed James's accident, it all came rushing back to me."

Aunt Mary stepped forward and gave Allison a hug. "I know it must have been painful, but I hope it helped you find some sort of closure."

Allison nodded as tears welled in her eyes. "It brought back all the fear and sorrow I felt that day, but it also helped me remember Mama."

"I'm glad."

Allison smiled, despite her tears. "I want you to know how much I appreciate all you've been teaching me. Getting to know you and your family has given me a taste of what life would have been like for me if my mamm had lived."

"Having you here has been good for us as well." Aunt Mary patted Allison's back. "We're all pleased that you've decided to stay longer."

"I just hope Papa's okay with it. I still haven't had a letter from him in response to my request. It makes me worry that he might say no."

"I'm sure a letter will come soon, and then your fears will be put to rest." Aunt Mary handed Allison a tissue. "Now dry your eyes and be on your way to town."

"I hope the bed-and-breakfast will be willing to buy some of my dolls," Allison said as she set her black outer bonnet in place over her white kapp.

"They've bought other things made by the Amish in this area, so I'm sure they'll be interested in your dolls, as well."

Allison smiled and scurried out the door. Thanks to Uncle Ben, she found her horse and buggy all ready to go. With a quick wave to Aunt Mary, Allison clucked to the horse and guided her buggy down the driveway. She was excited about taking some of her dolls to the bed-and-breakfast, but nervous about stopping at the harness shop to speak with Aaron. Would he be glad to see her? Would he be too busy to talk? Could they get their relationship back to where it had been before James's accident?

Allison thought of Proverbs 18:24, which she'd read that morning: *"A man that hath friends must shew himself friendly: and there is a friend that sticketh closer than a brother."* She wanted to be Aaron's friend, even if she couldn't be his girlfriend. She knew if he was grieving over James's death, he really needed a friend.

As Allison's horse and buggy proceeded down Highway C, she tried to focus on other things. It was a warm morning, already muggy and buzzing with insects. She'd been swatting at flies ever since she left her aunt and uncle's place.

Allison wondered what it would be like to spend a winter in Webster County. Since the Amish who lived here only drove open buggies, they would have to bundle up in order to be protected when the weather turned cold and snowy. Even so, she longed to stay in this small Amish community, where she could be close to the family and friends she had come to care about. What if, for some reason, Papa didn't want her to stay? What if he insisted she return to Pennsylvania at the end of summer?

Halting her negative thoughts, Allison guided the horse to turn at the entrance of the Hiltys' place. She stopped in front of the hitching post by the harness shop and stepped down from the buggy. It was time to see Aaron.

"I'm going up to the house to speak with your mamm, but I'll be back soon," Paul called to Aaron. "Is there anything I can bring you to eat or drink?"

Aaron looked up from a tub of dye and smiled. He hadn't had a chance to apologize to his stepfather for the harsh words he'd spoken the other morning, but he would do that as soon as Paul returned to the shop. "How about a couple of Mom's oatmeal cookies?"

"Sure, I can do that." Paul opened the door and had just stepped outside when Allison walked in.

"Guder mariye, Paul," she said. "I'm on my way to Seymour and thought I'd drop by and see Aaron a few minutes. If he's not too busy, that is."

Paul nodded. "Aaron's dying some leather straps, but you're welcome to talk to him."

As Allison moved toward Aaron, his breath caught in his throat. He waited for Paul to shut the door, then held up his hands, encased in rubber gloves that were dark with stain. "Better not get too close. This stuff is hard to scrub off. Just ask my mamm; she's had to deal with trying to get dye off my clothes, as well as my skin, ever since I was a boy and first came to work in this shop."

"I'll be careful."

"What did you want to see me about?" he asked.

Allison leaned against one of their workbenches. "We haven't had a chance to talk since the night of James's accident. I had wanted to speak with you after the funeral dinner, but Joseph said you'd gone home with your folks."

Aaron nodded.

She cleared her throat. "You've been acting kind of distant, and I'm wondering if something's wrong."

Aaron draped the piece of leather he'd just stained over a rung on the wooden drying rack and stood. Should he tell her what he thought about her reaction to James? Would it do any good to share his feelings?

"Are you upset about James?" Allison questioned.

He nodded. Maybe she had figured things out already.

"If you're feeling guilty because you said unkind things about James before he died, all you need to do is confess it to God."

Aaron's mouth dropped open. "What?"

"You seemed so glum during the funeral service. I wondered if it was because you felt remorse and wished you could have made things right between you and James before he died."

"I do feel bad for speaking against him," Aaron admitted.

"It's easy to let things slip off our tongue when we're upset. I should know; I've done plenty of it in the past—especially things I said to Aunt Catherine." Allison took a step toward Aaron, but he held up his hands.

"Stain, remember?"

"Right." Her smile seemed to light up the room. "So the reason you didn't say much when you took me home after the accident was because you felt bad about the way things had been between you and James?"

"Actually, I wasn't talking much because I was upset over *you* and James."

"Me and James?"

"Jah. The way you acted when he was thrown from his buggy made me think you had strong feelings for him."

Allison's mouth dropped open. "You thought that?"

He nodded. "You were determined to speak with James, and then you wanted to ride to the hospital in the ambulance with him. It made me believe—"

"I did care about James, but not in the way you think," she interrupted.

"How was it then?"

"I cared about his soul—where he would spend eternity if he died."

Aaron shifted from one foot to the other. Was Allison saying she had rushed to James's side in order to speak to him about God?

"I told James he could be forgiven of his sins, and then I prayed, asking him to repeat the prayer in his mind. I believe in my heart that James understood and accepted Christ as his Savior."

"I . . . I see." Aaron felt as if someone had squeezed all the air out of his lungs. If Allison wasn't in love with James, was it possible that she cared for him?

She stepped forward and touched his arm. "Are you okay? Have I said something to upset you?"

He pulled the rubber gloves off his hands and let them fall to the floor, then quickly reached for her hand. "I've been so dumb thinking you loved James." He lowered his gaze. "It's taken me a long time to deal with my feelings about my daed's death and how it affected my mamm. I was scared of falling in love, because I was worried if I got married, I might lose my wife, the way Mom lost Dad." He drew in a deep breath and lifted his gaze. "After talking to my mamm several weeks ago, I realized that God gave her a second chance at love with Paul and that it wouldn't be good for me to live my life in fear of the unknown."

"That's true."

"I've always told everyone that I'd never get married because I couldn't find the kind of woman I needed. But the truth is I've been too scared." He paused and moistened his lips. "Then you came along, and that all changed."

Allison's forehead wrinkled. "I . . . I'm glad you feel that way, but how can you think I'm the kind of woman you need? I can barely cook, and the things I enjoy doing most are considered men's jobs."

Aaron lifted her chin with his thumb. "That's what I like about you—you're not afraid to try some things other women might shy away from." He drew her into his arms, not even caring about what would happen if Paul stepped through the door. "I'm glad you came by today," he murmured against her ear.

"Jah, me, too."

"Catherine, you've got to listen to reason," Herman said as he pulled out a chair at the kitchen table and sat beside her.

She shook her head. "There is no need to bring Allison home early."

He held out the letter he'd recently received. "She wants to stay longer than originally planned."

Catherine shrugged. "She can do whatever she likes."

"But you're going to need her help," he argued.

"I'll do what I can for as long as I can." She took a sip from her cup of tea. "If I need any help, I'll ask some of the women in our community."

Herman was sure Sally's mother, Dorothy, and several other women would be willing to help out, but they couldn't be there all the time. Besides, Allison deserved to know about her aunt's cancer, and he was sure once she heard, she would want to return home.

"Can I talk to you a minute?" Joseph asked when he stepped out of the barn and spotted his stepfather heading for the harness shop.

"Jah, sure. What's up, son?"

Joseph hurried to his side. "I was wondering . . . ."

"You seem nervous. Is there something wrong?"

"Not wrong exactly." Joseph cleared his throat a couple of times. "It's just that . . . well, I know you and Aaron have been pretty busy in the harness shop lately, and I was wondering if you might need an extra pair of hands."

"You mean *your* hands?"

Joseph nodded. "My job at Osborn's tree farm is only parttime, and so's the farm work I do for the neighbors."

Papa studied Joseph intently. "Are you looking for full-time work? Is that what you're saying?"

"Jah. I need something steady and reliable. Something I can count on all year long."

Papa squinted as he gave his earlobe a tug. "You've never shown much interest in the harness shop before. You'd have a lot to learn."

"I know."

"Do you mind telling me why the sudden desire to work there?"

"I just told you—I need to find a full-time job."

"And why is that, Joseph?"

"Well, I—"

"Is there a woman involved in this decision?"

"Jah. I've asked Katie Esh to marry me, but her folks won't give their blessing unless I have a full-time job."

Papa's brows furrowed. "Is that the only reason?"

"What do you mean?"

"Don't they have any concerns about the fact that you and Katie are only eighteen?"

"I suppose they do, but—"

"Don't you think it would be better if you and Katie waited a few years to be married?"

"Katie and I are in love, and we want to be married as soon as possible."

"Even if you did have a full-time job, I don't think you're mature enough to be a husband right now."

Joseph's spine went rigid. In all the years Paul had been married to Mom, he'd never made Joseph feel as small as he did right now. "I'm not immature. I'm a hard worker, and I make good decisions."

"Do you now?" Papa gave his earlobe another quick pull. "Was it a good decision when you bought that very spirited gelding a few months ago and then it kicked one of the other horses because it has such a mean streak?"

"I had no way of knowing the horse was mean when I bought him."

"A knowledgeable horseman would have known. Would have asked more questions before buying such a horse."

Joseph grunted. "So you're saying I shouldn't marry Katie because I made one mistake when I bought a spirited horse?"

"I'm not saying that at all. I just think you need to wait a few years before you settle down to marriage and raising a family." Papa sighed. "If you really want to work at the harness shop, I'll have Aaron train you in his spare time, but that doesn't mean you have my blessing to marry Katie right now."

"Just forget it." Joseph kicked at the stones beneath his feet. "I'll find a job somewhere else."

Papa put his hand on Joseph's shoulder. "I didn't say you couldn't come to work for me. If you really want to work in the harness shop, then I'd like to have you here." He smiled. "Maybe someday, after I retire, you and Aaron can run the shop together."

Joseph compressed his lips as he mulled things over. *If I learn the harness business and prove that I'm hard-working and reliable, maybe Papa will change his mind about me marrying Katie.* "I'll think things over and let you know." He hurried away before Papa could say anything more.

• • •

As Aaron walked past the front window of the harness shop, he spotted Paul talking with Joseph. His brother appeared to be quite upset. So did Paul, for that matter. Surely they couldn't have had a disagreement. Joseph and Paul had always gotten along so well. For many years, Aaron had struggled with jealousy toward his brother because of his and Paul's special relationship. Easygoing, happy-go-lucky Joseph had stuck to Paul like sticky tape when he'd first come to work for Mom in the harness shop. Aaron could still remember the irritation he'd felt every time he'd seen Joseph sitting beside Paul, looking up at him with adoration. And Paul had seemed equally mesmerized with Joseph. Zachary and Davey, too, for that matter. It was as if Paul had taken their father's place right from the start. Back then, Aaron had thought Paul was buttering Joseph and Zachary up just so he could get close to Mom. He figured Paul was trying to worm his way into her heart so he could get his hands on the harness shop. But later, when Paul had taken more of an interest in Aaron and shown that he really loved Mom, Aaron had decided that Paul wasn't after the harness shop at all.

"I brought our lunches," Paul said when he stepped into the shop a few minutes later.

"Danki." Aaron took his lunch pail from Paul and placed it on the nearest workbench. "I saw you talking to Joseph outside. Is everything okay?"

Paul shrugged. "Jah, sure. Why do you ask?"

232

"Both of you looked kind of upset, and I wondered what was going on."

"Joseph asked if I might consider hiring him to work here in the harness shop."

Aaron's mouth dropped open, and his heart raced. Did Joseph want his job? Was he hoping to get his hands on the harness shop after Paul retired?

"You look surprised."

"I am. I mean, Joseph's never shown much interest in the shop before. He's usually avoided coming in here because he doesn't care for all the strong odors."

"I know, but some things change. People change." Paul thumped Aaron on the back. "We've got a lot of work right now. I think we should give your brother a chance, and I told him you'd be the one to train him."

Aaron's face heated up. "Me? Why me?"

"Because he's your brother, and I know you'll do a good job teaching him what he needs to know."

Aaron was getting prepared to argue the point, but the telephone rang.

"I'd better see who that is." Paul hurried over to his desk and picked up the phone.

Aaron slumped against the workbench. He had no appetite for lunch now. And he definitely did not want to train his brother to work in the harness shop!

Chapter 24

Allison awoke with a feeling of anticipation. Uncle Ben's barn raising was today, and Aaron would be here, along with most of the Amish men in their community. It would be a long day, and the men would be arriving soon, so she needed to hurry and get downstairs to help Aunt Mary and Sarah in the kitchen. Several women would be coming with their husbands, so they would have plenty of help throughout the day.

Allison headed down the stairs and met her aunt in the hallway. "Guder mariye," Aunt Mary said. "Did you sleep well?"

"Jah. And you?"

"I slept fine, except I'm wishing I had gone to bed earlier last night. I'll need a lot of energy to get through this day."

"I'll help wherever I'm needed."

"I know you will." Aunt Mary squeezed Allison's arm. "You've been a big help since you came here, and I'll be real pleased if your daed says you can stay longer."

Allison smiled. "Me, too."

"Oh, I almost forgot—when I was in Seymour at the chiropractor's yesterday, I was telling the doctor's receptionist about your faceless dolls. She has a friend who works at a gift shop in Branson, and she's interested in selling some of your dolls in her shop."

"That would be wunderbaar." A sense of excitement

welled in Allison's soul. She had never been excited about much of anything when she was at home. Maybe that was because every time she showed the least bit of enthusiasm, Aunt Catherine threw cold water on it. "I've got several dolls made up, so maybe I could run them by the chiropractor's office on Monday morning."

"I might go with you," Aunt Mary said as they entered the kitchen. "Then I can see if the doctor has time to work on my back. After today, I'll probably need another adjustment."

"If you're hurting, why don't you rest awhile and let me take over? I'm sure there will be plenty of other women here to help, too."

Aunt Mary shook her head. "I wouldn't dream of putting all the responsibility on your shoulders. I'll be fine as long as I don't lift anything heavy."

"We'll just have to see that you don't." Allison gave Aunt Mary a hug, grabbed her choring apron from the wall peg by the back door, and hurried to the refrigerator. There was so much to be thankful for, and she was eager to begin the day.

"How come you two are wearin' such scowls on your faces? Is it because you're not anxious to spend the day workin' up a sweat?" Zachary asked, glancing first at Aaron and then Joseph as they headed for the Kings' place in Aaron's buggy.

"I'm not wearing a scowl," Joseph mumbled.

Zachary nudged Joseph with his bony elbow. "I

would think you'd be wearin' a smug expression today."

"Why's that?" Joseph asked.

"'Cause your *aldi* will be there, and I'll bet you can't wait to see her." He snickered. "The same goes for you, Aaron. I'll bet you're in *lieb* with Allison, huh?"

"Knock it off, or we'll put you in the backseat," Aaron warned. He was in no mood for his little brother's teasing.

Zachary's forehead wrinkled. "Maybe I should have ridden with Papa and Davey."

"That might have been for the best." Joseph bumped Zachary's shoulder. "At least they'd be the ones putting up with you now, and Aaron and I would be riding in peace and quiet."

Zachary's right; I am in love, Aaron thought as he snapped the reins to get the horse moving faster. *But I'm not about to admit that to my little brother. I haven't even told Gabe yet how deeply I've come to care for Allison.*

Aaron thought about his best friend, who would soon become a father. At one time, the idea of having children had scared Aaron to death. Not any-more. Now that he and Allison had worked things out, he was hopeful they might have a future together. If they ever decided to get married, he hoped Allison would be willing to live in Missouri. He had no desire to move, especially not to an area where there were so many tourists. Of course, with

Joseph working at the harness shop, Aaron needed to accept the fact that Paul might give the place over to Joseph instead of him. If that happened, Aaron might need to move away so he wouldn't have to watch the shop that was supposed to be his be run by someone else.

"I'm glad we're finally here," Joseph said as they pulled onto the Kings' property. "You want me and Zachary to help you with the horse, or should the two of us start working on the barn?"

"I can manage on my own," Aaron replied. "I'll join you as soon as I get the horse situated in the corral."

"Okay." Joseph jumped down, and Zachary did the same. As soon as they had moved away, Aaron drove his rig to the area where several other buggies were parked. He'd just gotten the horse unhitched when Gabe showed up.

"Are you all set for a good day's work?" Gabe asked with a smile.

"Sure. How about you?"

"Jah. I'm happy whenever I'm building anything."

"I'm sure that's true. You've enjoyed working with wood ever since we were boys."

"I can probably get started on Rufus's dog run some evening next week," Gabe said. "Would that work okay for you?"

"Whenever you have the time."

"You look kind of down in the dumps today," Gabe commented. "Is there anything going on I should know about?"

Aaron grunted. "Is there anything you don't already know?"

Gabe slapped him playfully on the back. "Are you sayin' I'm nosy?"

"I'm not saying that at all. You just seem to have a way of knowing what's going on around our community."

Gabe chuckled. "Guess that's because so many of my customers like to share the local news."

"Jah, well, you need to be careful you don't blab everything you hear. Some folks don't like others knowing their business."

"Like you? Is that what you're saying?"

Aaron shrugged and led his horse into the corral.

"Are you going to tell me what's put such a sour look on your face this morning or not?"

Aaron closed the corral gate and turned to face his friend. "If you must know, my brother is coming to work in the harness shop."

Gabe's eyebrows lifted. "Which brother?"

"Joseph."

"But I thought he already had a job working at Hank Osborn's Christmas tree farm."

"He does, but it's only part-time, and he asked Paul about working in the harness shop so he'd have steady work." Aaron grimaced. "Paul said yes, and the worst part is, he wants me to train Joseph."

"So that's what's got you looking so down-in-the-mouth?"

"Right. If Joseph learns the harness trade, then he might be looking to own it some day."

Gabe's forehead wrinkled. "But it's been promised to you. Am I right about that?"

"That's true, but things can change." Aaron grunted. "Joseph and Paul have always been very close. I wouldn't be surprised if Paul doesn't decide to give the shop to Joseph instead of me."

Gabe shook his head. "I don't think that's going to happen."

"If it does, I'll probably move away."

"Where would you go?"

Aaron shrugged. "Maybe to Pennsylvania. There are plenty of harness shops there, so I'm sure I'd be able to find a job."

A slow smile spread over Gabe's face. "Does Allison Troyer have anything to do with the reason you would choose Pennsylvania?"

Aaron shrugged. "Maybe."

"I knew it! You're in love with her, aren't you?" Gabe thumped Aaron on the back. "By this time next year, you could be an old married man."

"We'll have to see how it goes." Aaron glanced around, hoping to catch a glimpse of Allison, but she was nowhere in sight. He figured she was probably inside with the women fixing snacks or getting the noon meal going. Maybe they could spend a few minutes together after lunch. If not, he would make a point to speak to her before he went home.

Gabe motioned to the group of men wielding hammers and saws. "I suppose we've gabbed long enough, so let's get to work!"

"Why don't you and I serve that table over there?" Allison suggested to Katie as she motioned to the wooden plank set on two sawhorses where Aaron and Joseph sat with several other young men.

"That's fine with me," Katie said.

When Allison set the plate in front of Aaron, he leaned over and whispered, "It's good to see you. Have you been working hard all morning?"

"Not nearly as hard as you. It's awful hot today. Have you been getting enough to drink?"

He nodded. "Sarah and Bessie have brought water to the crew several times this morning."

"Are you gonna pass those sandwiches over, or did ya plan to spend your lunch hour gabbin'?" Zachary, who sat across from Aaron, held out his hand. "I'm starvin' to death here."

Aaron grabbed a ham sandwich, plunked it on his paper plate, and handed the platter to the next man in line. "Maybe there won't be any sandwiches left by the time they get around to you, little bruder."

"Don't pay him any mind, Zachary," Allison put in. "There's plenty more sandwiches in the kitchen." She enjoyed this bantering between Aaron and his younger brother. It reminded her of all the times she and Peter had teased each other. Of course, whenever Aunt Catherine had caught them fooling around, they'd always been reprimanded.

Allison moved back to the serving table to get a bag of potato chips. When she returned, she was surprised to see that Aaron wasn't in his seat. Surely he couldn't have finished eating already. He hadn't even had dessert.

"*Psst* . . . Allison—over here."

When Allison turned, she saw Aaron crouched in the flower bed near the back porch. "What are you doing down there?"

"I spotted this and wondered if it was yours." He held a tiny white kapp between his thumb and index finger.

Allison squinted. It looked like one of the head coverings she had made for her faceless dolls. But how would it have gotten in the flower bed? "Let me have a look at that." She took the tiny hat from Aaron and studied the stitching. It had obviously been done by hand, not on the treadle machine. She knew immediately whose it was. "This isn't one I made. It belongs on the little doll my mamm sewed for me before she died." She slowly shook her head. "I don't understand how it got out of my room and ended up in the flower bed, though. I always keep the doll at the foot of my bed."

Aaron stood. "Maybe one of the kinner who came with their folks today wandered into your room and discovered the doll."

"I guess I should go inside and take a look." Allison started to turn around, but Aaron touched her arm.

"Uh . . . before you go, I was wondering if we could plan another day of fishing soon. Maybe we could invite an old married couple along as chaperones."

"You mean Gabe and Melinda?"

"Jah. We had fun with them the last time, don't you think?"

"Except for our little dunking in the pond," she said with a grin.

He chuckled. "We'll try not to let that happen again."

"When did you want to go?"

"Well, I was thinking—"

"Hey, Allison, the mail just came and there's a letter for you," her cousin Dan interrupted. He held the envelope out to her.

Allison took the letter. "Danki, Dan."

He stood there, as though waiting for something. "Well, aren't ya gonna open it? It could be important, ya know."

Allison glanced at the envelope. The return address was Papa's. Maybe this was the letter she had been hoping for.

She took a seat on the porch steps and was about to rip it open when Aaron said, "Guess I'll let you read your letter in private." He glanced at the picnic tables. "And I'd better get back to the table before all the food's gone."

"Oh, okay. I'll talk to you later then."

Aaron smiled and walked away.

Allison glanced at her young cousin. "Shouldn't you be eating your lunch, too?"

"I'm done."

"Then haven't you got something else to do?"

Dan shrugged his shoulders. "If I go back to the

242

table, Papa will see me. Then he'll expect me to haul more nails and stuff to the men." He wrinkled his nose. "Why can't they see that I'm capable of doin' some real work for a change?"

"I'm sure they appreciate any help you can give them." Anxious to read Papa's letter, Allison decided the only way she was going to have any privacy was to go upstairs. "I've got to run up to my room a minute, Dan. Why don't you ask Aaron or Joseph if there's something you can do to help them this afternoon?"

Dan's lips curved into a smile. "That's a good idea. I think Aaron likes me, so he might let me help him pound nails." He turned and darted away.

Allison hurried into the house and rushed upstairs to her room. As she took a seat on her bed, she realized that her faceless doll was missing. Aaron was probably right—one of the children here today had most likely come into her room, spotted the doll, and taken it somewhere to play.

She placed the little kapp on the table beside her bed and ripped open the letter from Papa:

Dear Allison,

I haven't mentioned this before, but your aunt Catherine has been having pains in her stomach for some time. Thanks to Sally's mom, she finally agreed to see the doctor. At first, the doctor thought the pain she was having was from an irritable bowel. But then he ran some tests, and a few weeks ago we got the results. There's no easy way to say this, but my sister has colon cancer, and the doctor says it's spreading quickly.

Allison clapped her hands over her mouth. Muffled words came out from between her splayed fingers. "Aunt Catherine is sick with cancer? No, it can't be."

She sat for several seconds, trying to digest what she had read. Aunt Catherine had always been a healthy woman. Even when Allison and the rest of the family had come down with a cold or the flu, Aunt Catherine had remained unaffected by the bug. Allison used to think her aunt was too mean to get sick.

Needing to know more, she turned her attention back to the letter:

I received your letter asking if you could stay in Webster County longer than planned. I'd fully intended to tell you to stay as long as you like, but now things have changed. You see, Aunt Catherine has refused to have surgery or undergo any kind of treatment. She asked me not to tell you about her illness and insisted that I not ask you to come home. At first I agreed to her request, but she's getting weaker every day and suffers with more pain. This morning she couldn't get out of bed because of the pain. Peter and I are fending for ourselves, but I'm hoping you will set your plans aside and come home as soon as possible.

Love,
Papa

Allison let the letter slip from her fingers as a cold chill rippled across her shoulders. "Oh, dear God, please don't let Aunt Catherine die before I get home. I need the chance to speak with her."

Chapter 25

As if in a daze, Allison made her way back downstairs. She found Aunt Mary in the kitchen with Katie's mother and a few other ladies from their community.

"I need to speak with you," Allison said, stepping up to her aunt.

"Certainly. What did you need?" Aunt Mary asked with a pleasant smile.

"Can we find somewhere private to talk?"

"Jah, sure." Aunt Mary led the way to her room and took a seat on her bed, motioning for Allison to join her. "What's this all about?" she asked.

Allison swallowed around the lump in her throat. "I got a letter from my daed today, with some very bad news."

Aunt Mary's eyes widened. "What kind of bad news?"

"Aunt Catherine has colon cancer, and it-it's spreading."

"I'm so sorry to hear of this."

"I've got to go home," Allison said with a catch in her voice. "Papa and Peter need my help. So does Aunt Catherine."

"We'll be sad to see you go, but I certainly understand." Aunt Mary clasped Allison's hand. "Maybe you can return to Webster County when things are better."

Allison shook her head. "I don't think things are going to get better. Papa says Aunt Catherine has refused all forms of treatment, so I'm sure it's just a matter of time before she dies." She drew in a shuddering breath. "I need to speak to her about Jesus. I need to be sure she's accepted Him as her Savior."

Aunt Mary nodded. "Jah, that's the most important thing."

"Could I talk to you for a minute?" Joseph asked Katie when she brought a jug of water out to him. "Someplace in private?"

"Of course." She motioned to the side of the house, where there was a shady maple tree. "How about over there?"

"That'll be fine."

Katie led the way, and Joseph followed. When they were under the tree, she turned to him and smiled. "Is everything okay?"

Joseph wiped the sweat from his forehead and grimaced. "I asked my daed the other day if I could go to work in his harness shop, and he said I could. But when I told him that I needed the job so I could marry you, he wasn't so pleased."

"How come? Doesn't he like me? Does he think I won't make you a good wife?"

"It's not that. Papa likes you just fine. He just thinks we're too young, that's all."

Katie swallowed against the burning in her throat. "I guess no one thinks we're ready for marriage."

"After thinking and praying about things, I think they may be right." Joseph reached for her hand. "To tell you the truth, I really don't want to work in the harness shop, but I would if it meant we could be married soon."

She shook her head. "I wouldn't want you working at a job you didn't enjoy. As much as I dislike saying this, I think it's best that we wait until we're both a bit older and you've found a job you really like."

He nodded and smiled. "Is it any wonder I love you so much, Katie Esh? You're exactly what I need."

She stared lovingly into his eyes. "You're what I need, Joseph Zook."

Aaron had just returned to the work site with a can of nails when he spotted Joseph heading his way. He figured this might be a good time to confront Joseph about working at the harness shop, since he hadn't been able to say what was on his mind as they'd traveled here this morning. Not with Zachary's big ears listening to everything they said.

"We need to talk," Aaron said when Joseph approached him. "Meet me over by the buggy shed."

Joseph's eyes narrowed. "What's up?"

"I want to discuss something with you."

"Jah, okay."

Joseph headed for the buggy shed, and Aaron did the same. He was relieved to see no one else was about.

"What did you want to talk to me about?" Joseph asked, leaning against the side of the shed.

"It's about working in the harness shop."

"Oh, that."

"If you really want to work in the shop, there's nothing I can do, but if you've got it in your head that you'd like to own the place someday, then I take exception."

Joseph's mouth dropped open like a broken window hinge. "Own the place? Ach, Aaron, no such thought has ever entered my mind."

"Then how come you asked Paul if you could work there?"

"Because I need a full-time job." Joseph grunted. " 'Course that's not so much the case now."

Aaron wrinkled his forehead. "I'm confused. What are you talking about?"

"As you've probably guessed, I'm in love with Katie, and we were hoping to get married soon."

"From the way you get all starry-eyed whenever Katie's around, I kind of figured you were in love," Aaron said. "But I had no idea you were thinking of getting married."

"Thinking and wanting is about as far as it's gone." Joseph slowly shook his head. "Her folks said I'd need to have a full-time job and that they thought we were too young to be thinking about marriage. When I mentioned it to Papa, he said pretty much the same thing." He shrugged and released a groan. "I figured after three negative votes, there wasn't much point in talkin' to Mama about it."

"Let me get this straight. You thought if you had a full-time job you'd be able to marry Katie?"

Joseph nodded.

"I have to agree with the others. There's a lot more to marriage than just being in love, Joseph."

"Humph! What makes you such an expert on the subject of love and marriage? Until recently, I've never seen you take much interest in any woman."

"Things are different now, and I need to be sure my job at the harness shop is secure—in case I should decide to marry."

"Well, you needn't worry about that, because I've changed my mind about working there. I've never really cared much for the smells in that shop, and spending eight or nine hours a day cutting and dyeing leather really isn't what would make me happy."

"What would make you happy?"

Joseph shrugged. "I haven't figured that out yet. But when I do, you'll be one of the first to know."

Aaron chuckled. "After Katie, you mean?"

"Jah. After her."

"I'm glad we had this little talk," Aaron said. "I feel much better about things, and now I'm free to ask—" Aaron stopped talking when he noticed Allison heading his way. He needed to get rid of Joseph so he could speak to her in private.

As if he could read Aaron's mind, Joseph said,

"Well, I'd better get back to the work site." He offered Aaron a wide smile. "See you later, big brother."

As Allison passed Joseph on her way to speak with Aaron, she hoped he wouldn't detain her with small talk. To her relief, he merely smiled and moved swiftly over to the work site. She hurried over to where Aaron stood by the buggy shed, hoping for the right words and praying she wouldn't break down in front of him.

"Allison, I was hoping I'd get the chance to talk to you again," Aaron said. "I just got some good news."

"I could use some good news about now," she said. "What's your good news?"

"Joseph was planning to work at the harness shop, but he informed me that he's changed his mind."

Allison had no idea why that was good news to Aaron, but she knew if she didn't say what was on her mind quickly, she might lose her nerve. "I came over here to tell you what was in that letter I got from my daed this morning."

"Did he give you an answer about staying on here longer?"

She nodded, as tears stung the backs of her eyes. "He said he would have been fine with the idea, but things have changed at home, so he couldn't give his approval."

Aaron frowned. "What's changed?"

"My aunt Catherine has colon cancer, and it's spreading to other parts of her body." She swallowed hard. "I'm needed at home to care for my family."

Aaron stood for several seconds, rocking back and forth on his heels. "I'm sorry to hear about your aunt, but couldn't your daed find someone to—"

Allison shook her head. "I'm not just needed to cook and clean for them. I need to go home so I can tell Aunt Catherine about Jesus."

Aaron looked at Allison like she'd taken leave of her senses. "She doesn't know about Jesus?"

"She knows *about* Him, but I don't believe she knows Him in a personal way."

"I see. Then I guess it's important for someone to tell her."

Allison nodded. "Aunt Catherine and I have never been close, and I'm not even sure she'll listen to anything I have to say. But I have to try, Aaron." Tears clouded her vision and dribbled onto her cheeks.

"You will write to me, won't you?"

"Of course. I'll write as often as I can."

"I'll write you, too." Aaron pulled her into his arms and gently patted her back. "Will you come back to Missouri?"

"I . . . I'm not sure. I want to, but I'll have to wait and see how things go." She sniffed. While she wouldn't tell Aaron, she believed that once she returned home, she would never see him again.

Chapter 26

As Allison stood with Aunt Mary in front of Lazy Lee's Gas Station on Monday morning, tears welled in her eyes and mixed with the raindrops that had begun to fall. The much-needed rain they'd been praying for was finally here, and it seemed fitting that the clouds overhead would add their tears to her own. Instead of taking her homemade Amish dolls to the chiropractor's office so the receptionist could offer them to a gift shop in Branson, Allison now waited for a bus that would take her home.

It pained her to leave Aunt Mary and her family, and it especially hurt to be going away from Aaron. It had been hard to tell him she was returning to Pennsylvania, and even more difficult to admit she didn't know when or if she might return to Missouri. Even though she and Aaron had promised to write to each other, it wouldn't be easy to carry on a long-distance relationship. She wished she could have offered Aaron a guarantee that she would come back, but there were no guarantees. She didn't know how long she would be needed at home, and if Aunt Catherine died, Papa would need someone to cook and keep house for him.

Allison could still see the forlorn look on Aaron's face when they'd said good-bye yesterday in front of the buggy shed. She had longed to say she loved him and ask if he would wait for her, in case she was able to return to Missouri. But that wouldn't have been fair. As much as it hurt, she would have to let Aaron go. He deserved the freedom to move on with his life and find someone else to marry.

"We'll surely miss you," Aunt Mary said, breaking into Allison's thoughts. "We'll be praying that God might offer a miracle for your daed's sister."

Allison nodded. "It would be wunderbaar if she was healed of her cancer, but as I've mentioned before, I'm more worried about healing for her soul."

"We'll be praying about that, too." Aunt Mary smiled and slipped her arm around Allison's waist. "I'll ask God to give you the chance to witness to your aunt Catherine, just as you did with James."

"Danki, I'm praying for that, too." Allison glanced over her shoulder. A part of her had secretly hoped Aaron would come to see her off this morning. But maybe it was for the best that he hadn't shown up. A tearful good-bye in front of Aunt Mary or anyone else waiting for the bus would have been too difficult.

"I appreciate your willingness to see if you can sell the dolls I'm leaving with you, and I'm also glad you gave Bessie permission to take my kitten," Allison said, hoping the change of subject might lessen her pain. "There wouldn't be much point in me taking the dolls with me, and since Aunt Catherine doesn't like pets, I couldn't take Shadow."

"I don't mind keeping the dolls or your cat," Aunt Mary replied. "But I do hope you will continue making faceless dolls when you get home."

Allison shook her head. "I doubt there'll be enough time for that, since I'll have so many chores to do. Not to mention that I'll be needed to help care for Aunt Catherine as she nears the end."

"I understand, but if you do find any free time, sewing might be good therapy for you."

"I'll have to see how it goes." Allison looked at the piece of luggage sitting at her feet. All the clothes she had brought to Missouri were inside the suitcase, but one important item was missing—the little faceless doll her mother had made for her before she died. It didn't feel right leaving without that precious doll; yet all that remained of it was the small white kapp Aaron had found in the flower bed.

After Allison had made a thorough search of the room, she'd resigned herself to the fact that someone had indeed taken it. She had questioned everyone in Aunt Mary's family and searched the house and barn, but the doll hadn't turned up anywhere.

"If you ever find the faceless doll my mamm made, would you mail it to me?" Allison asked Aunt Mary.

"Of course, and I'll ask everyone in the family to keep an eye out for it."

The rumble of the bus pulling into the parking lot brought a fresh set of tears to Allison's eyes. She was about to leave Webster County behind, along with so many people she had come to love. At least she was returning home a little better equipped to run a house, and for that she felt thankful.

While Allison's suitcase was being loaded into the baggage compartment, she turned and gave Aunt Mary a hug. "Danki for everything—especially for showing me how to find the Lord." Her voice broke and she swallowed hard. "Come visit us sometime if you can."

Aunt Mary nodded as tears trickled down her cheeks. "I'll be praying that you'll be able to come back here again, too."

"There's something I need to tell you," Herman said as he took a seat on the sofa beside his sister.

"What is it?" Catherine asked, barely giving him a glance.

"I wrote Allison a letter the other day and told her about your condition."

"Figured you would," she mumbled. "Never could trust you to keep your word."

Herman fought the urge to argue with her. Catherine always had to be right. He cleared his throat a couple of times. "The thing is I asked if Allison would come home."

"You did what?" Catherine's voice trembled, and her usually pale face turned crimson.

"Allison is needed here, and—"

"I told you I didn't want her help."

"I know what you said, but I also know that you can no longer keep up with things around here."

"Write her back and tell her not to come."

"It's too late for that; she called me the same day she

got my letter and said she's coming home. Fact is, she should be on the bus by now and will be here in a couple of days."

Catherine folded her arms and stared straight ahead. "Then I guess there's nothing more to be said."

As Aaron guided his horse and buggy into Lazy Lee's, he scanned the parking lot, filled with numerous mud puddles. There was no sign of Allison or her aunt out front. Had he arrived too late to say one final good-bye?

A vision of Allison's face popped into his head. He could still see her sad expression when she'd told him she was leaving. He could still smell the aroma of peaches from her freshly shampooed hair and hear the pain in her voice as she'd murmured, "I'll write you as often as I can."

Aaron pulled on the reins and halted his horse near the back of the station, where a hitching rail had been erected for Amish buggies. Maybe the bus hadn't come yet. Allison might be waiting inside, out of the rain. He jumped down from the buggy, tied the horse to the rail, and dashed into the building.

Aaron glanced around the place, noting the numerous racks of fast-food items and shelves full of oil cans, wiper blades, and other things the Englishers used on their cars. A man and a woman sat at one of the tables near the front of the store, eating sub sandwiches. But there was no sign of Allison or Mary. Could they have gone to the ladies' room?

"Has the bus come in yet?" Aaron asked the middle-aged man behind the counter.

"Yep. Came and left again."

"How long ago?" It was a crazy notion, but if the bus wasn't too far ahead, Aaron thought maybe he could catch up to it along the highway.

"It's been a good ten or fifteen minutes now," the station attendant replied.

Aaron's heart took a nosedive. He was too late. There was no hope of him catching the bus; it was well on its way to Springfield. He'd thought saying good-bye to Allison yesterday would be good enough, but this morning as he was getting ready for work, he'd changed his mind. With Paul's permission, he had hitched his horse to a buggy and headed for Seymour, with the need to see Allison burning in his soul. He needed to hold her one last time and let her know how much he loved her.

"You wantin' to buy anything?"

The question from the store clerk halted Aaron's thoughts. "Uh . . . no. Just came in to see if the bus had come yet."

"As I said before, you've missed it."

With shoulders slumped and head down, Aaron shuffled to the front door, feeling like a heavy chunk of leather was weighing him down. Would he ever see Allison again?

Chapter 27

"I want you to be prepared for the way things are at home," Allison's father said as their English neighbor drove them from the bus station to their home in his minivan.

Allison turned in her seat and faced her father. "What do you mean, Papa?" His grave expression let her know things weren't good.

"Your aunt Catherine won't accept any of the treatments her doctor's suggested, and she won't even talk about her illness."

"Why not? Doesn't she realize the treatments might prolong her life?"

"I think she's afraid of the negative side effects the treatments could cause." He pulled his fingers through the side of his hair. "To tell you the truth, I don't think she cares about prolonging her life."

"Oh, but—"

"This is her decision, and I've agreed to abide by it." He reached for Allison's hand. "She's irritable and tries to do more than she can. Then she exhausts herself and ends up unable to do anything except rest for the next several days. Peter and I can fend for ourselves when it's necessary, but we don't have time to cook decent meals or keep the place clean. And someone needs to be at the house to take care of my sister when she's having a bad day."

"Maybe she will rest more with me there to do the cleaning and cooking."

Papa nodded soberly. "That's what I'm hoping for, and I thank you for coming."

"You're welcome." Allison leaned her head against the seat and tried to relax. The days ahead would be full of trials. She could only hope she was up to the task.

"Wie geht's?" Gabe asked as he stepped into the harness shop.

Aaron pulled his fingers through the back of his hair. "I'm doin' okay. How about you?"

"Can't complain." Gabe moved toward the workbench where Aaron stood. "I came over to start working on Rufus's dog run. It's about time I got around to it, wouldn't you say?"

"I suppose."

"You don't sound too enthused. I figured you'd be desperate to get your mutt in a dog run."

Aaron gave a noncommittal shrug.

"You seem really *nunner* today."

"You'd be down, too, if the woman you loved had moved to Pennsylvania," Aaron mumbled.

Gabe shook his head. "Allison didn't *move* to Pennsylvania, Aaron. She lives there and had to return because her aunt is sick."

"I know that, but she was planning to stay here—at least longer than she'd originally intended."

"She's only been gone a few days. I wouldn't think you'd miss her so much already."

"Jah, well, how would you know what I'm feeling? You're married to the woman you love, and you know she'll be waiting for you when you come home every night." Aaron removed his work apron and hung it on a wall peg. It was past quitting time, and Paul had already gone up to the house. Aaron had figured he would stay and work awhile longer, hoping to keep his hands busy and his mind off the emptiness he'd felt since Allison left. Now that Gabe was here, he figured he might as well quit for the day. Truth be told, he was tired and didn't feel like working longer, anyway.

Gabe rested his hand on Aaron's slumped shoulder. "Don't you remember how things were with Melinda and me during our courtship? There was a time when I didn't know if she was going to remain true to the Amish faith, or if she would choose to go English and become a vet." He shook his head. "Don't think that wasn't stressful. Believe me, I know more of how you're feeling than you can imagine."

Aaron knew his friend was probably right, but it didn't relieve his anxiety any. It had taken a lot for him to get past his feelings about marriage and start courting Allison. Knowing they might never be together hurt worse than a kick in the head by an unruly mule.

"Have you had supper yet?" he asked, feeling the need to change the subject.

"Melinda and I had an early supper," Gabe replied. "But feel free to go have your meal. I'll get started on the dog run, and when you're done, you can join me. If you don't have anything else to do, that is."

"I'm not all that hungry, so I'll go inside and tell my mamm I won't be joining them at the table this evening. Then I'll come back out to help you with the dog run."

Gabe clucked his tongue. "You've got to eat, Aaron. Pining for Allison and starving yourself won't solve a thing."

Aaron knew his friend was only showing concern, but it irked him. He didn't want anyone's sympathy, and he didn't need to be told what to do.

As he opened the shop door and stepped out, a blast of hot, muggy air hit him full in the face. He grimaced. "Sure wish it would cool off and rain again. I'm sick of this sweltering weather!"

He kicked at the stones beneath his feet. *I hope I get a letter from Allison soon. I really do miss her.*

Allison thought she had prepared herself for this moment, but the sight that greeted her when she and Papa stepped into the house made her stomach clench. Aunt Catherine lay on the sofa with a wet washrag on her forehead and a hot water bottle on her stomach. Her skin had a grayish-yellow tinge, her eyes were rimmed with dark circles, and she looked skinny and frail. This wasn't the robust, healthy woman Allison had seen three months ago. It made her wonder how long Aunt Catherine had been sick and hadn't said anything. She might have been in pain for some time.

That could be the reason she'd been so crabby much of the time.

Allison approached the sofa, and her aunt struggled to sit. "That's okay. Don't get up on my account." Allison leaned over and took hold of Aunt Catherine's hand. Aunt Catherine squeezed it in return, but there wasn't much strength in her fingers. A tear trickled down Allison's cheek, and she sniffed.

"We'll have no tears around here. You shouldn't have come home." Aunt Catherine's words were clipped, and if it hadn't been for the knowledge that her aunt was hurting, Allison would have felt offended. "I told your daed not to write that letter, but he insisted on bringing you back to take care of me."

Allison wasn't sure if Aunt Catherine didn't want her here because she didn't like her, or if her harsh words were because she felt bad about Allison having to leave Missouri. It didn't matter. Allison was home now, and she had a job to do. Many times in the past she'd let Aunt Catherine's sharp tongue bother her, but with God's help, she would care for her aunt's physical and spiritual needs without complaint.

"Have you heard anything from Allison?" Melinda asked Mary as she and Katie stepped into Mary's living room for a quilting bee.

Mary nodded. "I got a letter this morning."

"How's she doing? I've only had one letter, and that was right after she first got home," Katie said.

"She's doing all right, but she's very busy keeping house, cooking, and taking care of her aunt."

"Is her aunt's health any better?" Melinda wanted to know.

Mary shook her head. "I'm afraid not. Allison said Catherine is still refusing any kind of treatment other than some pills for her pain."

"That's a shame," Melinda's mother, Faith, put in from across the room. "It seems that so many people have cancer these days."

"If only there wasn't so much pain and suffering in this world," Melinda said, taking a seat in front of the quilting frame. "It breaks my heart to see even the animals I care for when they suffer with some incurable disease."

"Sickness and death were brought into this world when Adam and Eve sinned," Vera Esh spoke up. Her eyes misted. "But someday, God will wipe away all our tears."

"And there will be no more pain and suffering," Mary said, reaching for her well-used thimble. "In the meantime, we can do our part to alleviate some of the misery our friends and family must endure by being there for them and lifting them up in prayer."

All heads nodded in agreement, and Mary lifted a silent prayer on behalf of her brother-in-law, Herman, and the whole Troyer family.

"If you keep jabbing that pitchfork the way you're doing, you'll put a hole in the floor instead of spreading straw in the places it needs to be spread," Peter said when he stepped into the stall Herman had been cleaning.

Herman set the pitchfork aside and straightened. "I guess I *was* going at it pretty good." He reached around to rub a sore spot in his lower back and grimaced.

"If you're back's actin' up, why don't you let me take over?" Peter offered.

"Actually, I think I'm hurting in here more than here." Herman touched his chest, and then his back.

"Because of Aunt Catherine, you mean?"

"Jah, that and the fact that Allison had to cut her time short in Missouri in order to come back and care for things here."

"I think the two of us could have managed okay on our own," Peter said. "It's Aunt Catherine who needs the most looking after right now."

Herman nodded. "I'm afraid it's only going to get worse. Have you noticed the determined set of my sister's jaw when she tries to do something? She attempts to cover up her pain, but I'm no *narr*."

"Of course you're not a fool, Papa."

Herman grimaced. "That sister of mine is hurting more than she'll admit, but I sure wish I hadn't had to ask Allison to come home. She's been so sad since she arrived. I don't think it's just because she feels bad about Aunt Catherine's condition, either."

"You think she's missing Aunt Mary and her family?"

"Jah, and maybe a few others besides."

Peter tipped his head to one side. "You don't think Allison found a boyfriend while she was there, do you?"

Herman shrugged. "I can't be sure, but from the way she's been acting, it's my guess that she's missing more than just her family in Webster County."

Peter stabbed a chunk of straw with the pitchfork and dropped it to the floor. "Allison hasn't had very good luck getting boyfriends in the past, so if she did find one while she was visiting Aunt Mary's family, she's probably none too happy about giving up that relationship." He stuck the pitchfork into the pile of straw again. "Want me to ask her about it?"

Herman shrugged. "She might not appreciate it, but if you feel so inclined, go right ahead."

"I think I will," Peter said with a nod. "As soon as I figure out the best way to ask."

Over the next several weeks, Allison established a routine. Up early every morning to fix breakfast so Papa and Peter could get out to the milking barn. Clean up the kitchen. Take a tray of hot cereal up to Aunt Catherine, who now ate most of her meals in bed. Do the laundry whenever it was needed. Dust, sweep, and shake rugs in every part of the house. Bake bread and desserts, while making sure that each meal was fixed on time.

Allison had to squeeze in a few minutes before bed at night to read her Bible. And she had been negligent about letter writing. She'd only written to Aaron twice, once to let him know she'd arrived home safely, and another letter earlier this week to tell him how her aunt was doing and that she missed him. She'd also written to Aunt Mary and Uncle Ben, as well as to Katie and Melinda. Aunt Mary had sent several letters in return, and she'd had two letters from Katie, but only one from Melinda. Allison figured that was because Melinda had recently given birth to a baby boy, which she'd learned about when she'd received a letter from Aaron last week. He had also said he missed her and had been praying for her aunt.

"I wish I could see that boppli of Melinda's," Allison said with a yawn. For that matter, she wished she could see all her friends and family back in Missouri—especially Aaron, whom she missed more than she was willing to admit.

A knock sounded on Allison's bedroom door.

"Come in," she called.

The door opened, and Peter stuck his head inside. "I was hoping you were still awake."

"I was just getting ready to read a few verses from the Bible before I go to bed," Allison replied.

"Mind if I come in so we can talk awhile?"

"Be my guest," Allison said, motioning him into the room.

Peter stepped inside and took a seat on the end of Allison's bed. "I'm worried about you, Allison."

"Why would you be worried about me? Aunt Catherine's the sick one here."

His forehead wrinkled. "I know that, but you've been working hard night and day. I'm afraid if you don't slow down some you're going to collapse."

She shook her head. "You sound more like Papa now, and not my little bruder."

"I'm not your little brother, Allison. In case you've forgotten, I'm two years older than you."

"I know, but you're my youngest brother, just the same."

Peter smiled, but then his face sobered. "I wish you hadn't felt it necessary to come home so you could take care of us."

"I love you and Papa, so I wouldn't have it any other way." She shrugged. "Besides, I wanted to be here for Aunt Catherine during her time of need."

Deep wrinkles formed in his forehead. "I don't think she's got long for this world, do you?"

Allison shook her head. "Short of a miracle, Aunt Catherine's going to die soon, and I want to be sure she knows Jesus in a personal way before she goes."

"How can you care so much after all the mean things she's said to you over the years?"

"The way I felt about Aunt Catherine changed after I accepted Jesus as my Savior."

Peter nodded slowly. "You have changed a lot since you came home from Missouri."

Allison stared at her Bible, lying on the table beside her bed. "I used to feel faceless, like my life had no purpose. But after Aunt Mary explained to me that God sent Jesus to die for my sins and that He does have a purpose for my life, everything changed." She smiled. "I'm planning to be baptized and join the church this fall."

"That's good to hear."

"Have you ever confessed your sins and asked Jesus to come into your heart, Peter?" Allison asked pointedly.

He nodded. "I made that confession before the People when I was baptized and joined the church."

"I guess the truth of God's plan of salvation never hit home with me until Aunt Mary explained things," Allison said.

Peter reached across the bed and touched Allison's arm. "Mind if I ask you a personal question?"

"What do you want to know?"

"I was wondering why you wrote and asked Papa if you could stay in Missouri longer."

Allison's face heated up, and she blinked a couple of times to keep her tears from spilling over. "I liked it there. I—"

"Did you fall in love with someone? Is that why you wanted to stay?"

She nodded slowly. If she spoke the words, she knew she would dissolve into a puddle of tears.

"I don't suppose you want to tell me who you're in love with?"

She shook her head. "It's over between us, so there's no point in even talking about it."

"That's okay; you don't have to." Peter stood. "Maybe things will work out so you can go back to Missouri after Aunt Catherine—"

Allison held up her hand. "Don't even say it, Peter. My place is here now, and it will always be so for as long as Papa needs me."

Peter opened his mouth as if to say something more, but he closed it again and hurried out of the room.

Allison reached for her Bible, feeling a strong need to read a passage or two before she fell asleep. *I don't want Aaron to get his hopes up about me going back there, because unless God provides a miracle, it doesn't look like Aunt Catherine will make it. If she dies, Papa will need me here more than ever.*

As Allison read John 3:16 and reflected on how God had sent His only Son to die for the sins of the world, she felt a sense of urgency. She had tried on several occasions to witness to Aunt Catherine, but every time she brought up the subject of heaven, Aunt Catherine either said she was tired and wanted to sleep, or became irritable and shouted at Allison to leave the room.

"Dear Lord," Allison prayed, "please give me the opportunity to speak with Aunt Catherine about You soon."

Chapter 28

By the first of November, Aunt Catherine had become weak she spent most of her time in bed. The pain in her body had intensified, and the medication brought little relief. Allison knew if she was going to get through to Aunt Catherine with the message of forgiveness, it would have to be soon. In desperation, Allison formulated a plan. She would make Aunt Catherine a faceless doll and attach a verse of scripture to it, the way Melinda's stepfather did with the desserts he baked to give to folks he felt had a need. Maybe the verse would touch Aunt Catherine's heart in a way Allison couldn't do with words.

Allison headed for the treadle sewing machine, which she discovered was covered with dust. It had obviously been some time since it had been put to use. Carefully, she cut out a girl doll, using the pattern Aunt Mary had given her. She also cut enough material to make a dark blue dress with a black cape and apron, a pair of black stockings, and a small white kapp. It made her think of the doll Mama had made—the one that went missing while she was in Missouri. She'd clung to the doll during her growing-up years, and even though she missed it, she realized what she missed most was not an inanimate object, but people— her aunt, uncle, cousins . . . and especially Aaron.

Allison closed her eyes and drew in a weary breath. She felt so tired and discouraged. Nothing she'd said or done had seemed to please Aunt Catherine. To make things worse, she missed Aaron so much she felt as if her heart could break in two. The only good thing that had happened in her life lately was that she'd been baptized and joined the church a few weeks ago. But even that positive happening hadn't filled the void Allison had felt since she'd left her family and friends in Missouri.

Should I continue to write Aaron letters? she wondered. *Or would it be better if I made a clean break?* Allison continued to ponder the situation as she sewed the doll. Maybe she should wait until after Christmas to make a decision. Or would it be better to do it now, while it was fresh on her mind?

"The letter can wait," she murmured as she slipped a piece of muslin under the pressure foot of the treadle machine. "Right now I need to concentrate on making this doll and deciding which verse of scripture to attach to it."

"Let's get these stalls mucked out now, and then we'll go outside and get that hay unloaded that we've got on the wagon," Herman said to Peter as they entered the barn.

"Good idea," Peter agreed. "The cows aren't as agreeable when they come in for the night and find dirty stalls."

Herman chuckled. "I think it would take more than a clean stall to put some of our cows in an agreeable mood."

"Jah—like Aunt Catherine. She's rarely in a good mood."

"She's got a good excuse for being grumpy these days," Herman said as he handed Peter a shovel.

Peter nodded as he began to muck out the first stall. "Remember when you and I talked about whether Allison has a boyfriend back in Missouri?"

"Jah." Herman lifted a clean bale of straw onto his shoulders and carried it to the stall.

"Well, I had a talk with her about that a few days ago, and I keep forgetting to tell you what she said."

"What did she say?"

"She admitted that she's in love with someone, but she wouldn't say who, and she said it was over between them." Peter grunted as he scooped a shovelful of cow manure into the wheelbarrow. "I think Allison believes her place is here now, caring for us. She's certainly doing a good job, too," he added.

"You're right about that. She may have left Lancaster County a tomboy, but she came home a woman, capable of running a household by herself." Herman set the bale of straw on the floor and grabbed a pitchfork. "I'm just sorry to hear she began a relationship that was over before it really had a chance to begin."

"When I mentioned her returning to Missouri, she said she felt obligated to us. She thinks once Aunt Catherine is gone, she'll be needed here even more."

Herman nodded. "We'll have to see about that when the time comes."

"What are you doing over there?" Aaron asked his youngest sister, Emma, as he stepped into the barn and discovered her huddled in one corner near some bales of straw. Since he'd heard their mother call Emma a few minutes ago, he figured the child must have sneaked off to the barn to play with the kittens when she should have been inside helping set the table for supper.

Emma jumped, like she'd been caught doing something bad, and she looked up at Aaron with both hands behind her back.

"What have you got that you don't want me to see?" he asked, taking a step closer.

She backed away, until her legs bumped the bale of straw. "Nothin'. Just girl stuff."

"What kind of girl stuff would you need to hide?"

She hung her head but gave no reply.

"Emma, hold out your hands so I can see."

Her shoulders trembled, and Aaron guessed she was close to tears.

"If you've got something you're not supposed to have, you'd better give it to me."

"I . . . I didn't mean to keep it. I was only gonna borrow it, but then—"

"Borrow what, Emma?"

The child sniffed, and when she looked up at Aaron, he saw tears in her eyes. "I borrowed this—from Allison Troyer."

Aaron's mouth dropped open as Emma extended her hands, revealing a faceless doll with no kapp on its head. He knew immediately it was the one Allison's mother had given her when she was a young girl. The one Allison's aunt had told him was missing.

"Why, Emma? Why would you take something that wasn't yours?"

Her voice quavered when she spoke. "I-I've asked Mama to make me a doll, but she always says she's too busy takin' care of Grandma and Grandpa Raber. I think she loves them more'n she does me."

Aaron's heart went out to Emma, even though he knew what she had done was wrong. He knelt in front of the little girl and gathered her into his arms. "If I had known you wanted a doll so badly, I would have asked Allison to make you one. She sews faceless dolls and sells them."

Emma opened her mouth as if to say something, but he cut her off. "As far as our mamm loving her folks more than she does you, that's just plain silly. Grandpa and Grandma have some health problems, and she wants to care for them during their old age. But you're her little girl, and she loves you very much." He patted her gently on the back. "Remember when you were in the hospital because of your appendix?"

"Jah."

"Mom and Paul . . . uh . . . your daed, came to see you every day. Fact is, during the first twenty-four hours after your surgery they never left the hospital. Did you know that?"

She hiccupped on a sob. "Huh-uh."

"Do you think they would have done that if they didn't love you?"

"I guess not."

Aaron took the doll from his sister. "This isn't yours, and taking it was wrong. You'll need to tell Mom what you've done."

Tears streamed down Emma's cheeks. "Do I have to, Aaron? What if she gives me a bletsching?"

Aaron gently squeezed her shoulders. "I haven't known our mamm to give out too many spankings over the years, but I'm sure you'll receive whatever punishment she feels you deserve. And if Mom knows how important having a faceless doll is to you, she'll either find the time to sew a doll or she'll buy one for you. Why don't you ask after you've told her what you've done?"

"I . . . I will."

Aaron stood. "I'll see that this doll is sent to Allison, and I'll be sure and tell her how sorry you are for taking it."

She nodded. "Jah, please tell her that, for I surely wish I hadn't done it."

He pointed to the barn door. "Run into the house now and set things straight with Mom. I'll be in shortly."

Emma hesitated, gave Aaron a quick hug around his legs, and darted out the door.

Aaron stared at the bedraggled-looking doll. "Allison will sure be surprised when I mail her this." He smiled. "Maybe I'll wait and send it to her for Christmas."

Allison crept quietly into her aunt's room, unsure if she would find her asleep or not.

The floor squeaked, and Aunt Catherine's eyes fluttered open. Allison smiled, but Aunt Catherine only stared at her with a vacant look. *Doesn't she know who I am? How close might she be to dying?*

"Aunt Catherine, I brought you something," Allison said as she approached the bed.

No response.

"It's a faceless doll, and I made it myself." She held the doll in front of her aunt's face.

Aunt Catherine moaned, as though she were in terrible pain.

"Are you hurting real bad? Is there something I can get for you?"

"I-I've always wanted one."

"What do you want?"

"A faceless doll." Aunt Catherine lifted a shaky hand as tears gathered in the corner of her eyes.

Allison handed the doll to her aunt, and the woman clutched it to her chest with a trembling sob. "My mamm wouldn't allow dolls in the house when I was a girl—not even the faceless kind."

"I-I'm so sorry." Allison's throat clogged with tears. Through all the years Aunt Catherine had lived with them, she'd never thought about how things must have been for her aunt when she was a child. Allison knew Aunt Catherine had grown up with seven brothers and no sisters, but she didn't have any idea the poor woman had been denied the pleasure of owning a doll. All this time, Allison had focused only on how mean Aunt Catherine was and how she'd never felt that the woman cared for her. Maybe if she'd shown love first, it would have been given in return.

"Wh-what's this?" Aunt Catherine asked, touching the slip of paper pinned to the back of the doll's skirt.

"A verse of scripture," Allison replied. "It's one

Aunt Mary quoted to me one day, and then I asked Jesus to forgive my sins. Would you like me to read it to you?"

Aunt Catherine's expression turned stony, and Allison feared she might throw the doll aside or yell at Allison to get out of the room. Instead, her aunt began to cry. First it came out in a soft whine, but then it turned to convulsing sobs. "I've sinned many times over the years." She drew in a raspy breath. "When I learned I had cancer, I wanted to die quickly, but now that my time's getting close, I'm afraid because I . . . I don't know where my soul will go. Oh, Allison, I'm so scared. I don't think I'll make it to heaven."

Aunt Catherine's confession was almost Allison's undoing. She took a seat on the edge of the bed and reached for her aunt's hand. "You can go to heaven, Aunt Catherine. The Bible says we have all sinned and come short of the glory of God. But He provided a way for us to get to heaven, through the blood of His Son, Jesus." She paused to gauge her aunt's reaction. Aunt Catherine lay staring vacantly like she had when Allison first came into the room.

"I used to feel faceless before God," Allison went on to say. "I know now that I'm not faceless. The Bible tells us in Jeremiah 29:13: 'And ye shall seek me, and find me, when ye shall search for me with all your heart.' " She smiled. "I had been searching for Jesus for some time, but it wasn't until I accepted Him as my personal Savior that I felt a sense of peace and purpose for my life. I have every confidence that if I were to die today, my soul would enter into the place where my heavenly Father lives."

"Heaven," Aunt Catherine murmured, as if she were being drawn back into the conversation.

Allison nodded. "Romans 10:9 says, 'That if thou shalt confess with thy mouth the Lord Jesus, and shalt believe in thine heart that God hath raised him from the dead, thou shalt be saved.' Aunt Catherine, would you like me to pray with you, so you can confess your sins and tell the Lord you believe in Him as your Savior?"

"Jah, I would."

Aunt Catherine closed her eyes, and Allison did the same. Allison prayed the same prayer Aunt Mary had prayed with her and that Allison had prayed with James. Aunt Catherine repeated each word. When the prayer ended, a look of peace flooded the woman's face. Allison knew that no matter when the Lord chose to take Aunt Catherine home, she would go to heaven and spend eternity with Him.

Chapter 29

As Allison headed down the driveway toward their mailbox in early December, she let her tears flow unchecked. Yesterday had been Aunt Catherine's funeral. Despite any negative feelings Allison had harbored toward her aunt in the past, she would miss her. Aunt Catherine had been given the chance to make peace with God, and for that Allison felt grateful.

Allison thought about Aunt Catherine's final days

278

on earth and the request she'd made one week before her death. *"Peanut brittle. Let me taste some peanut brittle,"* she'd said.

Even though her aunt had been too weak to chew the hard candy, Allison had honored the appeal. Using the recipe she'd found tucked inside Aunt Catherine's cookbook, Allison had made a batch of peanut brittle.

She could still see the contented expression on her aunt's face when she'd placed a small piece of it between her lips. *"Umm . . . good."*

Allison knew from that day on, whenever she ate peanut brittle, she would think of Aunt Catherine and the precious moments they had spent together over the last few months.

Allison glanced at the letter in her hand. She had planned to wait until after Christmas to write Aaron and tell him she would be staying in Pennsylvania. But why prolong things? Wouldn't it be better if she made a clean break so Aaron could move on with his life? Now that Aunt Catherine was gone, Papa needed Allison more than ever. As much as it hurt to tell Aaron goodbye, she knew it would be best if he found someone else.

Allison opened the mailbox flap, placed the letter inside, and lifted the red flag. With tears blurring her vision, she turned toward the house. *This is for the best—jah, it truly is.*

Aaron's hands trembled as he read the letter he had just received from Allison. She wasn't coming back to

Webster County. Her aunt had died, and her father needed someone to cook and clean for him.

"Doesn't Allison know I need her, too?" he mumbled. "I don't want to court anyone else. It's her I love."

Aaron thought about the doll Allison's mother had made and how he'd discovered his sister had taken it. He had planned to send the doll to Allison for Christmas, but he wondered if it would be best to put it in the mail now and be done with it.

As the reality of never seeing Allison set in, he sank to the stool behind his workbench and groaned. "It isn't fair."

"What's wrong, son? You look like you've lost your best friend," Paul said, moving across the room to stand beside Aaron.

"I have lost a friend." Aaron handed the letter to his stepfather. "Allison's not coming back to Missouri. Her aunt passed away, and she says her daed needs her there."

"I'm sorry about her aunt—and sorry Allison won't be returning to Webster County." Paul placed his hand on Aaron's shoulder. "You care for her a lot, don't you, son?"

Aaron nodded. There was no use denying it, but there wasn't much point in talking about it, either.

"From what I could tell when Allison was visiting for the summer, she seems a lot like your mamm," Paul said.

"She's the kind of woman I've always wanted but

never thought I would find." Aaron grunted. "I wish now that I'd never met her."

Paul pulled another stool over beside Aaron and took a seat. "This isn't an impossible situation, you know."

"As far as I can tell, it is."

Paul shook his head. "Have you forgotten that I used to live in Lancaster County?"

"No, I haven't forgotten. I remember when you first came here for your brother's funeral and decided to stay so you could help Mom in the harness shop."

"That's right. I thought I would only be here a few months—just until your mamm got her strength back after Davey was born. Then I figured I'd be on my way back to Pennsylvania, where I worked at my cousin's harness shop."

"But you ended up staying and marrying Mom."

Paul nodded. "That's right. I loved your mamm so much—and would have done just about anything to marry her." He squeezed Aaron's shoulder. "There is a way for you and Allison to be together."

"What way's that?"

"I could see if my cousin would be willing to hire you at his harness shop, and then you could move to Pennsylvania to be near Allison."

Aaron's mouth dropped open. He'd thought about moving to Pennsylvania once—when he believed Joseph might want to take over the harness shop. "I couldn't leave you in the lurch," he mumbled. "Mom's not able to help out here anymore, and there's too much work for one man. Besides, this shop is supposed to be mine someday. That's the way my real daed wanted it, you know."

"I realize that, Aaron, but what about what you want?"

"What do you mean?"

"Is owning this harness shop more important to you than being with Allison?"

Aaron didn't have to think about that very long. He loved Allison so much it hurt. "Well, no, but I still wouldn't feel right about leaving you to run the place all alone."

Paul pursed his lips, as though deep in thought. "Guess I could see if Zachary might want to work here—although he's never really shown much interest in the harness shop, and I'd have to train him."

Aaron thought about Joseph and how he had asked about working in the harness shop but suddenly changed his mind. Just last week Joseph had found a new job working at the local buggy shop. He liked it there and really seemed to have found his niche. Aaron figured it was just a matter of time before Katie received her parents' blessing to marry Joseph.

"What about asking Davey to work here?" Aaron suggested. "Do you think he might want to be your apprentice?"

Paul pulled his fingers through the ends of his beard and pressed his lips together. "Between Zachary and Davey, I'm sure one of them would be willing to take your place so you can be with the woman you love."

Aaron blew out his breath. "You really think it could work?"

"Don't see why not." Paul patted Aaron on the back. "When love's involved, there's got to be a way."

Aaron rubbed his chin thoughtfully. "Guess I'll have to give this matter some serious consideration."

"It wouldn't hurt to pray about it, too."

Aaron nodded. "I'll definitely be praying."

Paul started to walk away, but Aaron called out to him, "Can I ask you a question?"

Paul turned around. "Sure, Aaron."

Aaron rubbed the bridge of his nose as he contemplated the best way to say what was on his mind. "I've . . . uh . . . been thinking about the way I've been calling you *Paul* for a while, and I'd like to go back to calling you *Papa* again, if you don't mind."

Paul's face broke into a wide smile. "I don't mind at all."

"I'm glad to hear it, because I've come to realize that even though you're not my real *daed*, you love me and my *brieder* just like our real *daed* would."

Paul clasped Aaron's shoulder and gave him a hug. "You and your brothers are like real sons to me."

Chapter 30

For the next several weeks, Allison forced herself to act in front of Papa and Peter. Last week Sally had come for a visit and told her that she and Peter planned to be married soon. Allison was happy about that. Even so, whenever she was alone in the house, she allowed her grief to surface. With Peter soon to be married, Papa would be lonely and would need Allison more than ever. There was no way she would be able to return to Missouri; she needed to accept that fact.

But oh, how she missed Aaron and her family in Webster County. She missed making faceless dolls and spending time with Melinda and Katie. She even missed her cooking lessons and housekeeping chores. Of course, she had cooking and cleaning to do here, but it wasn't nearly as much fun as it had been under Aunt Mary's tutelage.

Allison stirred the pot of stew sitting on the back burner of the stove and sighed. If only she could forget about Aaron. Truth was she wished they'd never met, because it was too painful to find love and then lose it.

The back door slammed shut and she jumped.

"Sorry. Didn't mean to frighten you," Papa said, brushing the snow off his woolen jacket.

"I didn't think you'd be in so soon. Supper won't be ready for another half hour or so."

"That's okay. I'm not all that hungry yet." He ambled over to the sink and turned on the faucet.

"Where's Peter?" Allison asked.

"He went over to Sally's house for supper."

"So it's just the two of us?"

"Jah."

When Papa finished washing up, he pulled out a chair at the kitchen table. "Why don't you turn down the burner and come have a seat? I have a couple of things I've been meaning to give you." He motioned to the chair across from him.

Allison seated herself, curious as to what he had for her.

Papa reached into his shirt pocket and pulled out two envelopes. "This one is from your aunt Catherine."

Allison squinted at the envelope. "But how—"

"She gave it to me before she died—while she was still able to stay focused enough to talk, she told our bishop's wife what she wanted her to write." He handed Allison the envelope. "She said she wanted you to know a few things, but not until after she was gone."

"What things?"

"Why don't you open the letter and find out?"

Allison opened the envelope and read the letter out loud:

"Dear Allison,

It's never been easy for me to admit when I'm wrong, but there's something I need to confess. Remember when John Miller used to come around, wanting to spend time with you? Then just when you showed an interest in him, he quit coming around. That was my fault, Allison. I sent John away."

Allison looked over at Papa. "Why would Aunt Catherine have sent John away?"

"Because she was jealous."

"Jealous? Of me having a boyfriend?"

He nodded. "I think you'd better read on."

Allison focused her gaze on her aunt's letter again:

"I was jealous because someone was interested in you, which meant you had the possibility of marriage. I, on the other hand, was destined to be an old maid the minute my parents were killed in a horrible fire that destroyed our home and left me and my four younger brothers as orphans. I was the oldest and felt it was my duty to care for them.

"Jeremiah King had been courting me for several months, and he'd even hinted that he had marriage on his mind. Soon after my folks were killed, however, Jeremiah informed me that he'd found someone else he loved more than me. Turned out that someone else was my best friend, Annie. From that moment on, I vowed never to love again.

"I became bitter because I'd been jilted by the only man I'd ever loved, and I felt obligated to take care of my brothers. Then, when your daed lost his wife and asked me to move to Pennsylvania to care for his brood, my bitterness increased. That's why I've been so critical of everything you've done. I suppose I felt that if I couldn't be happy, I didn't want anyone else to be, either. So when John Miller started coming

around, I told him you didn't care for him and sent him packing.

"I know what I did was wrong, and I hope you'll find it in your heart to forgive me someday. I really do love you, Allison, and I thank you for showing me the way to salvation.

"With deepest appreciation,
"Aunt Catherine"

A lump clogged Allison's throat, and she blinked against stinging tears. "Oh, Papa, I had no idea any of that had happened to Aunt Catherine, or that John was seriously interested in me."

"How did you feel about him, Allison? Were you in love with John?"

"At the time I thought he was pretty cute, but I never really got to know him well enough to decide if I could love him or not." She shrugged. "It doesn't matter now, because John married Sharon Yoder, and they've moved to Illinois."

Papa reached for Allison's hand and gave her fingers a gentle squeeze. "One of the reasons I sent you to visit your aunt and uncle in Missouri was to get you away from my sister's bitter attitude. I could see how it was affecting you."

"That's true. Aunt Catherine and I never got along very well—not until her last days." She looked at the letter she'd placed on the table and sighed. "I wish Aunt Catherine would have told me all this to my face. We could have talked about it, and I would have said, 'I forgive you,' and I would have asked her to forgive me for the way I'd behaved during my growing-up years."

"I guess she didn't feel comfortable saying those things to your face, so that's why she asked our bishop's wife to write her thoughts down in a letter." Papa pulled a second envelope from his pocket. "This is for you, too—an early Christmas present."

Allison tipped her head. "What is it? A letter?"

He leaned across the table and handed it to her. "Take a look."

When Allison tore open the envelope, her mouth fell open. Surely this couldn't be!

Aaron held a piece of leather out to Zachary. "You didn't get it stained right. Now you'll have to do it over again."

Zachary's eyebrows drew together. "You're too picky, ya know that? I'll bet Papa will be easier to work with than you."

"That's what you think." Aaron ruffled his brother's brown hair. "Papa knows the harness business well, and he expects only the best. So you'd better learn to listen if you're going to work here."

Zachary leaned across the workbench and lowered his voice. "I would never admit this to Papa, but harness work ain't my first choice for an occupation."

"What would you rather be doing?"

"Well, since Joseph quit working at Osborn's Christmas Tree Farm, I've thought I might like to go to work there."

Aaron's eyebrows drew together. "If you'd rather work there, then why'd you agree to work here?"

Zachary shrugged. "Papa said you're in love with Allison Troyer, and I didn't wanna be the one blamed for keepin' you two apart."

Aaron grimaced. He still hadn't decided what he should do about going to Pennsylvania. He did love Allison, but he hadn't had a letter from her in several weeks, and in the one he'd received, she'd suggested he find someone else. She hadn't even said she missed him. Had she found someone else, or had he misjudged her feelings for him in the first place? Maybe it would be best if he forgot about her and made a fresh start with someone else.

Who am I kidding? he silently moaned. *There's no one I'd rather be with than Allison. Still, if she's not interested in me, then I guess I'll have to deal with it. Maybe I should tell Zachary he's free to take a job at the tree farm and just be satisfied working here for the rest of my life without a helpmate.*

The bell above the front door jingled, but Aaron didn't bother to go up front to see who'd come in. Paul was working at his desk, so he could wait on the customer.

A few seconds later, Paul called, "Zachary, can I see you a minute?"

Zachary looked at Aaron and shrugged. "Guess I'd best go see what the boss wants, or I'll be in trouble."

Aaron went back to work on the bridle he was making for Ben King and tried not to think about

Zachary's admission that he didn't really want to do harness work.

"Hello, Aaron."

Aaron looked up, and his breath caught in his throat. "Allison? Wh-what are you doing here?"

She took a few steps toward him. "I came to see you."

"But . . . I thought . . . I mean . . . I was going to . . . " Aaron knew he was stammering, but he seemed powerless to say anything intelligent. Allison looked so sweet, standing there smiling at him. He wanted to reach out and hug her.

"My daed gave me an early Christmas present—a bus ticket to Webster County, Missouri." She smiled. "I have to return for my brother's wedding in a few weeks, but then I'll come back here for good."

Aaron's heartbeat picked up speed. "You . . . you really mean that?"

She nodded.

"I thought you had to stay in Pennsylvania to care for your daed."

"I believed that, too, but after Peter and Sally are married, they've agreed to move in with Papa. Peter thinks it will be easier for him to keep working at the dairy farm if he lives nearby. Sally will quit her job at the Plain and Fancy Farm after she and Peter are married, and she told my daed that she'll be more than happy to take care of him and his house."

Aaron could hardly contain himself. "Do you know what this means, Allison?"

"I hope it means we can begin courting again—if you haven't found someone else, that is."

He shook his head and reached for her hand. "Never!"

"I'm so glad to hear it."

"It also means I can stay right here and keep working for Paul in the harness shop. Fact is, I'd be happy to work here even if I never get to call the shop my own."

Allison tipped her head and squinted. "What do you mean?"

"I was thinking about moving to Pennsylvania so I could be near you, but I wasn't sure you'd want me."

"Of course I want you, Aaron."

He pulled her into his arms and drew in a deep breath, relishing the pleasant aroma of her clean-smelling hair. "I'd even thought about showing up at your door and surprising you after the first of the year, but you've surprised me instead." Aaron pulled slowly away from Allison and moved over to the other side of the room. He took a small cardboard box from one of the shelves and handed it to Allison. "This is a special present for you."

"What kind of present?"

"Open it, and see for yourself."

She lifted the lid on the box and gasped. "My face-less doll! Oh, Aaron, where did you find it?"

"I found it in my little sister's hands, but I'll explain that later. Right now, I'd like to ask you a question."

"What question is that?"

"Will you marry me after we've had a suitable time of courting?"

Tears welled in Allison's eyes and threatened to spill over. "You . . . really want me to be your wife?"

"Jah, if you're willing."

She nodded and gave in to her tears, allowing them to trickle down her cheeks. "I'd be happy to marry you, Aaron, but there's one condition."

"What might that be?"

"That I'm allowed to work here in the harness shop with you."

Aaron chuckled as relief flooded his soul. "Now that's a deal I can't refuse." He drew Allison into his arms, thanking God for the way He had worked everything out and looking forward to spending the rest of his days on a journey of love with this special woman.

Epilogue

two years later

*A*llison sat in front of her treadle sewing machine, humming softly as she sewed another faceless doll. She glanced across the room, where her dark-haired, one-year-old daughter, Catherine, sat on the floor, playing with the doll Allison's mother had made many years ago.

She reached for the verse she planned to attach to the doll she was making. On each doll she sewed, she included a passage of scripture: *"Ye shall seek me, and find me, when ye shall search for me with all your heart . . . saith the* LORD*" Jeremiah 29:13-14.*

Aaron stepped into the kitchen and bent to kiss her. "How are my two favorite women?"

"We're doing just fine," Allison replied with a smile. "I was sitting here at my sewing machine, thinking how my coming to Webster County changed my life."

He swooped their daughter into his arms and took a seat in the rocking chair beside the stove. "Want to tell me and Catherine how your life has changed?"

"If I hadn't come here to stay with my mamm's twin sister, I might never have found the Lord as my Savior." She lifted the pressure foot and pulled the doll free, holding it up for her husband's inspection. "And I would never have learned to make these faceless friends."

He nodded. "Anything else?"

Allison left the sewing machine and reached for Aaron's hand. Then she placed both of their hands on their daughter's head. "If I hadn't moved to Webster County, I wouldn't be married to the new owner of Zook's Harness Shop, and I wouldn't now be the mamm of this sweet little girl I love so much." She chuckled and stroked the child's soft cheek; then she moved her hand to touch Aaron's bearded face. "Of course, I love Catherine's daed quite a lot, too."

"I love you both, too." Aaron grinned. "It sure was a nice surprise when my daed decided it was time to retire and turn the shop over to us, wasn't it?"

Allison nodded. "The Lord is good, and nothing He

does surprises me." She pointed to the doll nestled in little Catherine's arms. "I'm glad I no longer feel face-less before God." She smiled and blinked back tears of joy. "No matter how long I'm allowed to journey this earth, I pray that I can share the joy of the Lord with everyone who receives one of my little faceless friends."

Recipe for Aunt Catherine's Peanut Brittle

Ingredients:
- 2 cups sugar
- ½ cup water
- 1 cup white Karo syrup
- 1 tsp. butter
- 3 cups raw peanuts
- 1 tsp. vanilla
- 2 tsp. baking soda

In a kettle over medium heat, cook the sugar, water, and Karo syrup to the hardball stage. Add the butter and peanuts. Stir and cook just until mixture turns brown. Remove from stove. Add vanilla and soda. Spread over a large, buttered cookie sheet and cool. Cut or break into pieces and scrve.

Center Point Publishing
600 Brooks Road • PO Box 1
Thorndike ME 04986-0001 USA

(207) 568-3717

US & Canada:
1 800 929-9108
www.centerpointlargeprint.com